... he author of seven novels, including ... collection, *Pie...* ... *w*, *Granta*, *Harper's*, *Playboy*, and the *New Yorker*. He lives in Ithaca, New York, where he teaches writing at Cornell University.

Praise for *See You in Paradise*

"These stories are funny and moving, endlessly inventive and charmingly absurd. J. Robert Lennon can do anything on the page" Jess Walter, author of *Beautiful Ruins*

"J. Robert Lennon finds the uncanny hidden in the everyday. His dark, subversive stories are both hilarious and unnerving. *See You in Paradise* is smart, inventive and full of the fascinating particularities of various wayward humans" Dana Spiotta

Praise for *Familiar*

"J. Robert Lennon's beautifully written new novel bristles with menace and suspense – a terrific and disturbing read" *Daily Mail*

"This highly convincing nightmare reads like a thriller; Lennon is painfully truthful about grief and parenthood" Kate Saunders, *The Times*

"Tight in focus as well as in construction ... an otherworldly narrative" Leo Robson, *Evening Standard*

"Dazzling" Justine Jordan, *Guardian*

"The direct present-tense narration and instantly engaging plight prove an irresistible combination ... One of the clever things about the set-up here is how neatly it invigorates some of the drearier procedures of conventional fiction ... a meditation on family and identity likely to stir ... *Observer*

"Lennon is ... probe the psychology ... uses his

sci-fi vehicle to create eerie fiction. The notion of parallel universes becomes a metaphor for life choices and their results" Peter Carty, *Independent on Sunday*

"J. Robert Lennon's *Familiar* is so breakneck and harrowing, so grab-you-by-the-lapels astonishing, that you may not notice until nearly the end how many questions about your own life it makes you ask. Haunting, beautiful, a horror story about parenting, complicated – it's a wonderful book" Elizabeth McCracken

"A swerving, existential mystery … an allusive and mysterious novel … one of Lennon's finest" *New York Times Book Review*

"*Familiar* is as tightly wound as a great Alfred Hitchcock movie. He keeps *Familiar* balanced at a perfect pitch between allowing us to believe what has happened to Elisa is real and to think that she's had a mental breakdown brought about by anxiety and depression. In the scientific shadows, Lennon has executed a literary puzzle, a marvellous trick of the mind" *Los Angeles Times*

"A novel that imposes itself on the imagination from the opening sentences … Lennon's brisk prose is both vivid and precise; the dialogue is clear and authentic, often funny. In fact, considering that this is a deadly serious, often bewildering and affecting novel, *Familiar* is witty and satiric. It is obvious that its genius lies in Lennon's feel for metaphysical contradictions that consistently undercut the realism … a similar approach to the theme of parallel universes and altered experiences within shifting time frames has also been explored in novels such as Haruki Murakami's *1Q84* or Tom McCarthy's *Remainder*, neither of which achieves the unsettling mastery of Lennon's far shorter and infinitely superior novel" Eileen Battersby, *Irish Times*

"A stealthy and thought-provoking literary thriller … Lennon succeeds by setting his odd, uncommon narrative in intimate terms that delve into Elisa's sense of confusion" *Publishers' Weekly*

SEE YOU IN PARADISE

STORIES

J. Robert Lennon

These stories previously appeared, sometimes in a different form, in the following publications: *Electric Literature*: "Hibachi"; *Epoch*: "Farewell, Bounder", "Total Humiliation in 1987"; *Granta*: "Ecstasy"; *Harper's*: "The Future Journal"; *McSweeney's*: "The Accursed Items"; the *New Yorker*: "Flight", "No Life"; *Playboy*: "See You in Paradise", "The Wraith", "Zombie Dan"; *A Public Space*: "A Stormy Evening at the Buck Snort Restaurant"; *Salamander*: "Weber's Head"; *Weird Tales*: "Portal".

"Weber's Head" also appeared in *Best American Nonrequired Reading 2011*, and "The Accursed Items" appeared on the radio show *This American Life*.

First published in the USA in 2014 by Graywolf Press, Minneapolis, Minnesota

First published in the UK in 2014 by Serpent's Tail,
an imprint of Profile Books Ltd
3A Exmouth House
Pine Street
London EC1R 0JH
www.serpentstail.com

ISBN 978 1 78125 335 9
eISBN 978 1 78283 101 3

Printed and | on CR0 4YY

CONTENTS

PORTAL

It's been a few years since we last used the magic portal in our back garden, and it has fallen into disrepair. To be perfectly honest, when we bought this place, we had no idea what kind of work would be involved, and tasks like keeping the garden weeded, repairing the fence, maintaining the portal, etc., quickly fell to the bottom of the priority list while we got busy dealing with the roof and the floor joists. I guess there are probably people with full-time jobs out there who can keep an old house in great shape without breaking their backs, but if there are, I've never met them.

My point is, we've developed kind of a blind spot about that whole back acre. The kids are older now and don't spend so much time wandering around in the woods and the clearing the way they used to—Luann is all about the boys these days, and you can't get Chester's mind away from the Xbox for more than five minutes—and Gretchen and I hardly ever even look in that direction. I think one time last summer we got a little drunk and sneaked out there to have sex under the crabapple tree, but weeds and stones kept poking up through the blanket and the bugs were eating us alive, so we gave up, came back inside and did it in the bed like normal people.

I know, too much information, right? Anyway, it was the kids who discovered the portal back when we first moved in. They were into all that magic stuff at the time—*Harry Potter, Lord of the Rings,* that kind of thing—and while Gretchen and I steamed off old wallpaper and sanded the floorboards inside the house, they had this whole crazy fantasy world invented back there, complete with various kingdoms, wizards, evil forces, orcs, trolls, and what have you. They made paths, buried treasures, drew maps, and basically had a grand old time. We didn't even have to send them to summer camp, they were so . . . tolerable. They didn't fight, didn't complain—I hope someday, when the teen years are over with, they'll remember all that and have some kind of relationship again. Maybe when they're in college. Fingers crossed.

One afternoon, I guess it was in July, they came running into the house, tracking mud everywhere and breathlessly shouting about something they'd found. "It's a portal, it's a portal to another world!" I got pretty bent out of shape about the mud, but the kids were seriously over the moon about this thing, and their enthusiasm was infectious. So Gretchen and I followed them out across the yard and into the woods, then down the little footpath that led to the clearing.

It's unclear what used to be there, back in the day—the land behind our house was once farmland, and the remains of old dirt roads ran everywhere—but at this time, a few years ago, the clearing was pretty overgrown, thick with shrubs and brambles and the like. We figured there'd just been a grain silo or something, something big that would have resulted in this perfectly circular area, but the kids had uncovered a couple of stone benches and a little fire pit, so clearly somebody used to hang around here in the past, you know, lighting a fire and sitting on the benches to look at it.

When we reached the clearing, we were quite impressed with the progress the kids had made. They'd managed to clear a lot of brush and the place had the feel of some kind of private room—the sun coming down through the clouds, and the wall of trees surrounding the space, and all that. It was really nice. So the kids had stopped at the edge, and we came up behind them and they were like, do you see it? And we were like, see what? And they said look, and we said, where?, and they said, Mom, Dad, just look!

And sure enough, off to the left, kind of hovering above what had looked like another bench but now appeared more like a short, curved little staircase, was this oval, sort of man-sized, shimmering thing that honestly just screamed "magic portal." I mean, it was totally obvious what it was—nothing else gives the air that quality, that kind of electrical distortion, like heat or whatever is bending space itself.

This was a real surprise to us, because there had been nothing about it in the real estate ad. You'd think the former owners would have mentioned it. I mean, the dry rot, I understand why they left that out, but even if this portal was busted, it's still a neat thing to have (or so I thought at the time), and could have added a few thou to the asking price, easy. But this was during the economic slump, so maybe not, and maybe the previous owners never bothered to come back here and didn't know what they had. They looked like indoor types, frankly. Not that Gretchen and I look like backcountry survivalists or anything. But I digress.

The fact is, this portal was definitely not busted, it was working, and the kids had taken special care uncovering the steps that led to it, tugging out all the weeds from between the stones and unearthing the little flagstone patio that surrounded the whole thing. In retrospect, if I had been an expert, or even a well-informed amateur, I would probably have been able to tell the portal was really just puttering along on its last legs and would soon go on the fritz. But of course I was, and I guess still am, an idiot.

We all went over there and walked around it and looked through it—had a laugh making faces at one another through the space and watching each other go all funhouse-mirror. But obviously the unspoken question was, do we go through? I was actually really proud of the kids right then because they'd come and gotten us instead of just diving headfirst through the thing like a lot of kids would have done. Who knows, maybe this stellar judgment will return to them someday. A guy can dream! But at this moment we all were just kind of looking at each other, wondering who was going to test it out.

Since I'm the father, this task fell to me. I bent over and pried a stone up out of the dirt and stood in front of the portal, with the kids looking on from behind. (Gretchen stood off to the side with her arms folded over her chest, doing that slightly disapproving stance she does pretty much all the time now.) And after a dramatic pause, I raised my arm and tossed the stone at the portal.

Nothing dramatic—the stone just disappeared. "It works!" Chester cried, and Luann hopped up and down, trying to suppress her excitement.

"Now hold on," I said, and picked up a twig. I braced my foot on the bottom step and poked the twig through the portal. This close, you could hear a low hum from the power the thing was giving off. In retrospect, this was probably an indication that the portal was out of whack—I mean, if my TV did that, I'd call a guy. But then, I figured, what did I know?

Besides, when I pulled the twig out, it looked okay. Not burned or frozen or turned into a snake or anything—it was just itself. I handed it to Gretchen and she gave it a cursory examination. "Jerry," she said, "I'm not sure—"

"Don't worry, don't worry." I knew the drill—she's the mom, she has to be skeptical, and it's my job to tell her not to worry. Which is harder to do nowadays, let me tell you. I got up nice and close to the portal, until the little hairs on my arms were standing up, and I stuck out my index finger and moved it slowly toward the shimmering air.

Chester's eyes were wide. Luann covered her mouth with her fists. Gretchen sighed.

Well, what can I say, it went in, and I barely felt a thing. It was weird seeing my pointer finger chopped off at the knuckle like that, but when I pulled it out again, voilà, there it was, unharmed. My family still silent, I took the bull by the horns and just shoved my whole arm in. The kids screamed. I pulled it out.

"What," I said, "what!!"

"We could see your blood and stuff!" This was Chester.

Luann said, "Daddy, that was so gross."

"Like an x-ray?" I said.

Chester was laughing hysterically now. "Like it got chopped off!"

"Oh my God, Jerry," Gretchen said, her hand on her heart.

My arm was fine, though. In fact, it felt kind of good—wherever the arm had just been, it was about five degrees warmer than this breezy little glade.

"Kids," I said, "stand behind me." Because I didn't want them to see what I was about to do. Eventually we'd get over this little taboo and enjoy watching each other walk super slowly through the portal, revealing our pulsing innards, but for now I didn't want to freak anyone out, myself least of all. When the kids were safely behind me, Gretchen holding them close, I stuck my head through.

I don't know what I was expecting—Middle Earth, or Jupiter, or Tuscany, or what. But I could never in a million years have guessed the truth. I pulled my head out.

"It's the vacant lot behind the public library," I said.

———

I think that even then, that very day, we knew the portal was screwed up. It was only later, after it was obvious, that Gretchen and I started saying out loud the strange things we noticed on the family trip downtown. For one thing, the books we got at the library—obviously that's the first place we went—weren't quite right. The plots were all convoluted and the paper felt funny. The bus lines were not the way we remembered, with our usual bus, the 54, called the 24; and the local transit authority color scheme had been changed to crimson and ochre. Several restaurants had different names, and the one guy we bumped into whom we knew—my old college pal Andy—recoiled in apparent horror when he saw us. It was just, you know, off.

But the really creepy thing was what Chester said that night as we were tucking him in to bed—and how I miss those days now, when

Chester was still practically a baby and needed us to hug and kiss him goodnight—he just started laughing there in the dark, and Gretchen said what is it, honey, and he said that guy with the dog head.

Dog head? we asked him.

Yeah, that guy, remember him? He walked past us on the sidewalk. He didn't have a regular head, he had a dog head.

Well, you know, Chester was always saying crazy nonsense back then. He still does, of course, but that's different—it used to be cute and funny. So we convinced ourselves he was kidding. But later, when we remembered that—hell, we got chills. Everything from there on in would only get weirder, but it's that dog head, Chester remembering the dog head, that freaks me out. I guess the things that scare you are the things that are almost normal.

Anyway, that first time, everything seemed to go off more or less without a hitch. After the library we walked in the park, went out for dinner, enjoyed the summer weather. Then we went back to the vacant lot, found the portal, and went home. It's tricky to make out the return portal when you're not looking for it; the shimmering is fainter and of course there's no set of stone steps leading up to it or anything. Anybody watching would just have seen us disappearing one by one. In an old Disney live-action movie (you know, like *Flubber* or *Witch Mountain*) there would be a hobo peering at us from the gutter, and then, when we vanished, looking askance at his bottle of moonshine and resolvedly tossing it over his shoulder.

So that night, we felt fine. We all felt fine. We felt pretty great, in fact; it had been an exciting day. Gretchen and I didn't get it on, it was that time of the month; but we snuggled a lot. We decided to make it a weekend tradition, at least on nice days—get up, read the paper, get dressed, then out to the portal for a little adventure.

Because by the third time it was obvious that it would be an adventure; it turns out the portal wasn't permanently tied to the vacant lot downtown. I don't know if this was usual or what. But I pictured it flapping in the currents of space and time, sort of like a windsock, stuck fast at one end and whipping randomly around at the other. I still have no idea why it dropped us off so close to home (or so apparently close to home) that first time—I suppose it was still trying to be normal. Like an old guy in denial about the onset of dementia.

The second time we went through, we thought we were in old-time England, on some heath or something—in fact, after I put my head in to check, I sent Gretchen back to the house to fill a basket with bread and fruit and the like, for a picnic, and I told Luann to go to the garage to get the flag off her bike, to mark the site of the return portal. Clever, right? The weather was fine, and we were standing in a landscape of rolling grassy hills, little blue meandering creeks, and drifting white puffy clouds. We could see farms and villages in every direction, but no cities, no cars or planes or smog. We hiked down into the nearest village and got a bit of a shock—nobody was around, no people, or animals for that matter—the place was abandoned. And we all got the strong feeling that the whole world was abandoned, too—that we were the only living creatures in it. I mean, there weren't even any bugs. It was lonesome as hell. We went home after an hour and ate our picnic back in the clearing.

The third time we went through, we ended up in this crazy city—honestly, it was too much. Guys selling stuff, people zipping around in hovercars, drunks staggering in the streets, cats and dogs and these weirdly intelligent-looking animals that were sort of like deer but striped and half as large. Everybody wore hats—the men seemed to favor these rakish modified witch-hat things with a floppy brim, and women wore a kind of collapsed cylinder, like a soufflé. Nobody seemed to notice us, they were busy, busy, busy. And the streets! None of them was straight. It was like a loud, crowded, spaghetti maze, and for about half an hour we were terrified that we'd gotten lost and would never find the portal again, which miraculously had opened into the only uninhabited dark alley in the whole town. (We'd planted our bicycle flag between two paving stones, and almost lost it to a thing that was definitely *not* a rat.) Chester demanded a witch hat, but the only place we found that sold them wouldn't take our money, and we didn't speak the language anyway, which was this whacked-out squirrel chatter. Oh, yeah, and everybody had a big jutting chin. I mean everybody. When we finally got home that night the four of us got into a laughing fit about the chins—I don't know what it was, they just struck us as wildly hilarious.

Annoying as that trip was, I have to admit now that it was the best time we ever had together, as a family I mean. Even when we were freaked out, we were all on the same page—we were a team. I suppose it's perfectly normal for this to change, I mean, the kids have to strike out on their own someday, right? They have to develop their own interests and their own way of doing things, or else they'd never leave, god forbid. But I miss that time. And just like every other asshole who fails to appreciate what he's got while he still has it, all I ever did was complain.

I'm thinking here of the fourth trip through the portal. When I stuck my head through for a peek, all I saw was fog and all I heard was clanking, and I pictured some kind of waterfront, you know, with the moored boats bumping up against each other and maybe a nice seafood place tucked in among the warehouses and such. I guess I'd gotten kind of reckless. I led the family through and after about fifteen seconds I realized that the fog was a hell of a lot thicker than I thought it was, and that it kind of stung the eyes and nose, and that the clanking was far too regular and far too deep and loud to be the result of some gentle ocean swell.

In fact, we had ended up in hell—a world of giant robots, acrid smoke, windowless buildings and glowing toxic waste piles. We should have turned right around and gone back through the portal, but Chester ran ahead, talking to himself about superheroes or something. Gretchen went after him, Luann reached for my hand (maybe for the last time ever? But please, I don't want to go there), and before you knew it we had no idea where we were. The fog thickened, if anything, and nobody knew who had the flag, or if we'd even remembered to bring the thing. It took Luann and me half an hour just to find Gretchen and Chester, and two hours more to find the portal (and this only by random groping—it would have been easy to miss it entirely). By this time we were all trembling and crying—well, I wasn't crying, but I was sure close—and nearly paralyzed with fear from a series of close calls with these enormous, filthy, fast-moving machines that looked like elongated forklifts and, in one instance, a kind of chirping metal tree on wheels. When I felt my arm tingle I nearly crapped myself with relief. We piled through the portal and back into a summer evening in the yard, and were disturbed to discover a small robot that had inadvertently passed through along with us, a kind of four-slice toaster type thing on spindly anodized bird legs. In the coming weeks it would rust with unnatural speed, twitching all the while, until it was nothing but a gritty orange stain on the ground.

Maybe I'm remembering this wrong—you know, piling all our misfortunes together in one place in my mind—but I believe it was in the coming days that the kids began to change, or rather to settle into what we thought (hoped) were temporary patterns of unsavory behavior. Chester's muttered monologuing, which for a long time we thought was singing, or an effort to memorize something, took on a new intensity—his face would turn red, spittle would gather at the corners of his mouth, and when we interrupted him he would gaze at us with hatred, some residual emotion from his violent fantasy world. As for Luann, the phone began ringing a lot more often, and she would disappear with the receiver into private corners of the house to whisper secrets to her friends. Eventually, of course, the friends turned into boys. Gretchen bought her some makeup, and the tight jeans and tee shirts she craved—because what are you going to do, make the kid wear hoop dresses and bonnets?

As for Gretchen, well—I don't know. She started giving me these *looks,* not exactly pitying, but regretful, maybe. Disappointed. And not even in me, particularly—more like, she had disappointed herself for setting her sights so low. I'm tempted to blame the portal for all this, the way it showed us how pathetic, how circumscribed our lives really were. But I didn't need a magic portal to tell me I was no Mr. Excitement—I like my creature comforts, and I liked it when my wife and kids didn't demand too much from me, and when you get down to it, maybe all that, not the portal, is the reason everything started going south. Not that Gretchen's parents helped matters when they bought Chester the video game for his birthday—an hour in front of that thing and adios, amigo. Whatever demons were battling in his mind all day long found expression through his thumbs—it became the only thing that gave the poor kid any comfort. And eventually we would come to realize that Luann was turning into, forgive me, something of a slut, and that Chester had lost what few social graces we'd managed to teach him. Today his face is riddled with zits, he wanders off from the school grounds two or three times a week, and he still gets skidmarks in his tighty whities. And Luann—we bought her a used car in exchange for a promise to drive Chester where he wanted to go, but she gave him a ride maybe once—it was to, God knows why, the sheet metal fabricating place down behind the supermarket—and then forgot him there for four hours while she did god knows what with god knows who. ("It doesn't matter what I was doing! Stuff!")

But I'm getting ahead of myself. You'd think we would have quit the portal entirely after the robot fog incident, but then you're probably mistaking us for intelligent people. Instead we went back now and again—it was the only thing we could all agree to do together. Sometimes I went by myself, too. I suspect Gretchen was doing the same—she'd be missing for a couple of hours then would come back flushed and covered with burrs, claiming to have been down on the recreation path, jogging. I don't think the kids went alone—but then where did Chester get that weird knife?

In any event, what we saw in there became increasingly disturbing. Crowds of people with no faces, a world where the ground itself seemed to be alive, heaving and sweating. We generally wouldn't spend more than a few minutes wherever we ended up. The portal, in its decline into senility, seemed to have developed an independent streak, a mind of its own. It was . . . giving us things. Things it thought we wanted. It showed us a world that was almost all noise and confusion and flashing red light, with a soundtrack of something you could hardly call music made by something you maybe could mistake for guitars. Only Luann had a good time in that one. There was

Chester's world, the one that wheeled around us in pixelated, rainbow 3-D, where every big-eyed armored creature exploded into fountains of glittering blood and coins, and the one that looked like ours, except thinner, everything thinner, the buildings and people and trucks and cars, and from the expression of horror on Gretchen's face, I could tell where that one was coming from. And there was the one place where all the creatures great and small appeared to have the red hair, thick ankles, and perky little boobs of the new administrative assistant at my office. Gretchen didn't talk to me for days after that, but it certainly did put me off the new assistant.

And so before the summer was over, we gave up. The kids were too busy indulging their new selves and quit playing make-believe out in the woods. And Gretchen and I were lost in our private worlds of self-disgust and conjugal disharmony. By Christmas we'd forgotten about the portal, and the clearing began to fill in. We did what people do: we heaved our grim corporeal selves through life.

I checked back there a couple of times over the next few years— you know, just to see if everything looked all right. Needless to say, last time I checked, it didn't—the humming was getting pretty loud, and the shimmering oval was all lopsided, with a sort of hernia in the lower left corner, which was actually drooping far enough to touch the ground. When I poked a stick through the opening, there was a pop and a spark and a cloud of smoke, and the portal seemed to emit a kind of hacking cough, followed by the scent of ozone and rot. When I returned to the house and told Gretchen what I'd seen, she didn't seem to care. And so I decided not to care, either. Like I said before, there were more important things to worry about.

Just a few weeks ago, though, I started hearing strange noises at night. "Didya hear that?" I'd say out loud, and if I was in bed with Gretchen (as opposed to on the sofa, alone), she would rise up out of half-sleep to tell me no, it was just a dream. But it wasn't. It was a little like a coyote's yip, but deeper, more elongated. And sometimes there would be a screech of metal on metal, or a kind of random ticking; and if I got up and looked out the window, sometimes I thought I could see a strange glow coming from the woods.

And now, even in the daytime, there's a funny odor hanging around the yard. It's springtime, and Gretchen says it's just the smell of nature waking up. But I don't think so. Is springtime supposed to smell like motor oil and dog piss in the morning? To be perfectly honest, I'm beginning to be afraid of what our irresponsibility, our helplessness, has wrought. I mean, we bought this place. We own it, just like we own all our other problems.

I try to talk to Gretchen about it, but she doesn't want to hear it. "I'm on a different track right now," she says. "I can't be distracted from my healing." "Healing from *what?*" I want to know. "My psychic disharmony." I mean, what can you say to that? Meanwhile, I have no idea where our daughter is half the time, and I haven't gone up to Chester's room in three weeks. I can hear him up there, muttering; I can hear the bed squeak as he acts out his violent fantasies; I hear the menacing orchestral strings and explosions and tortured screams that emanate from his favorite games.

Problems don't just go away, you know? Problems get bigger and bigger and before you know it they're bigger than you are, and it's too late to fix them. Some days, when I've gotten a decent night's sleep and have had a few cups of coffee, I think sure, I'll just get on the phone, start calling people up and asking for help. A school guidance counselor, a marriage therapist, a pediatrician, a witch or shaman or wizard or physicist or whoever in the hell might know what to do about the portal, or even have the balls to walk down that path and see what's become of the clearing.

But on other days, days like today, when I'm too damned tired even to reach for the phone, the only emotion I can summon up is longing, for a time when the world was miraculous, when I couldn't wait to get up in the morning and start living.

I mean, the magic has to come from someplace, right? It's out there, bestowing itself on somebody else's wife, somebody else's kids, somebody else's life. All I want is to get just a little of it back. Is that so much to ask?

NO LIFE

In the sunblasted park, at the water's edge, a titan willow shades a circle of grass and lake. Beneath it the children can be seen wearing red tee shirts, white sneakers, and tan shorts. There are about twenty-five of them, from four years old to fourteen. A few brave the heat with a soccer ball; most are engaged in a game that seems to involve keeping a bunch of beanbags in the air. The grass is dead: it's late June and there hasn't been a day of rain in three weeks. Edward and Alison are watching from their car.

Edward is thinking that, from here, they all look pretty good. Scrubbed and uniformed, the children glance from time to time at the organizers grilling meat nearby, setting out foil-covered plates on a folding buffet table. The sight gives Edward a magnanimous, fatherly feeling. He thinks he'd better keep this feeling in check: You don't go hungry to the grocer's, he likes to say.

Alison is thinking: I don't want a white one. I don't want to be one of those people who has to have the right kind. Give me a black one or a Chinese one or something, they're all kids, they've all got good hearts, it doesn't matter.

Neither gets out of the car. Edward says, "Couldn't have picked a nicer day."

Alison sighs. "The grass," she says.

Then they notice the other couples. How could they have missed them? They're so conspicuous, each standing alone, far, far from the other couples, all of them perfectly still, watching. They're clean, neat, studiously casual: belted shorts and golf shirts for the men, sundresses and summer hats for the women: exactly the way Edward and Alison are dressed.

The children don't seem to notice. Some have been passed over a hundred times. Some have no hope at all, Alison is thinking, but they've come anyway, just in case. They're playing, just like normal children. They are normal children, she reminds herself.

"There," Edward says, pointing. A couple is making its move, heading for a spot beneath the willow where three children are playing a board game on the grass. As they approach, the man and woman bend over, readying themselves to speak. One child, a black-haired, dark-skinned boy, looks up.

The couple is intercepted by an organizer.

"Whoops," says Edward.

The organizers are wearing white tee shirts with an insignia on the breast. This organizer, a plump, youngish woman, has her hand stuck straight out to be shaken. The man and woman right themselves to clasp it. They are led to a buffet table and given name tags. The black-haired boy watches until he's handed the dice. Then he turns back to his game. The woman, narrow-faced, wan, thin-haired, continues to stare at the boy until her husband pulls her away.

"I can't do this," says Alison.

"It's a walk in the park," Edward tells her, then realizes the unintended joke and says, very loudly, "Ha!"

He gets out of the car; she follows.

The head organizer is named Greta. Edward misses the name when she introduces herself and ends up having to lean close to read her name tag. But not too close; he doesn't want her to think he's checking out her boobs, though of course he is. Consequently he reads it as "Great." Can that be right? She is tall and unbalanced, like a stack of colorful wooden blocks.

"I am simply thrilled to see you all here today," says Great. She has herded the couples onto a patch of grass that is burdened by direct sun, where they have been asked to sit. Behind them the children play, stealing glances. "A few guidelines. One, we have brought no forms to fill out, nothing like that. Today is just for kicks. If you hit it off with a particular child, let us know, and we can arrange a meeting. Two, don't talk about why you're here, please. The children already know, and they are a little nervous! So talk about something else—doggies, sports, airplanes, church."

Edward begins thinking about how he might incorporate all these subjects into a single sentence.

Alison thinks that the other couples look better qualified, wealthier, tougher than she and Edward. They probably have connections: she always believes all other people know one another. What if our child turns out to be religious? she wonders. A Baha'i? A Jain? There would be time to get books out of the library.

"And third, and this is most important, please: do not, under any circumstances, ask a child if he or she wants to come home with you, okay? Okay! Terrific!" Great claps her hands. The couples stand up.

———

Edward heads straight for the tallest child, an ugly, pale boy with stretched features: a long nose; narrow, slanted, almost Asian eyes; a pointed chin. He is sitting in the shade watching the other kids. Edward sits beside him.

"You don't want me, man," the kid says.

"Thanks for the tip," Edward tells him, and the kid looks surprised. "Why, what's wrong with you?"

"My folks were no good. Also people tried me out before and it didn't work."

"You were bad?"

The kid laughs. "Uh-huh."

"What'd you do?"

"Smoked weed."

"Mmm," says Edward.

"I never did it before. Their freakin' real son gave it to me, except they didn't believe me when I told them."

Edward reads the kid's name tag in an ironic, obvious way. Nate. "Oh, I believe that. Kids have no boundaries, Nate."

Nate stares at Edward for a moment. He says, "What's your name?"

"Ed."

"Do you let kids call you Ed or do they have to call you Mister something?"

"It's just Ed," Edward says. "Like Cher."

Edward thinks maybe he's gone too far. Nate is squinting at him like he's mad.

"Like who?" Nate says.

Alison watches Edward take off alone and feels sick to her stomach. They're in this together, she thinks. But she imagines what Edward would tell her if she said so: "We can cover more ground split up," he'd say, as if it were a scavenger hunt. And then she hears him say, "It *is* a scavenger hunt, Al." He calls her Al. Most of her boyfriends called her Allie, and the worst of them, a long-lashed pec-pumper named Lou, called her Alison, as if this formalized respect would fool her. Edward calls her Al and she calls him Edward. That happened on the first date. Al and Edward: it went through her head all night long. Then they got married and tried to have a kid for nine years. She didn't want the drugs; she was afraid of octuplets, and then what? Aborting some, but not others: that wasn't for her, it seemed so arbitrary. What if they killed the wrong ones? So adoption is it. It's the right thing to do. They read about the picnic in the paper.

A child comes to her, a tiny white boy. "Fow me dis!" he says, "fow it to me!" He thrusts a frisbee at her. She draws back, horrified, and it tumbles to the ground. The child picks it up and hands it to her again.

"Oh! I don't know . . ." It's a test! she thinks, taking the frisbee. It's a test and I'm flunking!

The child runs away to a small group of older boys. They are grinning with apparent mischief. "All right!" she calls out. "Get ready! Here it comes!"

She throws the frisbee, and it wallows in the air and falls ten feet short. "No!" the child says. "Wike dis! Wike dis!" He grabs the frisbee and flings it away, over the heads of the other children, and they chase it and are gone.

She wanders, watching Edward out of the corner of her eye. He is talking to exactly the wrong kid. She's done research. Adolescents and teens may already have developed beyond your ability to control them. Sometimes she suspects that Edward doesn't really want a child at all, and that this secret truth has rendered them infertile. She's not sure of the mechanics of the thing, but it is as easy to believe as what the doctor has told them.

At first their desire for children was as passionate and straightforward as a Labrador retriever, and as thoughtless. They liked each other and wanted to make more of themselves. They screwed with delightful abandon. Once it was clear things weren't working, though, sex became perfunctory. It seemed absurd and implausible, like Twister. They still have it, of course. Sex. They call it "it." "We should do it." Neither ever refuses, no matter how unappealing the prospect, because then there would be somebody to blame for their never doing it anymore.

They are most successful at it when he wears a condom.

Alison has been thinking these thoughts for a while before she realizes how she must look: slumped, agape, alone. She looks up, startled, at the scene around her. Predatory adults kneeling, touching, telling jokes. I don't know any jokes! she thinks.

Then she sees her child.

Really. He looks like her. He has her long fingers (curled around a plastic bat), her high forehead (sweating, like hers!), her coarse, raccoon-colored hair (though on him, tousled, gently curled, it looks charming). He is so obviously the one that it takes her several seconds to realize that he is already talking to some adults, older adults. Mature adults. The man wears boots and a bolo tie; narrow and bent, he looks like a hick. A rich hick. The woman is freckled and tan. It's over; the child has been claimed.

Still, her legs carry her toward the three of them.

"I don't want parents," Nate tells Edward. "I'm fine without them. Pretty soon I'll get out of high school and I'll take the money they give me at the home and buy a bus ticket."

The speech sounds rehearsed. "Where to?" Edward says.

"Vegas."

"What's there?"

"Everything, man. Girls. Money. I want to deal poker. You ever seen those guys? They're smooth."

"I agree."

Nate looks off across the park, squinting at the bright hills and water. It would be a piece of cake to live with this kid, Edward thinks. He'd be like a roommate. Because Edward doesn't want a baby anymore, really, the same way he doesn't want a sport-utility vehicle or a handheld computer. All the years of fertility brochures and pregnancy books, all the babies who pitch for mutual funds and radial tires and insurance policies and of course diapers and powders and creams: all of it has driven Edward to conclude that babies are a brand name, they are a product. They are conventional. They are what other people want you to have. To hell with them, with their big round heads and skinny asses and button noses. He'll take this: this guy.

All he has to do is find Al and introduce her to the kid. He scans the crowd. There she is, standing in the sunlight with a skinny sort of ersatz Texan and his wife. He stands up and brushes his butt off.

"Sit tight, Nate," he says.

"Whatever."

But as he draws closer to Alison and the Texans, he realizes it isn't going to work this way. In fact, it isn't going to work at all. That's because a child is there, among the three of them, a child of about five with the long, asking-for-it face of a chronic sinus sufferer. The child is holding a busted wiffle ball bat, whitened and creased in the middle, where it's been pounded against a tree. When Alison turns, her eyes are chaotically glittering, as if full of broken glass. She's in love.

Dammit, things ought to be simple. Nate fades away behind him like a Coke can tossed out a car window.

"Hi!" he says to the four of them and presses his palm against Alison's humid back. Nobody says anything except the doomed child.

"Hello."

Edward thinks he should probably introduce himself to the adults, but he has a feeling he's not going to like them. He bends over and says, "Who's in charge here? You, sir?"

The child says, "No, Mrs. Scott is," and points across the park to the tall woman, the one who looked like she might fall over. Great. Great Scott! Perfect! The boy is cowering, so Edward stifles his laugh. Raymond is his name. It's markered on his name tag in that new kind of printing they teach now, with little curlicues after all the letters, so that the children will find it easier to connect them someday, when cursive is taught.

Edward feels a willful hand on his shoulder. He allows it to pull him up into a standing position.

"Harlan Breece," says the Texan, "Linda Breece." Edward shakes the man's hand and gives Linda a little bow. Then Harlan Breece shakes Alison's hand, too. Edward tries goofily to shake Alison's hand, but she rejects him with a nervous smile. Everyone, actually, is smiling. Meanwhile Harlan is sizing them up, and after a moment he turns back to the boy, his face confident and calm. Edward sees that Harlan has deemed them not worth worrying about. His wife, seeing this too, relaxes, and a blush blooms briefly. Edward understands that a competition has begun. He turns to Alison.

"You ought to get into the shade," he says, for she is deep red and illuminated by sweat.

"I'm fine," she tells him brightly. "Raymond likes baseball. His favorite player is . . . who is it?"

"Sammy Sosa," says Raymond.

"Son," says Harlan Breece, "you ever been to a real baseball game?"

"No, sir."

"Well, somebody ought to do something about that."

"I want him," Alison says. They are in the car with the windows shut tight, the AC pumping hot air into their faces. The children are climbing into a bus while someone with a clipboard checks off their names. The event is over. The two couples talked to the boy Raymond for a good twenty minutes, not moving an inch, despite the blazing sun: a contest for which the heat-loving Breeces (genuine Texans, as it happens) were genetically predisposed. The Breeces revealed that they lived on the lake, that Harlan was a judge. They'd acquired a child once before, a foster child, as Linda had suffered a "female problem" that left her unable to conceive. The boy had gone back home after a year. The implication was that the separation had crushed poor Linda, and indeed, Linda looked the part, with her moist eyes and weak chin, and the heavy upper arms Alison tends to associate with deep sadness. The Breeces had sold their ranch to a developer and moved here, of all places, to the Finger Lakes.

All of this was spoken in code, of course, with occasional frank asides to Edward and Alison, whenever a nugget of information seemed like it might break their spirit. Judge. Money. Experience with foster children.

The teenager is getting on the bus now, the one Edward had been talking to. Alison says, "You could have been more helpful. Why were you talking to that young man?"

Edward's gaze follows the teen until he disappears. "Nate. I don't know. Nobody else was going to talk to him."

Though she knows it annoys him, she can't help sighing. Edward roots for the underdog. He buys cheap shirts from sale racks and votes for local crackpots every November. It's one of the things that, when she loves him, she really loves, and when she is angry at him, she finds intolerable. He is intolerable now, but already her intolerance is on the wane. She can't seem to get worked up about anything these days. It's a feature of their marriage: as sexual passion has faded, so has pride, so has resentment. Sometimes she feels she may vanish completely into an undifferentiated fog of vague love.

She isn't a crier—she prides herself on this—but she begins to cry. Edward pats her leg. The air is cooling down. In fact, it is suddenly ice cold. A chill runs through her. The tears shut off. Edward shuts off the AC.

"I'm thinking of a word," he says.

"Oh, God, not right now."

"No, let's do it. You know you wanna."

"I don't!" But she can't resist the game. They've played it on every road trip they've ever taken. They've played it naked. They've played it in elevators and on the Great Wall of China. She wipes her face, hangs her head, whispers, "Fallopian."

"After."

"Infertility."

He snorts. "Before!"

"Uh, gum?"

"Close, in a way. After."

"Itchy," she says, scratching her legs.

"Itchy comes after infertility."

"Edward, I just don't feel like doing this right now."

"It's between infertility and gum," he says quietly. "Something delicious."

"Hot dogs. Hominy?"

"Perfect for a day like this. A sweet, refreshing treat."

She turns to him. He is holding an invisible ice-cream cone and licking it lasciviously, his eyebrows rising and falling, his eyes rolling back in his head with simulated pleasure. He has not yet noticed the approach of Harlan Breece, who is walking bent over with his hands on his khakied knees, squinting in Edward's window.

Edward sees the shadow of the massive hat falling across the dash before he hears the tap on the window, not a tap actually but a small thud, as Breece is using his fingertip, not his fingernail. In fact, Edward notes as he rolls the window down, Breece has barely got any fingernails at all. They are as irregular and receding as his hairline. He counts this as a victory and is able to meet the Texan with a broad and truly genuine smile. A ten-gallon smile, he thinks, that's how we do it in Upstate New York! He realizes he is still holding the invisible ice-cream cone and releases it. Invisible ice cream splatters his thighs.

"Harlan, hello!"

"Hi there, Alison dear," Breece drawls, glancing past Edward, "and I'm ashamed to admit I've forgotten your name." Breece grimaces calmly at him.

"Edward. 'Big Ed,' if you like."

"You'll accept my apologies then, Ed, and hear me out. I'm pleased to tell you that Linda finds you both mighty charming, and she's asked me to extend an invitation to dinner up at our little lakeside cottage. We still got a little water left in the lake, in spite of this heat of yours."

We got a little water! Heat of *yours?* Edward loves it, an honest-to-God member of the privileged class, whose wife finds him and his wife mighty charming. Without turning to Alison, Edward says, "Well, we're real sorry about our heat, but we'd love to come take a gander at your water."

"Splendid," says Harlan Breece, and angles his brush-covered panhandle of an arm in through the window. Edward shakes the hand at the end of it. "When's good for you?"

"Just about anytime," Edward says as the first bad vibes reach him from Alison's side of the car. "It isn't like we need to get a sitter."

"Tomorrow? Eight?"

"Of course, sure."

The panhandle withdraws and returns, this time bearing a white slip of paper with a map printed on it. It dawns on Edward that Breece just happened to have this map on him, and probably has several more. You never know when you're going to need to invite somebody up to the shack for some pig's feet and moonshine. Edward accepts the map and gives it a game squint, then nods at Harlan as he rolls the window back up, his own pumping arm looking very working class, vulgarly utilitarian, like an oil derrick.

When the window is shut tight, he turns to Alison. "That oughta be fun."

"You will be alone," she says.

———

But he isn't alone when, the following night, they get into the car and point themselves north along the scenic Lake Ridge Highway. She meant it when she said it, but really, she would never abandon him. Of course the Breeces didn't find them charming, no doubt they found them odious. But tonight, none of it bothers her, because she knows that they, she and Edward, are going to win. Alison phoned up the agency first thing this morning from her desk at Spitznagel & Pinch Real Estate and told the girl that they wanted to "meet with the little boy Raymond." Take a meeting, she restrained herself from saying. And the girl said, "Oh, he is a cutie, isn't he, it's amazing nobody's whisked him home yet."

Nobody's whisked him home. Hanging up the phone, she pictured herself doing the whisking, ushering little Raymond into their car, into their house. The Breeces hadn't got him yet. During her lunch hour, she stopped at the library and learned that childless couples in their thirties are more likely to adopt successfully than those in their fifties, and she felt a cautious optimism. Thirties: that's us!

Or so thinks Alison. Edward, however, at thirty-seven, doesn't see himself as being in his "thirties." If pressed he would probably say he's "around twenty-five." That was his age when he met Alison, the age when he hung up his bong and shaved his beard. He regards marriage as a kind of deep freeze that perfectly preserves the version of Ed— Version 3.0, following Innocence (1.0), The End of Innocence (1.1), and College (2.0)—that got married. Sure, he's noticed a few little changes, the usual ones: the hair loss, the out-of-breath, the getting-fat. But these are minor setbacks, if they're setbacks at all. When he was a kid he'd get these hard fleshy growths on his fingertips, tiny numb extinct volcanoes, which lasted a good six months and went away on their own. That's how it is with these things.

But this morning, when he was sitting in the breakfast nook, looking out at the suburban street and the elementary school and the cafeteria workers ineptly parallel parking at the curb, he suddenly found it difficult to see. He didn't know what it was at first, a darkening, a fluttering, and for a moment he thought he was having a heart attack. Just for a moment! And thinking he was having a heart attack made his heart stand briefly, horrifyingly still, so that he seemed to be having another one. Then his focus shifted, and he saw that the bird feeder hanging from the eaves, suspended in the center of the window, was bristling with nuthatches. There had to have been twenty, flapping madly about the six seed-choked holes, and Edward laughed and instantly relaxed. Not a heart attack! Nuthatches!

They've got the dome light on and Alison is trying to read the map. "There's supposed to be a secondhand clothing place . . . and then a bridge . . . wait, two bridges, take the first left after the second bridge, not the left after the first . . . and then go 2.3 miles . . ." The map is absurdly, counterproductively detailed, so that if they miss a single landmark they'll be eating roasted possum off the end of a stick in the woods tonight. Still, somehow, they manage to find the place. The Breeces' driveway is a couple of ruts that snake through a half-reclaimed farm field and plunge into an untrimmed copse of box elders. And beyond the treeline: Taliesin. Or something like that. Massive, slabbed, lit like a pumpkin; you can see everything inside—the furniture and art and a gigantic fireplace—and right through the back windows onto the lake and the blazing sunset reflected there. Alison suppresses a wave of hatred for the rival real-estate agency that sold it: she could have bought a baby on the black market with that commission.

They park in a gravel lot the size of a tennis court. Theirs is the only car. It is Linda who comes to the door, looking awfully tall without Harlan. She leads them inside.

Harlan's in front of the fire (as they've got the AC pumping pretty hard in here) with a drink in his hand. A mesquite smell fills the room. "Harlan, dear," his wife calls out, and he theatrically snaps to attention and a grin spreads across his face, a wide face for such a thin guy. Edward notes a bear rug. Wow!

"Welcome, welcome!" says Harlan. He sets down the drink on a coffee table made of petrified wood and throws his arms wide.

"Howdy, pardner," Edward says, and imagines he sees a flicker of irritation on the judge's face. They shake hands. This time Harlan uses his free hand to seize Edward's forearm, so Edward does the same. For a moment the two men are locked in a Boy Scout Death Grip. It is Harlan who lets go. Edward notices Linda and Alison attempting to greet one another. Al is a handshaker, and he just bets Linda is a kisser. The two stare nodding at one another from a distance of several feet.

"What's your poison, Ed?"

"Does hizzoner drink tequila?" Edward says impulsively.

"Hell yes."

———

Linda is talking about their failed foster-child experiment. Alison listens with alarm. It is a sermon, really, a testimonial, delivered with the strained alacrity of an introductory economics lecture. There is no room for question or comment.

"He was the sweetest little boy, a little black boy," she says. "His momma was hooked on the drugs, and he never had no daddy to speak of. His daddy wasn't ever around—well, I suppose it could have been anyone. His momma went to prison because of picking up drugs at somebody's house with the little boy in the back seat. And well, Harlan and I saw him and we thought, He's the one. He had the sweetest kinky hair and his skin was so smooth and dark. Well.

"We brought him back to the ranch and gave him all the advantages, don't you know. He had a nanny of his own kind who was just as sweet as a biscuit, and we gave him riding lessons and Harlan took him out on the little golf course we used to have, just four holes. This was in the days before black boys played golf. And he went to a wonderful little school we found for him outside of Dallas, with children from all different races, they had the Mexicans and the Chinese and the Indians and all that. Well, we thought it would be just perfect. Except he had some trouble with reading, and they found out there was something wrong with his eyes, and also his ears, which explained why he didn't seem to be listening to what we were saying to him sometimes. If you ask me, it was the drugs, the drugs his momma took when he was in her belly. And then poor Angeline, that's the colored girl who was his nanny, she had to go back to Trinidad to take care of her momma, and the next one we got was a Mexican, name of Armada—"

"Amara," Harlan says, staring hard into his tequila. Alison can't help but notice that Edward's glass is empty and that his eyes are casting about for the bottle. There it is, right in front of Harlan. She watches as Edward leans right past him and grabs it around the neck.

"Of course," Linda goes on. It occurs to Alison that the Breeces cannot possibly have any friends here. She wonders why they left Texas at all, how Harlan managed to get appointed a judge in Lake County. Edward keeps drinking. She nudges him to let him know that she considers this unwise, and Harlan, raising his eyebrows in a flirtatious manner, seems to notice.

When the story peters out, they eat. It is DIY, black-bean-and-chicken fajitas. The salsa is out of a jar, a local store brand. The tortillas are cold and clammy and the chicken has had every last drop of moisture cooked out of it. It is a cursory dinner, clearly not the intended focus of the evening. Alison begins to wonder, with some concern, what the real focus is.

After dinner they drink some more, then Harlan gets up to take the plates to the kitchen. "A little thing I like to do for Linda," he explains. "Be a man, Ed, give me a hand here."

The two leave the room, balancing the plates in their arms. Edward is weaving dangerously. His shoulder bumps the kitchen doorway and Alison winces. She remembers the booze-soaked dinner parties they used to have, the giant vats of food, the shouted conversations during which not enough could ever seem to be said. And later, when the guests had gone, love. Their grad-student pals, with their retro eyeglasses and liter bottles of red wine, where are they now? Los Angeles, Costa Rica, Alaska. She and Edward were so smug about staying: real people stay put, they told themselves. And here they are, right where they wanted to be.

She turns back to Linda and has to stifle a gasp. The older woman has come to life: hands on her knees, she leans forward as if to impart a powerful secret. Her eyes glow orange in the firelight, her skin is flushed—and how did her neck get to be so long and muscled? She looks like . . . a cheetah.

Alison realizes that this is it. The moment. She is about to learn why they were asked here.

"Where is your bathroom?" she asks.

Startled, Linda coughs, licks her lips. A small smile arranges itself. She points to the stairs.

"Second door on the left."

———

In the kitchen, Edward drops the plates on the counter. For a moment he is disoriented enough to mistake the sound for a flying object, and he ducks. His brain stays where it was, though, and the room doubles. He blinks hard. When his vision is restored, the face of Harlan looms.

"I got a lot of good friends," Harlan says.

"Not me," Edward replies. He's trying to be funny, but suddenly this doesn't seem funny at all. Perhaps because it is true.

"People in law enforcement, people in the courts," the judge goes on, ignoring the interruption. "One particular friend of mine is located in Cambridge, Mass."

"Never heard of it." Harlan is very close, leaning right over him, giving off an odor. It's the smell of mentholated salve. Has he got arthritis? Edward feels sorry for the older man, sorry for the life he's leading here on the lake, in the house, with the wife. He's sorry for having come to dinner. The fajitas are a bitter ball inside him.

"Sure you have. You've been there."

"Have I?" says Edward.

"Yes, you have. You were there between the years of 1981 and 1987. You went to college there. Remember that?"

"Sheesh," Edward tells him. "I sure don't know. Do you think I could help myself to a glass of water?" Was it really that long ago? He still has dreams about college, in which important mail is waiting for him in his campus mailbox and he can't remember the combination.

Incredibly, Harlan moves even closer. "You had yourself a little business there, didn't you, Eddie?"

"I was an English major."

"You were in sales and distribution."

"Nah."

"Unfortunately your little business came to the attention of the Harvard administration. You were spared prosecution in exchange for your permanent absence from the campus. After that you got yourself enrolled at Tufts and slunk outta there a couple years later. Is this refreshing your memory?"

"You bet it's refreshing. I don't even need that water anymore."

Harlan attempts a grin, but the corners of his mouth don't seem to be cooperating. "Keep cracking those jokes, pothead," he whispers, and the whispers clatter around the gleaming disinfected kitchen. Behind Harlan, on the counter, Edward spies the takeout boxes from Taco Treat. Two of them, then four, then eight. Then just one. Oh dear. "Seems that your records with the agency lacked this important information. I took the liberty of updating them for you."

"The agency?"

"The adoption agency."

Something is welling up inside Edward, something acid and explosive, first in his churning stomach, then in his esophagus, then in his throat. How dare this man judge me, he thinks—but then again, that's what judges do. They make judgments! And then it's out of him and all over the room: hot laughter, cracking the air. Judgments! He falls against the counter, tears pouring from his eyes. Harlan has taken a step back. He's put on his workaday face, the one he must wear as he pretends to listen carefully to all the evidence. Edward is gasping for breath.

"What the hell?" Harlan says.

Edward pounds the counter, hurting his hand. It feels great! He can't seem to speak, but what would he say? The picnic, the Breeces, this house, it's all so fucking funny! Maybe he and Alison should give up on the sex and do this at night instead, get drunk and tell jokes.

But Harlan doesn't seem to get it, and he doesn't seem to like not getting it. He sets himself in a bearish crouch, and his lip curls under, and the fuzzy panhandle rears back. Yikes!

Edward finds himself on the floor, his legs splayed on the terra-cotta quarry tile, his back against the cabinets. Hey, how'd he get down here? The cabinets are light blue, with red lizards stenciled on them. The whole right side of his face seems to be throbbing, yet giggles are still coming out of him, like hiccups, involuntary and annoying. Harlan has cured Edward's indecision. There will be no adoption.

"You son of a bitch," Edward hears. And then he is yanked to his feet and flung through the kitchen door.

"You can find your own coat, asshole," shouts the judge.

Alison's feet are silent in the carpeted hallway. It's different up here, the walls are bare. When she shows a house, the upstairs hallways are always like this: hollow-core doors, shag carpeting, a life-swallowing softness. This is where she always loses the buyer, right here, as her enthusiasm leaves her.

If only enthusiasm meant anything to the State of New York. If only the sprawl and scatter of lived life was worth anything: then their house, their home, would be all the application they needed. But it was all too easy to see it through the eyes of the agency. The basement full of nail-riddled scrap lumber. The tangle of extension cords behind the sofa. The champagne stain on the living-room ceiling. All of it screaming *unfit*.

But this! Alison cannot compete with this. A blameless, immaculate hallway, erased of all evidence. As if in cahoots with her heart, her bladder grows heavier.

The second door on the left. There it is, the only one open. A dim light shines from inside. She can hear voices in the kitchen, Harlan's and Edward's, exchanging confidences. It's so easy for men, she thinks, so hard for women. Men of any class have football and fishing to discuss; women have nothing. Or worse, they have children. Or worse still, no children.

She enters the bathroom and sees a bed. Obviously she's made a mistake. She peeks out into the hall: second door on the left. No, it was no mistake. She's exactly where Linda wants her. The bedroom walls are painted bright blue and red, and there is a small desk with a colorful computer on it, and there is a boom box and shelves stacked with comic books. The wallpaper is patterned with cartoon characters. There's a Buffalo Bills throw rug.

Instinct tells her to leave immediately, to grab Edward's arm and yank him out of the house. But she still has to pee. She spins and walks stiffly into the hall. She tries each door until she finds the real bathroom, a dimly lit fun house of globe lights and gilt mirrors.

Then she happens to glance down the stairs and sees the back of Linda's head, the tight, ugly coif, and she changes her mind.

She goes back into the boy's room. There is a Knicks trash can in the corner by the desk. She pulls it out a little and looks down into it, at the pale, blurred oval at the bottom, her face.

Can she do it? That is, physically? There is only one way to find out. It was hot enough today for her not to have worn panty hose, and that makes it easier.

Crouched over the can, she is amazed at the loudness of it, like rain on a corrugated tin roof.

———

He's drunk, she drives. They aren't fighting; that will happen later. What they're doing now is thinking. Alison is thinking, To hell with adoption. Give me the drugs. If I get pregnant with eight babies, they can kill six. It's worth it to me. I will populate the world with bold, honest, sloppy people like myself. And if Edward can't deliver, I will use another man's sperm, from a lab. She is amazed that she can remember the doctor's phone number: if she had to, she could pull over at a convenience store and leave a message with the answering service. She feels fecund and powerful and reckless and correct in everything. Every thought is gilded, and sharp as a dagger.

Meanwhile, Edward is having a fantasy. He and Alison have gone back to college. They live in a dorm, with roommates who never go out: for Edward, a brooding bicyclist who always leaves sweaty towels lying around; for Alison, an angry feminist with tangled hair. How hard it is to be together, and how sweet. They meet in dark and lonely places for whispers and for sex: an abandoned carrel in the engineering library, the woods behind the physical plant, a supply closet in the business school. They talk about what it will be like someday when they're married and have a house of their own: a place all to themselves, where they'll never be bothered by other people. They'll make love in every room. They'll confess their deepest secrets, or better yet, they won't have any.

Edward is asleep when they get home. Poor Edward, lolling half-conscious in the passenger seat, reminds Alison of a mannequin. No, a dummy: a marriage-test dummy, with a heart-shaped target on his chest where he keeps getting pounded. She unbuckles his seat belt and shakes him, but he refuses to wake. All he will do is quietly moan. So she leaves him there, in the car. Later on, showered, cold-creamed, nightgowned, she'll lie in their bed not sleeping, her fingers on her belly, waiting for the sound of the door.

SEE YOU IN PARADISE

Brant Call was a pretty nice guy. He lived in a small rented house on a quiet street in the town where he went to college. He always shoveled his walk when it snowed and he always said hi to passing neighbors, and though he was young (he'd graduated only a couple years before) he acted like he was thirty-seven, and everybody liked him for it.

And Brant liked that everybody liked him. When somebody told him how much they liked one or another of his good qualities, he reacted by striving to enhance that quality, so as to become nicer still. Nobody ever pointed out his bad qualities—which included gullibility, impatience, and a creeping smugness—because they thought it might upset him, and in this they were right. In Brant's world, people did not point out others' bad qualities. He grew up in the suburbs, hauled old ladies' trash cans to the curb, and was named after a beach in New Jersey. He was not introspective. It didn't occur to him that being universally liked might be a bad thing, or even illusory.

He still worked at the college he'd attended, as managing editor of the alumni magazine of the business school. The year Brant started working there, the magazine had been rated one of the top five business school alumni magazines in America, and he took pride in this honor, though he didn't have much to do with it. He referred to the magazine as "we," as in, "We gotta up our donations this year," and occasionally when he did this the person he was speaking to became confused and had to ask whom he meant by "we." He said this very thing once to a woman about whom the magazine was running an article, and the woman tilted her head, smiled microscopically, tucked a blond lock behind a pink ear, and said, "We you, or we who do you mean?"

The woman was named Cynthia Peck. She was a senior at the college and her father owned one of the fifty largest corporations in America. The article was to be a rich-heiress's-eye view of the business school, in which Cynthia would be portrayed as being in training to assume her rightful position (as Leyton Peck's only child) at the helm of Peck, Inc. Brant had volunteered to write it himself because he hoped to secure a big honking donation for the magazine, and the editor-in-chief agreed because he thought Brant's niceness might actually cause this to happen. And so, at the end of an hour-long interview, during which it became clear that Cynthia Peck was not going to be at the helm of anything complicated in the near future, he made the comment about having to up the donations. And when she said, "We you, or we who do you mean?," he said, "We me, or I mean we us. The magazine. I was wondering if you, or rather your company—or I mean your dad's company, might consider donating some, you know, money, so we can go on doing what we're doing in terms of work, which is being one of the top five business school alumni magazines in America."

Cynthia Peck's tiny smile became a slightly larger smile, and then a kind of smirk, and when the lock of hair fell over her eye again she didn't move it. Instead she peered around it, discreetly licked her lips, and said, "Are you trying to ask me out?"

Brant almost said no. Instead, he tried to blush, and found that, to his surprise, his face was already hot and his head already half-turned away, and he said, "Well . . ."

"Well what?"

"Well, I guess I am. You want to go out?"

"Be more specific."

"To dinner?"

"More specific."

"My place?"

"Try again."

"A restaurant."

She raised her eyebrows.

"Seven Sisters?" he said, because this was the only place in town anybody could conceivably take the daughter of one of the richest men in America, a Frenchy sort of sit-down place up on the hill with turrets and flags and prices that could make your hair stand on end. And indeed, the name made her sit up straight and nod her head in congratulations, and she said, "When?" and he said, "Uh, tonight?" and she said, "Friday," and he said, "Friday." He asked if he should pick her up around eight and she said eight thirty, and he asked if she wanted to go anywhere afterward and she said We'll see. Then she handed him a little card with her name, address, and phone number printed on it, and walked out the office door.

Later on, the editor-in-chief asked him how it went and would they be getting the money, and Brant, in response to both questions, said "I have no idea."

Looking at her over dinner, Brant realized that he found Cynthia pretty attractive, though she was generally known on campus as "The General's Horse" because of her bulky frame and equine features: a broad nose, an elongated face, and wide-set eyes. But her face was open and expressive, if not entirely intelligent, and she had nice hair, a sexy walk, and a terrific bosom, the exposed cleft of which, invitingly peeping out from behind two unbuttoned folds of silk, he tried the entire evening to keep his eyes off of. They talked about the college, about roommates they'd had, about New Jersey, where both of them had grown up (vastly different New Jerseys, sure, but they both used to drive an hour to visit the same mall). In fact they got on just great, and after dinner they went back to her place and made out for the better part of an hour, and Brant got to stick his hand down her bra and the back of her underpants.

A sort of courtship followed. Brant and Cynthia were seen around together, holding hands and smooching on benches. The magazine got its donation, and Brant asked for and received a raise. Six months went by, and graduation was coming, and Brant considered buying Cynthia an engagement ring. Ultimately he decided against it: he had to prove to her, somehow, that he didn't want her money. The problem was, of course, that he did want her money, and this seemed wrong to him, though he was certain he would want her whether she was rich or not. Of course, her being rich was part of what made her who she was, and was the reason he met her in the first place, and so trying to extricate her wealth from his affection was pointless—and yet he tried it anyway.

In May Brant got his suit dry cleaned and went to her commencement. It took place in the football stadium. The speaker was Ellen DeGeneres. This had been a controversial choice for many reasons, but she didn't talk about being a lesbian or about being on TV, and everyone seemed very calm and attentive. For most of the speech, Brant scanned the rows of seniors with the binoculars he'd brought along. When he finally found Cynthia, she was whispering and giggling with her friends. He watched her whisper and giggle for the rest of the ceremony.

That night her father threw a party at Seven Sisters. Brant had rented a tux, but when he arrived he realized that nobody else was wearing one. So he went home and put his suit back on and re-arrived, this time late. There were ten large round tables filled with people just getting started on their glasses of wine, and one of them contained an empty chair. Next to the chair was Leyton Peck, and on his other side sat Cynthia, looking not just attractive but really pretty, her skin ruddy from the sunny commencement, her eyes subtly made-up, her lips lipsticked. She saw him and motioned him over, and he took his place next to her father.

Peck was in the middle of a story to which everyone was intently listening, their shoulders thrown forward over their plates, their faces frozen into expectant grins. Peck spoke in a cigar-roughened baritone, his hands curiously out of sight beneath the table, which Brant felt privileged to know was the result of prematurely blossoming liver spots. This small bit of inside information enabled him to listen to the story with something approaching the appropriate level of attention.

". . . and so I say to the guy, 'Look, I know this task sounds boring, but the reason our company has the number one industrial coatings division in America can be summed up in two words: Quality Control. So what I need you to do is keep your eye on each patch of paint through every stage of the drying process.' The guy nods, like he's getting it all, so I keep on talking. 'Drying doesn't just happen, there are a series of crucial aridity thresholds that are passed, and during each of them any number of microscopic fissures can appear. These fissures close quickly, but they negatively impact the long-term stability of the coating. So I want you to get your face right up on there and make sure no cracks appear and disappear. If any develops, you mark it there on your patch diagram, and below each crack you detect, I want you to mark its duration, have you got that?' Okay, sure, the guy's nodding, nodding, it all sounds very important to him, right? So I tell him, 'Each of these cans behind you represents a production run, I need you to test every one of them, the paint dries hard in two and a half hours, so you'll be able to do three a day. So get to work.'"

Peck looked around the table, faintly smirking, for several seconds before he delivered the punch line. "The guy watched paint dry for two and a half months!"

Brant laughed along with everyone else, but mostly he watched Cynthia laugh. He was shocked to discover that he had never seen her laugh before (not with true abandon, anyway—giggling didn't count), which is to say that he himself had never made her laugh. Well, why not? He was funny, right? Couldn't he do a wide range of voices, including Old Jewish Lady, Old Black Guy, and Duck? Wasn't he good at sneaking up on squirrels and then shouting "Booga-booga-booga?" Didn't he own the entire run of *Monty Python's Flying Circus* on DVD? He could, he was, he did! But he had never seen Cynthia like this: her hands clutching her cleavage, her mouth gulping air, her eyes wrinkled shut like a prizefighter's. She looked . . . indecorous. He was loath to imagine what kind of hideous air-guitar faces he made when they were porking, but as for Cynthia, she always looked serene, sleepy, disappointingly pleased, as if there might be a hidden camera somewhere recording the moment for inclusion in some kind of X-rated home furnishings catalog. This was entirely different, this elasticized guffaw, and he didn't much care for it. She looked like Seabiscuit, for crying out loud.

It took a couple of seconds for the hilarity to wane and for the guests to realize that they would now be expected to amuse themselves. During this awkward silence, Peck turned to Brant and, loudly enough so that others should hear, said, "You must be that Brant."

"Yes!" Brant replied brightly.

The two stared at each other for a moment, and in that moment Brant saw his chance with this man roar past, flag-waving revelers shouting out its bunting-underslung windows, and recede into the distance. It was gone before he even knew what it was, a distant speck leading a dust cloud.

Peck was smiling at him. Brant had seen this face before, of course, in flash photographs in magazines or pen-and-inked onto the front page of the *Wall Street Journal;* it was familiar but unmemorable, like a second-rate old pop song. And the eyes: you'd expect the eyes of a man like this to be direct, penetrating, alive: but instead they were furtive, blurred, facing in slightly different directions. The skin was sallow, blotched, creased; the cheeks cadaverous. But the forehead! This, Brant thought, was what did all the work, this gleaming hemisphere that looked like it had been dragged here by a glacier. It bore neither hairs nor pores, this wall, and behind it the killing thoughts cozied up against one another. As Brant gazed at it the mouth beneath it opened and words came out. "Perhaps we ought to shake hands, Brant."

"Oh, sure!"

Peck took Brant's hand, but took it limply, making Brant's strong grip, intended to express a marriageable masculine confidence, instead seem like a withering critique of the old man's waning virility. Peck actually winced, and Brant jerked his hand away. "Uh, I ought to thank you, sir, for the—"

"Please," Peck said, secreting the hand back under the table, "there's no need to grovel. Now, Brant."

"Yes, sir?"

"You're diddling my daughter."

"Yes, sir."

"You're thinking of marrying her, right?"

"Uh, yes."

"Getting yourself a piece of the family fortune?"

"Well, that's—"

"Don't be ashamed, Brant, that's how I got started on mine. I took one look at Cynthia's mother, at that stunning horse face and that glorious udder, and I said to myself, there's a twenty-four-carat cunt if I ever saw one. You can believe I got in there but quick."

There was nothing Brant could say to this; if he protested, he would be branded a liar; if he agreed, he would be a prick. If he said nothing, he would be a weakling. He said, "Uh huh!"

"But I'm not a pussy, Brant, and neither are you. I had to work for my supper, and so will you. I did my time at her father's company, and so will you."

"I will?"

"Yes. You're going to man the home office."

"I am?"

"Yes. You're going to become chief of operations at headquarters." Brant didn't get it. He said, "In New York?"

Peck laughed—it was what he wanted to hear. "Guyamón."

"Guyamón?"

"It's a lesser Bermuda. A tax dodge. We have to have an office there. Staffed by a staff of one. The job is currently occupied, but if you say yes, he's fired." Peck removed a cell phone from his pocket—a rather large one by present standards, mid-nineties vintage, a charming affectation. "If you say no, you can get the hell out of my daughter's graduation party, and if you ever again so much as fondle a tit I'll have all your arms broken. And don't think I can't do it."

Brant looked past him to Cynthia, who, though while theoretically engaged in a conversation with an avid middle-aged couple, was glancing his way, her eyebrows expectantly arched, her mouth tilted in a hopeful, nervous smile. He had to admit that, for the whole night up until now, he had not been feeling super about Cynthia. The party had cast a tawdry light upon her; she did not seem worth all the hoopla, which in turn felt excessive, striving. But now, after staring at her father's creepy mug for minutes on end, Brant experienced a loosening of critical faculties, and saw Cynthia as lovely and strong, and remembered her playfulness, her sexual enthusiasm, and her beautiful car, and suddenly he felt that he could not do without her. Something about her laugh, the one her father had drawn from her, made him hesitate, but it wasn't enough. He wanted her. Hell, he loved her! He turned back to her father. He said, "I'll do it."

"Great," said Peck, without much enthusiasm, and pushed two buttons on the phone. "Serkin? Peck. You're fired. The plane leaves at seven p.m. Thursday. Get on it, or you're stuck. Goodbye." He pushed another button, and then two more. "Book Brant's flight," he said, and hung up.

"Go home," he said now to Brant, tucking the phone back into his jacket pocket.

"Home?"

"To pack. You're leaving tomorrow. A car will pick you up at noon. Good luck." He cleared his throat and fell upon his meal, which had been placed before him by a napkin-draped arm.

"But don't I—"

"Go," muttered Peck through a mouthful of broccoli. "Don't worry about the details. A packet will be waiting for you in the car. Go ahead, smooch your honey and vamoose."

He rose, went over to Cynthia. "I have to go," he whispered in her ear.

"So you said yes?"

"Yes."

"Oh, Brant!" she said, and craned her neck to kiss him. When he hazarded a glance at her father, he could see that he was paying no attention at all.

———

He left a message for his boss on voicemail. "I'm sorry," he explained, "Peck's making me take this job. I'll send you an email." But he wondered if there would even be email on Guyamón, or restaurants, or television. He would miss restaurants and television—would miss delivery food, football. But surely Guyamón had these things—it was the Bahamas, it was a tourist destination. Probably there would be cool mixed drinks served at rattan taverns on the beach. There would be friendly natives in colorful shirts, and drunk Americans, and crazy birds that made crazy sounds. "Don't worry about your apartment," a voice had said on his answering machine when he got home from the commencement dinner. "Don't worry about anything. It will all be taken care of. Bring only those things you can't do without." For Brant, these were: his "property of" shirt from the business school, his Bob Marley CDs (and wasn't Guyamón near Jamaica? Maybe he ought to have an atlas), a picture of his mom, a picture of Cynthia (presented to him on his birthday, it was taken by a famous fashion photographer Brant had never heard of and tucked into a neat silver frame), and a toothbrush. He brought along three suits and seven shirts, as well. All the next morning he tried to get in touch with Cynthia, but she wasn't home. He left five messages. His boss called him and pleaded. He called his mother and sister, both of whom told him he was nuts. That was okay. In fact it was great! He felt, briefly, as if he were on the threshold of a fabulous future. "We thought he was nuts, but in the end, Brant was right."

A dented Lincoln picked him up; the driver wore an old-fashioned driver's hat and called him sir. He checked in at the airport, got on a plane, and flew first to New York, then Nassau. There, a gangly black man wearing aviator sunglasses (and why not?, he was an aviator) led him across a steaming tarmac to a little four-seater with a picture of a turkey stenciled on the side.

"What's with the turkey?" Brant shouted over the buzz of the engine, a buzz that seemed somehow insufficient.

The pilot pointed to his ear, shrugged.

In an hour they were above Guyamón, circling what appeared to be a volcano. Smoke was issuing from it in long windless streaks. The air was hot as hell, even in here. Brant was pitting out big time. It was evening. They landed on a cracked strip of concrete, the pilot swearing all the way in. Brant shuddered in his seat and conked his head on the roof.

"Hey, man," he asked the pilot as he got out. "That thing's inactive, right?" Meaning the volcano.

The pilot laughed good and long.

There was a car here, a jeep actually, US Army issue as far as Brant could tell, repainted with what looked like yellow latex housepaint. The driver was a fat white man wearing a spotless white shirt and a gigantic straw hat.

"You gonna need a hat for that bald patch," he said.

"I don't have a bald patch," said Brant. "Do I?"

The drive took half an hour. They traveled a mudded and potholed road to the base of the volcano, then turned right and edged around it. There were a lot of trees and ferns, except in the places where fresh lava had mowed them down. In places the lava covered the road and the jeep bumped jauntily over it. At last they arrived somewhere—a small stretch of paved cement before which stood a long row of cinder-block huts, about fifteen in all. They'd been built twenty or so years ago, and since then had been treated variously, some clearly abandoned and the windows and doors removed, some dolled up like vacation cottages. The jeep stopped in front of a middling one, its terra-cotta roof cracked and mossed, its walls in need of paint. The driver didn't bother turning off the engine. He handed Brant the key. Brant took it, then waited for instructions.

"You're supposed to get out," the driver said.

"What then?"

"Then I leave."

When the jeep was gone, Brant stood before the door, sweating. He put the key in the lock and turned it. The door creaked open.

The place had been ransacked. The mattress was slashed, stains that appeared to be red wine covered the walls. A dresser that stood at the foot of the bed seemed to have been urinated in. And in the middle of the floor sat a small pile of human feces, holding in place a handwritten note that read:

ENJOY THE TROPICS, WHORE!

———

A few days later, though, Brant was feeling pretty good about the whole thing. The cottage was equipped with a telephone, a computer, a fast internet connection, and satellite TV. He had spent most of his time so far watching baseball games, talking to friends in America, and enjoying pornography. He'd never liked pornography before, he hated to cave in to such base desires, but there didn't seem to be any girls here, and nobody he knew was likely to burst in on him, and so, from the computer's tiny speakers could be heard, at all hours of the day, the quiet moans of nude actresses as they masturbated before the masturbating him. Three times daily a little truck came clanking by, and the denizens of the cottage row—six in all—would amble out of their dens and eat the food their respective companies had paid for. There were burgers and french fries and imported beers. There were omelettes and apples—apples!, in the Bahamas!—and Dove bars and club sandwiches. The six men were always in, because they all had to answer the phone if it rang, although the phones never rang. After the truck left, they would stand around and talk, clutching their brown paper bags of loot. They didn't introduce themselves to Brant, but included him in their conversation as if he'd been there for a hundred years.

"See the Yanks?"

"Nah. Drooling over Nudie Village."

"Ya see the chick with the giant thatch?"

"Hell yeah!"

"What'd'ya get today?"

"Ham."

"Everybody got ham."

"I got yesterday's Molson if anybody wants it. I hate Molson."

"Hell yeah I want it."

"What'll you give me then?"

It took Brant a couple of days to find the courage to jump in, but once he did he was one of the guys. He caught a few names—Ron, Kevin, Pete. Pete was a cheerful man of thirty, thick around the middle, with dark eye bags that seemed genetic, rather than circumstantial. He held down the fort for an agribusiness conglomerate. One afternoon Brant was left alone with him after the others had gone home. He said, "So, does anybody go to the beach? Like, on breaks?" For he was allowed breaks, one hour out of every eight, and he had Sundays off. Sunday was tomorrow, his first here.

"There's a path out back. But it isn't much of a beach. Like ten feet, the rest is rocks."

"Is there a bar or something? In town?"

"No town. But there is a bar."

"Wanna go sometime?"

The question seemed to send shooting pains into Pete's head. He winced. "Ah, it's kinda far, and there are no girls."

"Oh."

So on Sunday Brant went to the beach, and Pete was right, it sucked. The rocks were sharp, and everything stank of fish. He went home, dejected. It had only been four days, and he could feel himself, his personality, shrinking to more or less nothing. He was Friendly Brant! He needed to greet passersby, to shake their hands! He wished there were some leaves to rake, some weatherproofing to do. But there wasn't any weather here. A little rain, a little sun. A little rain, a little sun. By noon he had already jerked off twice and played forty games of Donkey Kong. He decided to go visiting. He washed his hands and walked down to Kevin's place. Kevin had seemed okay to Brant, he told a joke once after Breakfast Truck, he had a nineties beard.

He knocked. "Yo, Kev!" he said.

From behind the door came sort of a muffled mumble that Brant thought was an invitation to enter, but when he opened the door Kevin was busy covering his and another man's (Brant hadn't gotten his name) naked sweating bodies with a sheet.

"Buzz off, asshole!"

"Sorry, dude!"

So much for dropping by. He had begun to prepare himself mentally for another encounter with his girl of the hour, Mandy Mounds, when he heard an unfamiliar noise coming from inside his cottage. What the hell was it? He opened the door and found that the noise, a kind of urgent, grating buzz, was the sound the phone made when it rang. The phone! It was ringing! Brant cracked his knuckles. Showtime!

"Hello?"

"I got a surprise for you!" The voice, though drunk, was recognizable as Cynthia's. It was coming to him through a haze of crackling interference.

"Hon bun!"

"I am having something delivered to your door," she said. Something about her tone seemed almost sinister, like the duplicitous sexpots in James Bond movies. He had to admit he liked it.

He said, "Where are you? You sound so far away." Duh!

"I'm on my cell. In a—whoop!—car."

"Isn't it illegal to talk on the phone while driving?"

"It's illegal to drive drunk, too, dummy. But I'm not driving."

"So what are you sending me?"

"Sposeta be a surprise."

"Is it delicious?"

"Yyyyes!"

"So you eat it?"

She snorted. "No, dipshit. You do." And with that she hung up.

Well. That was unproductive. He figured if she was sending the present now, he'd get it in what, two weeks? He opened up his browser and a couple minutes later Mandy Mounds filled the room with her delighted squeaking. He'd just got his shorts off when his door flew open and Cynthia came roaring in, hiking her sundress up to her waist. "You got yourself all ready!" she said, climbing on, and for ten or so minutes it was difficult to distinguish the sounds she made from the ones coming out of the speakers. Then they were finished and lay on the bed, unable to stop perspiring. At the computer desk, Mandy Mounds said, "More! More! More! More!"

"'Scuse me," said Cynthia, and she staggered naked across the room to switch off the computer. But first she paused, turning her head this way and that, checking out the competition. "I got better legs," she said.

"Sure."

"And her boobs look like saddlebags."

He didn't have much to say to that. She turned everything off. "I bribe Daddy's people. They bring me down here whenever I want." She hopped back onto the bed, sending him several inches into the air.

"But this is the first time you've been down here."

"Right. Hey, you wanna go to town?"

"There is no town."

"Who told you that?" she said.

They went to the other side of the volcano. The fat white guy drove them there. The little jeep shuddered and rumbled around lava flows and fallen trees, tossing them from side to side, against the doors of the jeep and each other. Cynthia laughed the entire trip, until they arrived at a little tent pavilion at the edge of what would have been a tourist paradise, if any tourists were there. Instead there were handsome black people in loose-fitting clothes, dancing to the music from a little amplified calypso band, and beyond them was a bar that was little more than a rusted metal cart covered with bottles and plastic cups, and beyond that was a dirt road leading to a lot of little houses. Cynthia paid the driver with a thick stack of bills, which he folded and stowed like a pro, and told him to wait. He said, "I'll be easy to find," and lurched into the fray.

They danced and drank all afternoon, and then ate parts of some kind of giant pig roasting on a spit, and they ate some kind of spicy thing wrapped up in leaves, and some sort of reeking but impossibly sweet fruit, and then they danced and drank some more, and the people, the villagers, didn't seem to mind them being there. Cynthia paid for everything and then some, handing people money at the slightest pretext, the band for playing something more up-tempo, the bartender for giving her a clean cup, a random bystander for letting her get ahead in the roasted-pig line. Soon after dark she took Brant by the hand and led him into the woods, where she fell to her knees at the base of a palm tree and puked, and then when Brant bent over to help her up, he puked as well. Then they sort of fell over on their way back, then they seemed to be asleep for a while, then they got up and found the jeep, which the driver was asleep in. They woke him up and he drove, drunk, back to the cottage row. Cynthia and Brant stumbled into his cottage and collapsed on the bed and woke up at noon. They tried sex but were too queasy to finish.

All day Brant lay half-in and half-out of sleep. At some point he opened his eyes to find Cynthia staring at his face, as if looking for something she'd misplaced. When he woke again, she was gone. Brant noticed the voicemail light blinking on his phone. He picked up the receiver, supporting himself with a trembling hand, and punched in his code.

The first message said, "If you aren't there in fifteen minutes, you're fired."

The second message said, "If you aren't there in ten minutes, you're fired."

The third said, "Five minutes."

The fourth: "You're fired. Your ride leaves at seven PM. Miss it and you're stranded."

It was 7:35.

———

Back home, behind his desk at the alumni magazine, the sounds of neighing, whinnying co-workers interrupted his concentration, causing him to forget the phone numbers he was dialing, to fumble his pleas to donors. He had to stand up in his cubicle and address the crouching, tittering crew in a strained voice: "Look, you guys, it isn't funny, okay? I was stranded for almost a week with no home, and I don't think I would be laughing right now if it was you it happened to." He thought about quitting—that would show them—but the thoughts never got much past the vengeful-fantasy stage. Besides, you never got anything out of losing your cool. People respected you for taking their shit. He just decided to take it, and he took it, and eventually, though when, he couldn't have told you, the whole thing would just up and blow away.

The day after she left, he was awakened by his replacement, a man, or rather a guy, about his age, deep-voiced, clean-cut, sweating respectably little in his white oxford shirt. "I beg your pardon," he said. "I was under the impression that this was to be my cottage."

Brant had not given his next move much thought, beyond stopping by one of the other cottages and asking how often the plane came. Not very often, he learned. Now, he gathered his things and shoved them into his bag while the new guy checked out the computer. "May I erase these files?" he said, clicking around aimlessly.

"No," said Brant. "If you do, the computer will melt."

He took his suits—never removed from their garment bag—and slung them over his shoulder. Then he walked around the volcano to the pavilion, looking for the locals' party. It took all day to get there, and when he arrived he found that the tent had been taken down, and everyone was in their houses. He sat on the paving stones where he had danced a few nights before, and panted, his tongue thick and dry as a towel. He almost cried, he was so sad. Eventually he got up and knocked on somebody's door and blurted out the whole story, and the family that lived there gave him a drink of water and let him sleep on their floor.

They were nice, this family—a man, a woman, two little girls. They spoke English but rarely spoke. They sat around all day making things—the man, thin and dark and thickly bearded, carved driftwood into interesting little sculptures, and the woman, who might have been the hottest human being Brant had ever seen, embroidered miniature tapestries that served as the facing for the macramé shoulder bags that the girls made. Every once in a while they all paused for a meal—fish and fruit, delicious beyond imagining, which they shared with him—and in the evening they watched the sun set, visited their neighbors, drank banana homebrew, and generally had a good, solid time. Each morning a man burdened by giant army duffels arrived on a bicycle, and forms were filled out and exchanged, and the things the village produced were stuffed into the bags and taken away to be sold to tourists.

Through all this, Brant did basically nothing. He had a fever and the shits, slept in the daytime, and lay awake nights gasping for breath. He slept on the floor next to the girls' bed and listened to their indecipherable whispers, to their quiet laughter as they talked themselves to sleep. Eventually, his host told him that the plane would come the following day, and the jeep would only go as far as the cottage row (he called it the Business Village), so he had better get back. Brant thanked the family profusely; he told them he would repay their kindness. "Like, in money I mean," he added. "American dollars."

The man smiled. "No need for that."

"Seriously, no, I will."

The man shook his head. "Don't worry. We are rich."

"Yes, of course," Brant said, shaking his hand, "I can see that your lives are very rich here. Thank you."

"No," the man said. "I mean, we are rich. Your corporations pay us money. The cottages are ours." He smiled. "I could, what is it you say, I could buy and sell you many times over."

"Oh," Brant said, dropping the man's hand.

"Oh," the man repeated in apparent mockery, though his voice, his face, retained their earnestness.

Brant walked all the way back, fortified by a canteen of water the family had provided. When he got to his old cottage, he knocked and entered. His replacement was sitting in the swivel chair, watching a Mandy Mounds video. His hand shot out and turned off the screen. "What do you think you're doing!" he shouted.

"Relax."

"This is my cottage!"

"I'm just gonna sit here by the fan until the jeep comes, all right?"

"No you're not!" the replacement said, his arms flailing. He had cut off his chinos and the sleeves of his shirt.

I should have shat on the floor, Brant thought, while I had the chance.

In the end, he sat next to the road and dozed. The sound of the jeep woke him up. The fat guy unloaded the sack dinners and demanded money for the ride to the airport. Brant forked over what he had left. He was back home by morning, his house (thankfully, he had retained the lease) exactly the way he had left it. He took a shower, curled up in the hot and musty bed, and slept until the middle of the next day.

And that, he decided, was that. He got his job back, having after all secured the magic donation from Leyton Peck—who had not, contrary to Brant's worst fears, reneged on the deal. He reclaimed his cubicle, endured the jokes, and tried to forget about Cynthia. He stayed off the internet and enjoyed the cool fall weather.

At some point guilt got the best of him and he tried to write a thank-you note to the family who had helped him through that terrible week. He managed a few lines about how grateful he was and how maybe someday they would meet again and stuffed it into an envelope, and then sat at the kitchen table trying to figure out how the hell to address it. He got as far as—

> The family
> First cottage
> Behind the volcano
> Guyamón

—before muttering "Fuck it" and tossing the whole thing in the trash. And then he had a change of heart. He reached into the trash can, picked out the crumpled paper, and smoothed it flat; then he dropped it into the recycling bin. After that he felt a hell of a lot better.

HIBACHI

Five months after Philip and Evangeline were married, Philip dropped his briefcase and four folders worth of loose papers in a pedestrian crosswalk and was run down by an old woman in a large car who had failed to notice his crouched form in the road. The car's fender—it was an SUV, a Chevy Tahoe—struck him just below the left shoulder, and he was knocked over and dragged forty yards down the street, resulting in the loss of much of the skin on his right arm. At this point Philip had broken only his humerus, collarbone, and several ribs, and might have been spared further injury had the driver noticed he was there. But she didn't, and at the next corner the car loosed its grip on Philip, and he was thrown under the back right tire. The tire crossed him from hip to shoulder, breaking more ribs, all the bones of his right arm, and his spine. He was rushed to the hospital and remained unconscious for several days; when he woke, he was told that he was unlikely ever to walk again. Meanwhile, the woman who had run him down had continued on to Home Depot and bought three rhododendrons, a box of thirty-gallon trash bags, and a bottle of orange-scented kitchen cleaner, and when the police tracked her down, she snubbed them, apparently thinking they were collecting for the benevolent association. Eventually she would be given a two-hundred-dollar fine and a one-month suspension of her license. It was two months before Philip had even the strength to sit in the electric wheelchair Evangeline's health insurance had almost, but not quite, covered, and another four before a settlement came through that, to Philip's mind, could only be called modest.

Philip was forty-one; Evangeline was forty-three. They had no children and wanted no children. He was an accountant. She was an accountant. They both went by their full names and corrected anyone who mistakenly called them Phil or Angie. But such an occurrence was infrequent, as they had few friends. They lived in a small house on a quiet street one neighborhood over from the posh part of town, and by the time Philip had grown adept at maneuvering his wheelchair around the house, Evangeline had had a ramp constructed for his ingress and egress. Even so, winter had begun, and it was April before Philip ventured out.

When he did, Evangeline was at work, and his batteries ran out six blocks from home. The policeman he hailed was one of the two who had arrested the woman who ran him over, and on the way back to the house, with the wheelchair awkwardly wedged into the trunk of the cruiser, this man said to Philip, "You got a raw deal."

"I suppose I did," Philip replied.

"I'm sure you heard," he went on, "but that lady's nephew won the lotto and she moved to Florida."

"No," Philip replied, "I hadn't heard that."

The policeman carried him, fireman-style, into the house, laid him down on the sofa, and gamely saluted before leaving.

———

It would be fair, if not entirely accurate, to say that Philip's accident and special needs put a strain on the marriage. Certainly, they were anxious now. But they had not been married long enough to know what normal was for them. They slept in the same bed, but never made love—Philip's doctors disagreed on his prospects for sexual potency, and there had so far been no sign of its intruding upon their lives. That said, they had had little sex before the accident, either. Both of them claimed to enjoy it while in its throes, but neither had ever relished the negotiations, preparations, and embarrassments necessary for its initiation. They had friends—Bob from Evangeline's office and his wife, Candace; Roy from Philip's office and his wife, June—but after a few awkward bouquet-clutching visits to the hospital, Bob, Candace, Roy, and June disappeared, and nobody had come to the house since Philip returned to it wheelchair-bound. Occasionally Evangeline called them and left messages. Philip didn't have the heart to tell her to stop. They did both like eating out, but had not got around to doing it much before Philip was hurt. They had liked to read on the sofa after dinner in the evenings, and they still did, but Philip was more comfortable in his chair, and usually became extremely sleepy at about eight thirty, after which his head would slump onto his chest, and his book would fall from his hands onto the floor. He had been reading the same crime novel since he came home from the hospital.

Evangeline was a tall, modestly attractive woman with prematurely gray hair, a full face, the figure of someone ten years younger, and the eyeglasses of someone twenty years older. Philip, before his accident, had stood at about five feet seven, but gave the impression of strength, owing to a broad upper body and narrow hips, and a strong, plain, blocky face. In fact, he had never been especially confident physically, and always believed he was about to develop back pain like his father's, though he never did, until now, of course, when it was the least of his worries.

They only went on seven dates before they married, in a civil ceremony at the county courthouse. They had first kissed on the second date, gone to bed on the fourth, and gotten engaged on the sixth, and when, at their wedding, their families and coworkers had asked them who had proposed to whom, neither was able to come up with a definitive answer. It was the first marriage for both of them and, seventeen months after the wedding and a year after the accident, they both appeared certain that it would be the last.

———

Because their first anniversary, owing to Philip's recovery, had been inadequately observed, he decided to take Evangeline out for their year-and-a-half. He hired a driver to bring them to and from the restaurant so that she wouldn't have to drive him, and he practiced getting in and out of the car by himself, so that she wouldn't need to do that, either.

The restaurant he chose was a new one in town—a Japanese hibachi steakhouse just off the highway, near the mall. Upon first glance, the place didn't look promising, with framed posters on the walls and plastic willow branches arranged halfheartedly in vases on the chipboard tables. Six hibachi grills filled the far side of the room, arranged in groups of two and bracketed by countertops, where dining spectators were to sit. Philip and Evangeline were seated—with great fussing and wringing of hands over Philip's wheelchair, so eager was the staff to avoid pissing off their first cripple—between a small family glumly celebrating a teenager's birthday and a pair of college-age lovebirds with their arms wrapped around each other.

Orders were taken, and the hibachi chef came out—a tall Asian man (though not, Philip believed, Japanese) whose hat made him appear taller still—pushing a sturdy wheeled cart of brushed aluminum. On the cart were arranged their uncooked meals, as well as a mountain of butter, squeeze bottles of various liquids, coffee-mug-sized chrome spice shakers, and a canister of utensils.

A familiar dread came over Philip, the same one he felt whenever he was about to witness any kind of performance, whether on a stage or at his front door, behind the book of Mormon. He turned to his wife to express his feelings but was brought up short by the expression on her face: one of rapt attention and giddy anticipation.

It would have taken a trained eye to detect these emotions, but a trained eye was what Philip had, and he kept his mouth shut.

For the chef's part, he maintained an expression of mock dignity and spoke not at all. Philip understood that women probably found him very attractive. He began his presentation by squeezing some kind of clear liquid onto the grill's clean steel surface, then setting it on fire with a cigarette lighter. The flames shot up two feet and Philip reared back. Everyone laughed. The college girl screamed and snuggled deeper into her lover's arms.

Next he placed an egg on the grill where the flames had been and spun it with his thumb and middle finger. He drew a spatula from a holster on his belt—the belt was leather, with metal sheathes for his tools, giving him the air of a culinary Batman—and scooped up the spinning egg. He tossed it into the air; caught it, still spinning, on the spatula's end; tossed it again. Finally, he lobbed it toward the college girl, then shot out a long-fingered hand without looking and plucked it from the air inches from her face.

Her scream this time was truly earsplitting. Philip hated her, the way he had taken to hating random people since the accident: hated the scream, the lipstick, the giant breasts. He hated the boyfriend and his wounded masculine laugh, huh-huh-huh. But Evangeline—Evangeline was concentrating with all her might, her lower lip gently held captive between her teeth.

The chef flung the egg into the air, bisected it against his spatula, flipped the shell into the trash. He scrambled the egg, spooned rice on top, spun his knife in the air—and by the time he caught it, a pile of green onions had materialized on the grill for him to chop.

It went on like this for ten minutes. The guy was big on throwing. Chicken breasts, steaks sailed through the air. A rain of shrimp, a fusillade of squash. Sauce bottles he lobbed from hand to hand and back into their holsters. Metal glinted and chimed. There was a lot of winking, especially at the teenager's nervous mother, and a lot of spinning around to catch things left suspended. When the cooking was done, the food rocketed onto the plates, and not a morsel was spilled. The diners clapped, the chef bowed. He scraped the grill free of debris, scrubbed it, and, with a final, comically deep bow, wheeled his cart away.

Philip had to admit that his meal was very good, fresh and unadorned. He didn't especially want to see the floor show again, but the food he liked. When they were through eating, they left, and in a wild, impetuous gesture of magnanimity, Philip tipped nearly 20 percent. Their driver, unfortunately, had to be hunted down; they discovered him behind some shrubbery, smoking with a waitress from the Applebee's next door. He brought them home and once again Philip tipped, though not so much this time around. Then they went inside and went to bed.

The mattress conveyed to Philip the information that Evangeline lay awake, staring at the ceiling. She rarely said much, but tonight she had said nothing at all, not since they left the house. He glanced at her. In the light from the street, he could see that her cheeks were flushed, her forehead slightly wet. She exuded the tense stillness that came over her when she was trying to keep her breaths even, to trick her body into sleep.

"Did you enjoy dinner?" he asked.

"Yes," was her immediate answer.

"We should do that again."

She managed a nod.

After a moment, and with considerable effort, Philip turned his body to face her, and snaked his hand up underneath her nightdress to cup one breast, then the other. After that he slid his fingers between her legs. She didn't resist, but she didn't help him out, either. It was warm and dry down there, and stayed that way. He thought perhaps he felt something, himself—some kind of faint stirring or itch? At times he experienced ghost sensations, dreams his body entertained while it slept. But maybe this was the real thing. He shoved a hopeful free hand into his pajama bottoms: no dice. Evangeline, having evidently read his mind, trained upon him a kind, pitying look. "Thank you, dear," she said. Probably she was referring to the dinner.

The next day, everything was back to normal. Philip returned to the half-time, halfhearted work his firm now offered him, perhaps out of pity; Evangeline returned to the office. Months passed in much the same sort of stasis they used to, with the exception that, every once in a while, Evangeline assumed an expression of squinting intensity, as though she was looking at something very small and very far away. But he didn't ask what she was thinking of. Once, while wheeling past the recently expanded bathroom, with its widened door, chrome support hardware, and disinfected-daily bathtub stool, he heard a small surprised sound escape his wife, a kind of chirp or hoot, which reverberated on the tile like a gunshot. It was repeated seconds later, longer this time, drawn-out, a coo. When she came out a couple of minutes later, smoothing her dress with her long fingers, she didn't look any different.

Her birthday was approaching. Philip trolled his usual internet haunts to find something for her that might result in some kind of reaction. Kitchen supplies, he thought—she uses them daily, and not without pleasure. At least he would get to see his gift in action, see it making her infinitesimally happier. He browsed a commercial kitchen retailer, noticed the chef's hats, remembered their night out. Typed "Hibachi" into the search box. Hit enter.

There it was! The Oiled Birch and Stainless Steel Professional Hibachi Kitchen Island and Accessory Kit, fourteen hundred dollars plus freight delivery. His finger hovered over the mouse button. Philip was no good at gifts—he usually bought Evangeline jewelry, because it was something that men were supposed to buy for women, though he had never seen her wear any of it, nor any other jewelry, either. It was months after giving her earrings that he noticed her ears weren't pierced. Even the leather eyeglass case he had gotten her had gone unused; her glasses were only ever on her bedside table or her face.

And so the accountant in him, which almost entirely filled his broken self, told him not to pull the trigger on the hibachi set. It was expensive and untested; its size would prevent Evangeline's being able to pretend it didn't exist. And if it was a mistake—surely, it was?—it would have to be rectified. And able-bodied Evangeline would be the one to whom this responsibility would fall.

Nevertheless, he did it. He clicked that button, signed off on the exorbitant shipping charge, and let out a long, light-headed breath.

The following week, a DHL truck pulled into the driveway and a slim, large-headed, babyish man with gangly, flopping arms hand-trucked several enormous cardboard cartons onto the front stoop. The man was sweating and panting and stared unabashedly at Philip's strapped-down legs as he handed over the plump electronic signature tablet.

While Philip signed his name, the man asked, "So what happened to you?"

Being asked this was so unusual that Philip stared, briefly, in incomprehension before answering, "I got run over."

"You got somebody to unpack this for you, right?"

"No," Philip said, handing back the tablet.

"What is it, like a grill?"

"Sort of."

The guy stood there, nodding. It dawned on Philip that the man's arm-flopping was actually a kind of tic. The unoccupied arm was twitching and flexing, the hand pale and dead-looking at its end. He couldn't have been thirty, but his chin was underslung with loose flesh, which was misted over by a few days' beard stubble, gray like a mold. He glanced at his watch.

"Can you help me, maybe?" Philip asked him.

"Whaa, with this?"

"I can't open it. I can't even stand up."

The man looked at his watch again, and suddenly began to chew a nonexistent stick of gum. "Hunh," he said. And then, unexpectedly, "Yeah hell sure."

No UPS driver would ever have even bothered stopping to chat, let alone open packages, but that's what this guy did. He hung around for a good hour and a half, unboxing and assembling the hibachi set as Philip looked on in wonder. All the while he chewed his lack of gum (wasn't this supposed to be the purview of very, very old men?) and maintained a steady stream of random chatter, touching upon barbecuing (good eatin' but not worth the effort), neighbors (annoying), dogs (indispensable, but annoying), cats (not worth a shit), women (can't live with 'em etc.), alcoholic beverages (a curveball here—"a real destroyer of families"), fathers (all bastards), and finally (via a story about his own father stealing the cushions off his neighbor's porch furniture as a practical joke, and the neighbor calling the cops, and his father actually spending the night in jail) back to neighbors. And as it happened, both the man's arms, though equally floppy, were entirely functional, brilliant in fact, assembling the hibachi in a blur of flesh and metal, while the instruction manual lay untouched on the counter.

It was even more impressive in person than on the web site. It filled the kitchen like a car someone had parked there. The dully gleaming brushed-steel cooking surface, outlined by a grease channel and then by a six-inch expanse of waxed hardwood; the attached stainless accessory trays, with their cargo of squeeze bottles and seasoning shakers and cleaning and cooking implements; the galvanized tent overhead, suspended upon four sturdy posts, which housed the state-of-the-art whisper-quiet exhaust system, as efficacious at the displacement of air as (so said the manual) "a small aircraft engine"—all of it gave the impression of power, efficiency, professionalism. It looked like the real thing. Philip hoped to hell Evangeline liked it.

To the DHL delivery man he offered his profound thanks and a fifty-dollar tip. The former was accepted, the latter refused. "Nah, nah, I could get in hot water over that."

"You won't get in hot water for being two hours behind schedule?"

A squint, a nod. "Yeh, that's true," he said, taking the fifty bucks. He turned to leave. "Yeh, so, sorry about the legs! Hope you get better."

"I won't, I'm afraid."

This seemed to anger the man. "Hey. Miracles happen." And he was gone.

Philip wheeled himself across the house and into the kitchen. It was strange and slightly frightening, being alone with the hibachi—the thing seemed faintly, subtly alive, like a killer robot from space. He took stock of the transformed room: the gleaming refrigerator, humming in the corner; the oven and dishwasher; the coffeemaker and toaster and bread machine and all the other useful stuff he could only reach and operate with great and humiliating effort—they now seemed to be in collusion with the hibachi, in a concerted effort to make him feel very small and weak and soft. But he was thirsty, so he attempted to wheel himself carefully around the hibachi in order to reach the sink. There was perhaps half an inch of clearance on either side of his chair, and his knuckles aligned perfectly with the sharp flange of aluminum that supported the hibachi's oaken rail. But then he had to avoid a cabinet knob on his left, overcompensated, and felt the skin flaying off two of his right knuckles. For crap's sake. Well, he'd develop calluses. He finally reached the sink, where he filled a glass with water and left the tap running gently and pinkly over his bleeding hand.

It was there that Evangeline found him. He hadn't heard her footsteps, only the little gasp that escaped her as she entered the room. He turned off the water, wrapped a dish towel around his fingers, and backed out to sit beside her. Her hand fell to his shoulder. She was standing very straight and tall, gazing with preternatural alertness through her thick glasses, her eyes roaming over the hibachi, taking in its stunning alien solidity. "Oh," she said. She stepped forward, ran her hands over the wood, the steel. She lifted each utensil out of its holder, opened the drawers, found the utility belt and hat. These she removed and put on, adjusting the belt around her waist, smoothing out her dress underneath it. She slipped the utensils— the long two-tined fork, the chef's knife, the oil and teriyaki sauce— into the belt and let her hand travel over them, not quite touching, as though testing their aura.

She looked very sexy. The belt accentuated her hips, and with her hair bundled underneath the ivory chimney of a hat, years had dropped from her face. Already tall, she now appeared, from his vantage point, to be some kind of giant, some impossible avenging force. She was smiling at him, a smile simultaneously of pity and gratitude, and he smiled back.

"I hope you like it."

Her only response was a nod.

"Happy birthday."

But already she was trying to figure out how to operate the thing, opening the double doors underneath and adjusting the valve on the propane tank. Philip tied the dishrag fast around his hand and wheeled out carefully, trying not to make any noise. He closed the kitchen door behind him and went to the living room to read.

———

For much of a week he saw little of her. She went to work, returned from work, and headed straight for the kitchen, and from behind the closed door he heard all manner of scraping, clanking, hissing, and sizzling. The house smelled wonderful at six, when he was hungry, and the food she placed before him at the table was fresh and flavorful, every bit as good as what they'd eaten at the restaurant. But at ten, eleven, twelve midnight, burning onions were the last thing he wanted to be smelling, and he wished that she would shut the thing down and come to bed.

When she finally did, however, his patience was rewarded—at least this is how he chose to see it—by a strange new phenomenon. She strode into the dark bedroom, shucked off her clothes, showered, and then crawled into bed beside him, naked. She had never used to sleep naked. Philip had, in fact, never been in bed with a woman who slept naked. In any event, her nakedness was, for three days, otherwise uneventful; but starting on the fourth she began, and there was no way around recognizing that this was what she was doing, masturbating. Not the furtive sort that an unsatisfied spouse might wish to keep from his or her mate: no, she levered herself against him, then reached down and touched herself, emitting into his ear noises of pleasure he had not heard from her for a long time, if ever.

The first time she did this, he was simply shocked, and said and did nothing. He pretended, in fact, to sleep. But on the second, he hazarded a glance in her eyes, which were wide open and staring, and the two of them gazed at one another with great intensity for the three minutes the experience lasted. The next night they kissed, and the night after that she tried to get him going, too. She undressed him, touched him, kissed him, and though his blood quickened, his palms perspired the way they had before the accident, he could feel nothing where it mattered, and he wept.

Somehow, though, it must have gratified her, because she persisted night after night, and slowly his humiliation drained away—part of it, anyhow—and he was able, at last, to enjoy this new intimacy, however limited, however unsatisfying it had to be. During this ritual, they never spoke, and they said nothing about it during the day, either, and it was like a secret between them, a secret not from the world outside, which they had never been open to anyway, but from each other, and from themselves. It was strange and, at least to Philip, not quite right. But life was much better with it than without.

A couple of weeks after the hibachi arrived, Evangeline informed him that they were going to have a dinner party.

"Why?" he couldn't help asking.

"I've taken the liberty of inviting Bob, Candace, Roy, and June. They're coming here on Friday night."

For a moment, Philip thought, Who? Then he remembered their old acquaintances, and the question again turned to Why? The answer, for the moment anyway, did not reveal itself in Evangeline's face. Her eyes blinked behind her thick smeary eyeglasses. Her smile could be described as beatific. She looked and sounded nothing like the woman he had come to know from their marriage bed. "There is nothing you need to do," she went on, continuing to ignore his question, "other than enjoy the show."

"The show?"

She patted his hand and went back to her book.

On Friday, their guests arrived at the promised hour, simultaneously but in separate cars. Bob was a round man with a round face who nevertheless was considered handsome, and by and large was. He had thick hair without any gray and large, deep, newscaster eyes, which always focused just over Philip's head. His voice was deep and his manner authoritative. His wife was taller than he was, but in contrast to Evangeline seemed frail and tentative, despite being the youngest among them. When confronted with any awkwardness, Candace had a tendency to turn her head to one side, squint, and quietly tsk. Roy and June, on the other hand, were quite similar in appearance and manner, stocky and loud. They liked to tell jokes, which they got off the internet. They slapped each other's knees when amused, usually by the jokes they told. To their credit, they were the ones who had persisted the longest in visiting Philip during his recuperation, though in his presence they mostly talked with each other.

Now these four were arrayed around the living room, holding glasses of wine and looking uncomfortable. "Please sit anywhere," Philip had told them, and Roy had replied, "Except for your chair, right!" and roared with laughter. He and June were chuckling randomly and reassuring one another with pats on the leg, and Bob kept holding up his wineglass to the light. Every now and then Candace coughed, her mouth a thin flat line. Philip recalled all his previous evenings with these people, the hours of mild boredom and unintentional ostracization, and he wondered if he ever would have seen them again even if he'd never been injured. Probably not. It occurred to him, perhaps for the first time, that he didn't actually like having friends. He liked to be alone. This is why he liked being an accountant—there was no greater pleasure than being alone with the numbers, putting them in order, making them add up. Actually, no—the only pleasure as great was Evangeline. She made him feel the same way: as though all was right with the world, as though everything added up. He wondered how she had persuaded their guests to come, after all this time. He wished she were here now, in this room with them.

Where on earth was she?

The kitchen door banged open. There she was: bent half over, in a ploughman's stance, wheeling the hibachi before her. It was very large, too large to move really, and it gouged the wall and pushed an ottoman into an end table, setting the vased flowers upon it into a treacherous wobble.

"Would you like help with that, my dear?" Bob asked her, rising to his full height, and Evangeline ignored him, and eventually he sat down again. The hibachi stood before them now, its exhaust tent forming a proscenium inside which she stood, white-apron'd and white-hatted, her gaze settling briefly upon each guest. She nodded, and everyone but Candace nodded back.

From somewhere underneath the grill Evangeline produced five bamboo trays, five plates, and five sets of utensils wrapped in a napkin. The trays were affixed with wooden bracing that swung down to make a little table. Philip had no idea where they had come from. She distributed the trays, placed a plate upon each tray, a rolled napkin beside each plate.

When she set Philip's place, she winked.

"Well, look at this!" June cried.

"Perhaps," Bob muttered, sounding uncertain, "we would be more comfortable at table?"

"What's this 'at table'?" Roy said. "What language are you speaking, Bobert?" He guffawed. June guffawed.

"It's a common expression," Bob replied.

"A common expression is 'put your money where your mouth is,' or 'you get what you pay for,' not 'at table'! 'At table'!" Roy laughed, and June laughed, and soon they were both caught up in hysterics. Bob was leaning slightly forward, his brow furrowed, and Candace continued to cough. Philip again wondered why Evangeline had invited them over. He hoped it wasn't for his sake.

By now she had fired up the propane tank and was smearing oil over the surface of the grill. Roy and June were still giggling, but Bob had grown curious and leaned forward for a better view. Philip recalled, with a small shudder, the onlookers who had observed him lying there, broken on the pavement—long after 911 had been dialed, long after the reassuring words had been spoken, people just stood over him, staring at his ruined legs, twisted underneath him, had watched his face contort in pain. On the edge of unconsciousness, he had lain there, thinking, For chrissake, you idiots! What in the hell are you standing there for? It wasn't that he hated them for it, or that he even minded. What did it matter to him? All he wanted at the time was not to die. But he didn't understand them. He didn't understand people at all.

Except Evangeline—he understood her, a little. He was so grateful to have her. He was so very much in love with her.

For a minute there, he hadn't been paying attention. But what she had done was to spin the egg on the cooking surface, just like the guy at the restaurant, and then toss it into the air, and catch it in the hollow of her hat. And, like the guy at the restaurant, she let it fall from there, and allowed her spatula to split it in two, and she caught the eggshell with one hand and scrambled the egg with the other, the very same way he had. And she grabbed from her caddy a canister of salt, and a canister of pepper, and tossed them from hand to hand, so that they tumbled in the air, spilling just the right amount of their cargo onto the egg, and Philip did not remember the restaurant chef even attempting to do that. And she brought out a bowl of steamed rice and fried it, and sprinkled on sesame seeds, and squirted on soy sauce and teriyaki, all with a balletic, nearly acrobatic, precision, and he realized that his wife had discovered something in herself she never knew was there—she had mastered her body.

By now everyone was rapt, staring at Evangeline in awe and, quite possibly, admiration. She threw her spatula down on the surface, hard, at such an angle that it bounced up, flipped over once, then again, and tucked itself neatly into her apron belt, which she had been holding open with her fingers to admit it. Again, Philip had not seen this trick at the restaurant, and he joined in their guests' shocked applause.

Now she brought out the onion half. Philip knew what was coming, he had seen it already, but he couldn't help grinning at the prospect of watching Evangeline do it. She balanced the onion half on its edge, launched the butcher knife from her belt, spun it in the air before her, and brought it down on the onion once, twice, three, four times. She hollowed each ring with the knifetip, flicking the inner layers onto the rice pile, and she stacked the shell into a dome, with a tiny hole on top. She sheathed the knife, reached behind her for the oil, and squeezed it into the onion half. And then, with a motion so swift and subtle it was hard to be certain it had happened, she pulled a wooden match from a pocket, scraped it against the exhaust hood, and set the onion alight.

The looks on their faces! They couldn't believe what they were seeing! A tower of steam and fire, gushing out of the onion! Poor Candace reared back as though Evangeline had released a mountain lion from a cage; she collapsed into her husband, burying her hatchet face into his meaty shoulder.

And it was a good thing, too, because it was at Bob's big bald head that Evangeline launched the first flaming onion ring. It traced an arc of oily smoke across the living room and came to rest just above his left eye. He barely had time to flinch. The burning ring stuck there, and for a terrible moment flared up, singeing his combover and leaving what would obviously be a painful and unsightly scar. He screamed, smacked the onion ring onto the carpet, and gawped at Evangeline with the expression of a big, miserable child who has just been called fatty by his own mother.

By the time it registered on the faces of Roy and June that something bizarre had occurred, the missiles intended for them had already been launched. The first caught June in the breast, where an embroidered silk rose brooch likely spared her from injury; nevertheless she squealed as if stabbed. Roy took his ring on the cheek, though it bounced off, leaving only a greasy smear. He said, much as though he were reading it from a script, "Ouch!"

It was not clear why Candace was spared. Evangeline was poised to strike, with Candace's burning ring perched on the end of the knife; and Bob, having stood up in shock, left his wife exposed and cowering in her chair. Perhaps it was some kind of solidarity between quiet women; perhaps it was nothing more than pity. In any event, the onion never flew. The knife clattered onto the grill. Evangeline's venom was spent. She bent down, turned off the heat, and walked calmly out of the room.

Leaving Philip alone with their stunned and injured guests, his mind racing. "Let me get you a cold washcloth," he said to Bob, whose soft hand was cupped underneath the wound, as if something, his mind perhaps, might fall out. But Bob held out the other hand to stop him, and without another word walked out the door, Candace following close behind.

"Roy, I'm sorry," he said, turning, and in spite of everything Roy's eyes still harbored a hint of humor. He would have a good laugh about this, sooner rather than later, but for now he put his arm around June (whose eyes betrayed nothing but hurt, and whose protecting hands concealed her charred rose) and led her out the door.

Alone in the living room, Philip set to cleaning up. He folded up the trays, put away the plates and silverware, maneuvering his chair with what he was beginning to realize was expertise. He wiped down the grill surface and threw away the ruined food. All of this took him a good twenty minutes, during which he strove not to think about what had transpired. When he was finished, he looked around for something else he could do in order to avoid going to Evangeline. But there was nothing. He took a deep breath, navigated around the hibachi, and rolled into the bedroom.

She was there, still in her apron and hat, lying supine on the bed. He wheeled over to his side, unbuckled his restraints, and hauled himself up beside her.

"I don't know what came over me," she said.

"It's all right."

Her eyes were dry. She was looking at the ceiling. "We're going to lose our jobs."

After a moment's thought, he said, "I'll be able to keep mine. It'll be enough." It wouldn't, of course—he worked under contract; she was the one with the salary, the benefits. And his medical bills remained high. But none of that seemed to matter.

"I was so angry," she said, and he could hear the resignation, at long last, beginning to creep into her voice.

He was supposed to have been angry, too. He had gone to a psychiatrist after the accident, and she had told him, week after week, that the anger would come out eventually, in some form or other, and that he had to be ready for it. Over and over the woman told him this, but it just didn't happen. And the psychiatrist seemed to lose enthusiasm for him, and eventually he stopped going to see her. Was it wrong to be able to absorb so heavy a blow with such perfect equanimity? Was it wrong to need no one but Evangeline, and to be glad for it, to be grateful for the excuse to renounce all others?

Philip took his wife's hand. "Thank you," he said, because he didn't know what else to say.

She turned to him and, as though she hadn't heard, cried, "Please don't leave me!"

"I will never leave you," he replied, as if there was even the slightest chance he would do such a thing. "I will always be here." He couldn't go anywhere on his own, anyway. And that was fine with him. He didn't need to walk to love her. He didn't even need to make love to her. He didn't need anything he didn't have.

He was hungry, but they didn't move. She slept through the night with her hat on.

ZOMBIE DAN

They figured out how to bring people back to life—not everybody, just some people—and this is what happened to our friend Dan Larsen. He had died falling off a yacht, and six months later, there he was, driving around in his car, nodding, licking his pale, thin lips, wearing his artfully distressed sport jackets and brown leather shoes.

Dan's revivification was his mother's doing. Yes, it was his father, Nils Larsen, who greased the right palms to get him bumped up in the queue, but his mother, Ruth, was the one who had the idea and insisted it come to pass, the one who called each and every one of us—myself, Chloe, Rick, Matt, Jane, and Paul—to enlist our emotional support as friends and neighbors and decent, compassionate Americans. When Dan revived, she explained, he would need to rely upon the continuing attention and affection of his loved ones, and it was all of us—his old high school chums—whom he would need the most.

Of course we agreed, how could we not? Dan's mother brought

us all together in the living room of the Larsen penthouse—a place of burnished mahogany, French portraiture, and thick pink pile carpet, which none of us had ever imagined we'd see again—and told us what was about to happen. We stared, petits fours half-way to our gaping mouths, and nodded our stunned assent. A thin, bony, almost miniature woman of sixty with an enormous dyed-black hairdo like a cobra's hood, Ruth Larsen gazed at each of us in turn, demanding our fealty with hungry gray eyes. The procedure would take several days, and then Dan would need a few weeks to recuperate—could we be counted on to sit at his bedside, keeping him company in regular shifts? Why yes, certainly we could! Were we aware just how important a part of the revivification process it was to remind the patient of his past, thus effecting the recovery of his memory? And did we know that, without immediate and con-stant effort, the patient's memory might not be recovered at all? And so would we commit ourselves to assisting in this informal ther-apy by enveloping Dan in a constant fog of nostalgia for the entire month of March? Sure, you bet!

Excellent, Mrs. Larsen told us, her papery hands sliding over and under each other with the faint, whisking sound of a busboy's crumb brush.

What remained unspoken that day, and went largely unspoken even among ourselves, in private, as we waited for Dan to be brought back to life, was that we had pretty much gotten over Dan since the funeral, and could not be said to have greatly missed him. Indeed, by the time Dan reached the age of twenty-five, the year of his death, we had basically had all of Dan we could ever have wanted. He was, in fact, no longer really our friend. The yacht he'd fallen off of be-longed to some insufferable blueblood we didn't know—that was the crowd Dan had taken to running with, the crowd he'd been born into, and all parties concerned had seemed satisfied with the arrange-ment. Dan's being dead was no less acceptable to us than his having drifted out of our circle.

But Ruth Larsen didn't know this, and so we were the ones she called upon in Dan's time of need. Either that, or the insufferable bluebloods had refused. At any rate, we agreed to do what Mrs. Larsen demanded, and for better or worse he would be our friend once again.

———

The discovery of the revivification process had resulted, initially, in great controversy. Surely, the naysayers wailed, not everyone who died could be brought back to life. What would separate the haves from the have-nots? Science offered one answer. To be eligible for revivification, you had to die a certain way. Drowning was best. Suffocation. Anything that resulted in a minimum of harm to the body, other than its being dead. Freezing wasn't too bad, and a gunshot wound, if tidy, could be worked around. Electrocution was pushing it, as was poisoning. Car crash, cancer, decapitation, old age? Right out.

But still, who then? Who among the drowned, the frozen, the asphyxiated, would get to come back?

The rich. Naturally.

Riots had been predicted, the burning of hospitals and medical schools, the overthrow of the government. None of it materialized. The rich had been getting the goodies for millennia—why should that change now? People shrugged and got over it. After all, it wasn't like the rich could live forever now. They would still die—it was just that now they could get a second chance in certain circumstances. And the rich had always gotten second chances at everything. No, the fact that they could be brought back to life was no big deal, and when you thought about it, not even very surprising.

Besides.

Besides, once the process started becoming commonplace, once people had gotten a look at the revivs, had talked with them, touched them, slept with them, it became clear that, as a general rule, they were a little bit off. You could miss it if you weren't paying close attention, but they were definitely not quite right. They had, for instance, a way of walking, a kind of sway, an instability. Their hips seemed to ratchet back and forth, like the platen of a typewriter. Their fingers had a habit of twitching or suddenly clenching. Their jaws moved with a bovine circular motion, whether or not they were eating—and when they did eat, they were fussy, often choosing a single item from a varied dish and pushing the rest aside, like children. They had a watery way of speaking and a faraway look in their eyes, but when you asked them, with irritation, if they had heard even a single word you had said, they were able to regurgitate your side of the conversation with pedantic thoroughness, all in a deadpan monotone that made everything you said sound foolish and dull. And they rarely advanced any ideas themselves, no intellectual abstractions, no opinions, not even suggestions for where to eat dinner or what movie to see. They were robust, it seemed, healthy-looking, upright, but passionless—you would never see them jump for joy or raise their voices in anger. They seemed to have a normal sexual response, all the parts worked and if they liked you they would do what you suggested and appear, in some detached way, to get off. But the expected and hoped-for moans, screams, and grunts just did not happen.

Also, they smelled different. A bit spicy. Not at all bad—better, in fact, than regular people. But it was different all the same.

So if you asked a random person from the street whether, if they choked to death on a Jolly Rancher, they would like to be revived, the answer was generally yes. But not an especially enthusiastic yes. "Sure," accompanied by a shrug, was the common response. By and large, revivification was thought to be something weird rich people did, something along the lines of hymenoplasty, or owning an island. It was impressive, but maybe it wasn't exactly a great idea.

———

You weren't, it turned out, supposed to call revivs *revivs*. Political correctness dictated that, if you had to refer to them, you should call them *restored-life individuals*. But, the argument went, since they were not disabled, any specialized term was an insult, and it was best to say something like "Ronald has gotten a second chance at life," or, "Francine has recovered from her fatal trauma." Better still to keep mum—to just pretend there was nothing amiss, because really there wasn't. Everything was totally normal. Calling somebody a *reviv* was a lie—every person is just a person, and that's all there is to it.

You were never, in any circumstances, supposed to call them *zombies*. This was, however, the most commonly employed term.

"My God," Chloe said, after that first long day at Dan's bedside. "He's a fucking zombie." The six of us were sitting around a table at the closest bar to the hospital, a too-well-lit place with vinyl settees separated by terra-cotta planters full of ferns. The settees were too low for the table, and we had to reach up to get our drinks, which we needed very badly.

As it happened, the meeting at Dan's mother's apartment was the first time we'd all been together in many years. Our manner with one another was familiar and weary. As teenagers, we had been inseparable; now we were grown, and had grown apart. Not completely apart, of course. We knew too much about one another for that: the broken homes, the crazy relatives; the dramas of self-discovery, the dirty secrets. The myths we armored ourselves with, out in the world, were worthless here, among people who had witnessed their genesis; and allegiances and estrangements had arisen and retreated among us more times than anyone could count. Chloe and Matt were once an item, as were Chloe and Paul. Rick and Jane had once seemed destined to spend their lives together, but they had broken up, and now Jane had married Matt. Paul and Rick had spent a drunken, carnal week together in a cabin upstate, and now Paul was in a relationship with a man twice his age, a painter from Long Island, and Rick had a girlfriend in Brooklyn. Chloe evidently had a boyfriend—they lived in New Haven—but I had long carried a torch for her, and she and I had managed a few moony glances at each other over the course of the day. I had a good feeling about Chloe. Hearing her call Dan a fucking zombie sent a pleasurable itch across my back. She had always been vulgar.

"I'm afraid you're right," Paul groaned.

Matt sighed, shaking his head. "How did we ever get into this mess?"

"It's my fault," said Jane, who always blamed herself for everything.

Rick said, "Let's just tell Ruth to go to hell."

"Oh, we can't do that," I said.

"Fuck, no," Chloe agreed, offering me a sly glance from the corner of her eye.

The group parted at the subway station. I lived nearby and could walk. Instead of following the others to the trains, Chloe grabbed my hand. "Let's go to your place."

"Don't you have a boyfriend?" I said.

"Feh," she said, with a shrug, and we walked off arm in arm.

———

As the days passed by, Dan slowly came around. He looked pale, and there were bandages on his head and neck where the revivification fluids and electrical current had gone in, but his eyes were clear and he followed us with them as we moved around the hospital room. Chloe and I had taken to sharing one another's shifts.

"Let's make out," she said one morning.

"He's watching us."

"So?"

She sat on my lap and we snogged as a cool polluted wind blew through the open window. I hazarded glances at Dan, who gazed at us intently, blinking. His soundless mouth opened and closed. Without solid food, his doughy countenance had given way to a new and slightly frightening chiseled look.

"I think he's trying to talk."

"Who?" Chloe said.

"Dan."

She tossed her hair over hear ear and winked at Dan. "Zombie Dan," she said. "Do you remember sex?"

A small groan seemed to escape him. Or maybe it was a noise from outside.

"How about boobs? Do you remember boobs?"

"I'm sure he remembers boobs," I said, trying to nip this one in the bud.

"Here," Chloe said brightly, hopping down from my lap. I awkwardly adjusted myself with a sweaty hand. Chloe stood beside the bed, unbuttoning her blouse. Dan stared. He seemed excited, though not in an especially lascivious manner. Before he died, women's breasts had always rendered him speechless; he tended to ogle. It had always irritated me when this resulted in his getting laid, which was most of the time.

But now his excitement seemed purely empirical, like that of a scientist gazing in sober wonder at the test results scrolling across a computer screen. Chloe unlatched her bra and did a little dance. "Remember, Dan? Boobies?" She scat-sang the stripping song.

"Okay," I said. "That's probably enough."

"It's therapy," she said. "We've got to get his motor running." She leaned over, bringing her chest about six inches from Dan's stunned face. "Here ya go, pal, get a good look."

Neither of us was prepared for the speed with which Dan's hands shot out from under the sheets and clamped themselves onto Chloe's breasts. She yelped. I gasped and jumped out of the chair to pull her away. But she warded me off. "No, no," she said. "I think it's all right. Look at the little bastard go." Dan had settled into a firm, somewhat mechanical knead, palpating Chloe like a masseuse-in-training. He scowled, licking his lips. A sound escaped him.

"Was that a word?" Chloe asked.

"Oh my God," I said.

"Stizz," said Dan.

"It was a word!"

"Niztizz!"

"Oh, listen!" Chloe cried, turning to me. "He's talking! He's saying 'Nice tits'!"

It was true. He was quite coherent now. Clearly he was remembering—"nice tits" was a thing he always used to say.

We called Ruth Larsen, who since the procedure had spent far more time than we had expected sitting around the family apartment.

She claimed to be attending to Dan's business affairs. But a zombie didn't have any business, and it seemed clear that she was really spending her time drinking. Chloe had been encamped in one of the many guest rooms at chez Larsen and could attest to the woman's dissolution, which involved a lot of vituperative mutterings and slow, self-indulgent groans. A nurse had told us that her reaction, upon seeing her child show the first signs of renewed life, was to run crying from the room. We hadn't seen her around the hospital since, though she insisted that she habitually sat with him through the night. The nurses, upon hearing she had told us this, had rolled their eyes.

"He what?" Ruth barked in response to the news.

"He spoke," I repeated. "He looked out the window and said, 'Nice day.'" This was the lie Chloe and I had agreed upon.

"It's cloudy."

"Maybe he thought that was nice."

A silence hung between us. I cleared my throat.

"Do you want to come see him?" I said. "Chloe and I are here now."

"What is she doing there? This isn't her shift."

"We're sharing," I said.

Mrs. Larsen sighed. "I'll be there in an hour," she said.

It was a very long hour. Now that Dan was responsive and alert, he was uncomfortable to be with. Also he appeared to want to feel up Chloe again. He stared at her restowed rack, blinked rapidly, and emitted a trickle of inarticulate mumbles which occasionally, startlingly, broke out into intelligibility. "frummarfladmmbabaamummumm-boxturtle," he said. "Gunnuunnnununnnufrenchfries. Hoffoffofoff-ffagaggaafucker-salassalassallaaaapeanut, peanut, peanut." He licked his lips, which would prove to be a permanent tic.

"I'm going out for a smoke," Chloe said quietly.

"All right," I replied.

"Mummahumummacigarette," Dan said.

"You want a cigarette?"

"Ummacigarette."

She reached into her purse, removed a pack, and slid out a cigarette. Dan leaned forward. She placed it in his mouth.

"It's backwards," I said.

"Like he knows."

Dan relaxed into his pillows. The cigarette dangled from his lip like a dead branch from a maple tree. He seemed relieved and his blinking slowed.

When Chloe returned, it was with a slightly unsteady Ruth Larsen, who gripped Chloe's arm for support. The first words from her mouth were "Jesus Christ."

"Hi, Mrs. Larsen," I said.

A change came over Dan when his mother walked into the room. He sat up again, and the cigarette went erect in his mouth. He brought up his hands, much as he had when Chloe took her shirt off, and his fingers groped and twitched. He scowled.

"What did you do to him?" Mrs. Larsen demanded.

"He just got like this," I said weakly.

"Fudder. Fudder! Prmbnmnshn."

"Daniel!" she bleated. "Stop that nonsense immediately!"

In response, Dan let out another "Fudder" and sprang out of bed. We all jumped back. Mrs. Larsen screamed a little scream.

After weeks of his being dead and days of him lying insensibly in the hospital, Dan's sudden mobility struck us all dumb with astonishment. He tottered around the room like a child, bracing himself against the table and chairs. His gait was stiff and rubbery, but he made it to the window and looked out. He turned, his cigarette clenched between yellow teeth. "Fudder!" he growled. His mother cringed.

"You're scaring your mother, Dan," Chloe scolded.

She shouldn't have called attention to herself. Dan turned to her. His face relaxed, his eyes grew misty, and the wet cigarette fell out of his mouth. "Tizz," he sighed, flecks of tobacco sticking to his chin, and he lunged forward and embraced Chloe, lifting her off the ground. She let out a yelp. His hands found her behind, engaging it in a desperate clutch. "My God," Ruth Larsen said.

"Dan," I offered, "put her down, please."

"Sazz. Nisazz."

"Thank you, Dan, that's enough," Chloe gasped. It seemed to get through to him. He set her on the ground, and she gently pushed him away.

"Peanut," he said. "Fudder."

"What have you done to him?" his mother again asked us.

"Mrs. Larsen," Chloe said, her face red, "we'll be taking a little break now. I think you need some quality time with your son."

"I—"

"He needs you, Mrs. Larsen." She motioned to me with a thin, pale finger. "Let's go," she said, panting.

I followed. She led me right to my apartment and into bed, where we went at it with giddy èlan. When we were through we lay together, tangled in the sheets, breathing slow and even breaths. It was a relief to be alone, after the day's shocks and embarrassments.

"How long do you have off work?" I asked her.

"Just this week."

"Me too."

I waited a moment before asking, "What should we do then? I mean, the two of us."

She didn't answer immediately. I assumed she had dozed off, so I nudged her and asked again. Her response was a sigh. "I heard you the first time."

"Sorry."

"Let's not talk about that now."

"Okay."

"Let's just be quiet."

"Okay."

"Good."

———

By week's end, Dan could almost pass for normal. He was allowed to go home, and his doctors paid him visits there. They were surprised at his speedy recovery and expressed this surprise with smug, proud ejaculations, piquant little hmms and huhs, which they de-

livered while nodding. Dan returned them in kind, an unlit backwards cigarette dangling from his mouth, his fingers clenching and
unclenching at his sides. His speech was coherent but strange, as if
run multiple times through translation software. The doctors asked
him questions and recorded the answers on dictaphones.

"Please describe your tenth birthday party."

"Hmm?" Dan replied.

"Daniel, the caboose?" his mother spat. "The magician?"

"Hmm, ahh, yes. Motherpaidaman. Parkingthecaboosein-
CentralPark. Eatingicecreaminside, yes. Mymanyfriends. Yes. Andthe-
magicianwithhisrabbit. Ofcourseyes. Fudder. AndChloewiththe-
quartersinherears."

Chloe giggled. It was true, the magician had removed quarters
from her ears, as a trick. All of us had been there, at that party, and
all of us were here now, crowded around the fireplace.

"Peanut. JanekissedMattbehindthefountain. Yesss."

"I did?" Jane said suddenly.

Matt turned to her. "You don't remember? How could you
forget?"

Her face crumpled. "I'm sorry, darling."

"But how the hell did Dan know?"

Dan, however, had gone on reminiscing. "Mmmmmremmmmm-
memberitwell," he said, nodding. The cigarette bounced on his lip.
"Andmotherfatherfighting. Mothersayinghowcouldyou. Andwith-
thatwhore, she said, yesss."

Ruth's eyes grew wide.

"Andfatherfantasizingmurderingherinhersleep, yess. Fudder.
Watchingthemagicshow, dreamingofslittingmothersthroat, yessss."

Nils Larsen was not home. Upon Dan's arrival he had left suddenly, and wisely, on a "business trip" from which he had not yet
returned. Everyone else, though, was staring at Zombie Dan in horror. He seemed to notice not at all. He was standing beside the fireplace, leaning against the mantel, rubbing his chin. Every once in
a while his tongue shot out and licked his lips. The cigarette sagged
but never fell.

"AndofcourseRick, fudderfudder, Rickwasstealingmoney. From-thehousekeeper. Yess. Stealingmoneyfromherpurse. Stealingabottle-ofmedicine. Tryingtogethigh, yessss, andthehousekeepertoldRick's-mother. ThatRickwasstealing. Andhismotherfiredher. Fudderpeanut, yesss."

"What!" Rick said, leaping to his feet.

"Sotrue, sotrue. Attheparty, Rick, feltsoguilty, yesss, nicetits, yesss. Butheforgot, everyoneforgot, everythingisforgotten."

Rick was slowly lowering himself back into his chair, his face crumpled like an old newspaper. Jane threw her arms around Matt, as if for protection. The doctors amplified their hmming. Pencils scratched on little pads. Beside them, Paul gazed expectantly at Dan, his face livid with masochistic excitement.

"Do you remember, Danny? Do you remember what I was thinking?"

Dan ground his jaw, seemed to sniff the air. "Skidmark. Skidmark. Youpoopedyourpants."

Paul's face blazed with delight.

"AndChloedearChloe," Dan said, seeming to study a corner of the ceiling.

Chloe sat up straighter.

"ChloeChloe, alwayslovedhersoverymuch. Betsywasmygirlfriend, yesss, JenniferAmyPaulaNancy, but Chloe, fudderfudder, Chloemy-secretlove. Yesss."

"Oh, my," Chloe said.

Dan turned and looked at her and smiled. The cigarette tipped up and for a brief moment he looked quite a lot like FDR.

"Peanut," he said. "Nice ass."

Chloe had gone pink. "Thank you, Dan."

Ruth Larsen stood up suddenly. "I want you all out of here. All of you. Now!"

Jane obeyed immediately. She pulled Matt to his feet and began to drag him toward the apartment door. He appeared lost as he stumbled after his terrified wife. Paul followed, a wry smile in place on his lips, and Rick slouched after, his face shattered.

I glanced at the exit, hoping that Dan wouldn't notice me. I motioned to Chloe, and she got up from her chair, but she headed for the hallway and for the room where she had been staying. I offered a questioning look, but she only winked. I supposed she wasn't going back to New Haven just yet. Meanwhile Mrs. Larsen was shouting at the doctors. "Liars! Liars! You didn't tell me they could do this!"

A squirrelly-looking man in thick glasses was nodding, and stroking his plasticine goatee. "Yes, well," he said. "Yes, well, we're still researching this particular . . . unexpected . . . ah . . . quirk . . ."

"Hmmm, DoctorGiles," Dan said, gesturing with his cigarette, "youreallyshouldhavethatlookedat."

"Pardon me?"

"Thethingonyourback, hmm, couldbefudderprecancerous . . ."

The little man's eyes widened as he backed out the door, his coterie of associates encircling him like a hedge.

"Out!! Out!!" screamed Ruth Larsen.

I wanted to go after Chloe. But instead I turned and left.

———

I went back to work. I was a graphic designer for a natural-products company. It wasn't something I'd ever intended to do—I'd begun there as a copy editor—but when the previous graphic designer had quit to move to Wyoming and raise pigs, I temporarily plugged the gap. Temporarily turned to permanently, though I was still making my old salary. My boss, Patty, had rejected eight drafts of my new herbal douche label and was now demanding changes to my ninth. We sat alone in the conference room with the reeking remains of lunch pushed to one side, and she squinted at the proofs, curling her nose in disgust.

"It's too girly," she said.

"It's for girls," I offered.

"Not for girly girls. For womany women."

"You want it womanier?"

"Womanier, yes."

When I spoke to anyone at work, for any reason, this was usually the kind of conversation that resulted. I missed the crass directness of Chloe. I yearned for her, in fact. I masturbated in the men's room on our floor with a cardigan sweater over my head, in protection against the surveillance camera. And of course I called Ruth Larsen's apartment several times a day. Nobody ever answered. I even looked up Chloe's boyfriend in New Haven and called him to see if he'd spoken to her. "That sick bitch can go fuck herself," he replied. Matt and Jane hadn't seen her—"We would both like to put this behind us forever," Matt said sternly, seeming by "this" to mean, among other things, me—and Rick's girlfriend wasn't letting him come to the phone. Paul just laughed at me. "Don't be a fool," he said. "You don't want her." I didn't have the guts to ask why not.

I spent my afternoon womaning up the douche label with some elegant Edwardian script and digitized sprigs of ivy. Then I went home. There was a message on my answering machine—a woman's voice. She had left only a number, and an unfamiliar one at that. I called it. Ruth Larsen answered. It sounded like she was out of doors—I could hear traffic and voices.

"Meet me at the Homburg Bar," she said, and gave me an address downtown. "We have business to discuss."

"What kind of business? Have you seen Chloe?"

Mrs. Larsen tsked and let out an impatient sigh. "All in good time," she said.

———

What, then, is the soul?

No, really. If there was one issue revivification raised that could not easily be resolved, it was this. If you believed in the soul, in heaven or hell, in eternal life, what did revivification tell you? On the face of it, not much. Revivs often could remember their death trauma and the events leading up to it, and they had no trouble remembering their return to life. But in between was a blank. None of them ever remembered a single moment. They didn't even seem to have noticed the passing of time—there was death, and there was life, and nary a wisp of a dream intervened between the two.

One school of thought held that the revivs disproved the existence of the soul. They remembered nothing, the argument went, because there was nothing. When you're dead, you're dead. The restoration of life, then, was no big deal—it was like starting up a car. God was nowhere shaking his shaggy head in divine disapproval. There was only man and nature and eternal oblivion.

There was another school of thought, however, that regarded revivification as proof of the soul's existence. The evidence was that the revivs were different. Something, the argument went, was missing. That thing was the soul. The revivs were zombies. Their souls were in heaven, or in hell, and what limped around on earth was an empty shell, a machine.

I had never been much for religion, but the second school certainly seemed to have a lot going for it. When asked to describe their revived friends and neighbors, when asked to choose a word that best characterized this new breed of human being, just about everybody said the same thing.

Soulless.

The Homburg was a hole in the wall, or more accurately, in the ground. It was in a basement underneath an art gallery, and had a cement floor, its concavity sloping toward a central drain, like a locker room shower. The walls were tile and the lights harsh and bare—yet the room was murky, its corners lost in darkness. Mismatched tables wobbled here and there, occupied by bored-looking hipsters, and I wondered how on earth someone like Ruth Larsen had heard about the place.

I saw her bony hand first—beckoning from a corner booth that was partially concealed by a curtain—and then her equally thin face, peering out from behind the fabric. I went to her. She had already ordered me something—a whiskey, neat.

"I'm sorry," I said. "I don't drink whiskey."

"Drink it." Her eyes were sunken and red and underslung with postman's sacks, and her cowl of hair drooped like a broken umbrella. I did as she asked, dispensing with the drink in a single gulp.

"Gahhh," I said.

"Now," she muttered, peering once again behind the curtain, "let's get to business."

"Mrs. Larson," I said. "Please. Can you just tell me if you've seen Chloe?"

She nodded. "Yes. I have seen Chloe. She is still in my house," she spat. "She has quit her job and spends her days having sex with Dan."

"Um," I said. "Oh."

"They drive about in his convertible, eat at restaurants, attend parties, and hump all night in his bedroom."

"Okay . . ."

"On my husband's dime."

"I see."

I suppose I knew all along that this was going on. But why him? Why Zombie Dan? He was without any redeeming qualities whatsoever. I hung my head. A little bit of whiskey seemed to be left in the bottom of my glass, and I held it upside down over my mouth for long seconds as it found its way out.

"I suppose you're wondering what Dan has that you don't. I suppose you're thinking he's not a real man. That he's a zombie. That he has no soul."

"Sort of," I admitted.

"You're full of anger."

"I am pretty angry," I said.

"Rage. You're enraged. Well, I am here to tell you that I am, too."

"You are?" I asked her.

"Yes, I am. And I bet you're wondering why. Well, it's because that thing is not my son." Her long finger emitted a faint, damp rattle as she waggled it in my face. "It is not my Daniel. It is a monster, and it must be stopped. It can read my thoughts. It remembers things about me that I worked very, very hard to forget. It is an offense against nature."

"Well," I said. "I wouldn't call—"

"Those smug quacks! They knew it all along! All they wanted was another test subject—it's all part of their stinking quest for knowledge." She leaned closer. Her fingers, horribly dry, brushed my wrist. "It's true about zombies, you know. They do eat brains." She bit her lip, as if the thought had made her hungry. "Their souls are gone, so they want yours, and mine. They can steal them, right through thin air!"

She peered once more behind the curtain, then reached into her handbag. "And that," she said, bringing out a small silver pistol and setting it on the table, "is why you're going to kill him."

I let out a little yelp. "Whoops! No, no, sorry . . ."

She shushed me, seizing my arm. "I paid to bring him here, and I will pay to send him back."

"But that's murder!"

Slowly, she shook her head. "That's where you're wrong. Killing a human being is murder. Killing a zombie is a public service. Especially one with dangerous powers. My son is dead, and his body has been stolen by a monster. A monster that is fucking your girlfriend."

"I don't think shooting Dan will get Chloe to like me again."

"Chloe isn't going to like you again anyway, you idiot," she growled. "That's not the point."

I felt very strongly that I ought to leave, but something kept me there, even aside from Mrs. Larson's death grip. Perhaps it was the whiskey. I felt slightly dizzy and very much open to suggestion.

"Did you slip something into my drink?" I asked.

"Yes, dear. Liquor." She seemed to relax a bit and released me, leaving pale throbbing stripes on my numb wrist. I slowly dragged it into my lap. "You were about to ask me," she went on, "what the point was of killing that . . . creature in my home."

"What's the point?" I obliged.

"Do you," she asked me, "love your job?"

"I hate my job."

"Do you love your employer?"

"I can't stand her."

"Would you prefer never to have to work again? Would you like to invite your employer to perform a sex act upon herself?"

I pictured a scenario of this variety, one that would beg to be followed up with an all-natural douche. I said, "I'd like that, yes."

She pushed the little gun an inch closer. It made a sound like fingernails scraping the lid of a coffin.

"We'll take care of everything," Mrs. Larsen whispered, leaning close. "We have means. People like us always get a second chance. And now we're giving you one."

Slowly, gently, I reached out and picked up the gun.

———

In the taxi on the way to the apartment, I tried to get it all straight in my head. If the existence of the revivs meant there was no God, then revivs were as human as anyone else, which meant that killing one as wrong. But if the revivs, by their very soullessness, proved that God was real, then it was all right to kill them, because they weren't human. But, given this logic, the existence of God made killing okay, and his nonexistence made it a sin. Somewhere I was missing something. I watched the buildings of the Avenue heave by outside as darkness brought their corners into sharp relief, and I considered just how unimportant it was—what I was about to do—to almost all of humanity, and how very much peculiarity the world seemed capable of absorbing.

I got out at the Larsens' building and walked to the elevator. The doorman nodded at me, glancing at my jacket, which was tugged down on one side, from the gun's surprising weight. I managed a nervous smile.

There was no one else in the elevator, no one else to slow down the ride. I stared at myself in its mirrored wall. I didn't look like a killer. I wasn't a killer. I was merely going to set things right: the balance of nature, the balance of my checking account. I cleared my throat, though I didn't have anything to say. I didn't intend to speak to Zombie Dan, just put him out of his misery.

He answered the door before I even reached it. The doorman had called ahead, of course.

"Ah, hellothere, comein, fudderfudder. Wewerejusttalkingabout-you."

"Um. You were?" He grabbed me by the arm and pulled me into the apartment.

"Good evening," Chloe said. She was standing in the hallway in a bathrobe, rubbing a towel on her hair. She turned to Dan. "You've got this under control, honey?"

Dan nodded. "Nicetizz." I reached for my pocket and found Dan's hand there, waiting for me. His other hand already contained the gun. His tongue gently dragged along his top, then bottom, lip; he seemed to have found a stylish way of executing the tic. "Fuddernevermindthis," he said. "Mypoormother. Dreamingnightandday. Peanut. Ofmydeath."

"Oh," I said.

"Shealreadytried. MattnJane. AndRick. NotPaul, shesafraidof-homos, fudder."

"Is that so?"

He was leading me into the living room. The gun he tossed onto the pink shag. I winced as it hit the ground.

"Donworry, fudder, Itookoutthebulletsthismorning. Now." He sat me down on a comfy chair, removed a cigarette from a pack in the pocket of his sport coat, and inserted it backwards into his mouth. "Wehavealot. Totalkabout. Niceass."

"We do?"

His eyes were not blank, not empty. There was something in them, something new and strangely comforting. I felt, under their scrutiny, very small and inert, like a pebble, perhaps, or a scrap of paper. Dan's smile was crooked and not quite under control, and the unlit cigarette twitched on his lip.

"Whyyeswedomyfriend." He blinked, and blinked again. "Such-asyourfudder. Father. Forinsssstance."

"I never knew my father," I said. Behind him, Chloe could be seen sauntering barefoot into the kitchen in a cotton sundress and cardigan. She caught my eye and gave me a little wave. She seemed different, too. More confident. Gentler. I longed for her.

"Ofcourseyouknewhim," Zombie Dan said, crossing his legs. "Thefishingtrip. Whenyouweresix."

"I never went fishing with my father," I said. "He left my mother when I was too young to remember. He was . . . abusive. It led to her breakdown." I'd said this so many times before, to so many people: therapists, girlfriends. But for the first time it didn't sound quite right.

"Butyouseethatswhereyourewrong." The cigarette stood at attention, wiggling at me like an accusing finger. "Fudderfudder. Itwasyourmother. Whodrovehimaway. Nizass. Thefishingtrip, hetoldyouthis. Butyoudidntbelieve, fudder."

"That's not true!" I said. My underarms were slick with perspiration and I had to pee. I thought about the phone conversation I'd had earlier. With my boss. When I was trying to get a cab. The terrible things I called her. The suggestions I made to her about what to do with her douche label. I sunk a little deeper into the comfy chair.

It was in a cabin of course, a log cabin. In the Adirondacks. It had a shag carpet and smelled like spray deodorant, and we ate all-beef franks raw from the plastic package.

"Damn," I said.

"Donworryoldbean," Zombie Dan said, leaning close and resting a cold hand on my knee. "Thislife, fudderfudder, ismerelyascrim. Betweentheconsciousmind. Andthesoul. Tits. Andnowwepull. Backthecurtain. Cigarette?"

"I don't smoke," I said.

His response was a stiff, sad smile. He reached into his pocket, took out a cigarette, and proffered it, backwards, to the vicinity of my face. Chloe's head poked out from the kitchen door.

"Go on," she said to me brightly. "It feels so good to let go. Just give him what he wants." And she disappeared with a wink.

Where was he now, my father? Far away, no doubt, maybe with

some other family. And my mother? Right where I'd last seen her, in her sad, sagging house upstate, four hours away. Too bitter, too angry, too crazy, really, for me to visit. A card at Christmas, a card on her birthday. If she was so terrific, why had I changed my phone to an unlisted number? Why did I shudder at the very thought of her? My life, I could see now, had been a lie. I supposed that I had always known—why else would I have lived it so leadenly, in denial of its impermanence, insulated from its deepest pleasures and agonies? Like I wasn't really alive at all.

I looked deep into Dan's eyes. His hand was steady. His tongue darted out and licked his lip. I opened my mouth and let him place the cigarette there, a sacrament.

A STORMY EVENING AT THE BUCK SNORT RESTAURANT

The Buck Snort Restaurant is empty of customers. This is not unusual for any Thursday night, but on this night, to any reasonable observer, it would seem nearly inevitable. The storm outside is severe; few travelers would dare risk the roads. A hurricane of this magnitude hasn't reached so far north and west into New Jersey in generations. Trees have been uprooted and have crushed the roofs of houses; power lines are down, spitting sparks into yards and alleys. Most informed and mobile residents of the area have left: by and large, these are affluent people, people who work elsewhere. Sensible, responsible people. This particular corner of the county, however, is as poor as it was a hundred and fifty years ago, when its first itinerant farmers, Civil War veterans granted land by the federal government, set up operations and—due in part to the clayey soil, in part to their own ineptitude—failed to thrive. The nearest town is called Banner, but the Buck Snort is not in any town. It would be a roadhouse, but it lacks a liquor license. It's a low, brown wooden building surrounded by a cracked asphalt parking lot. The sign that announces its existence is painted on wood and hangs by two rusted hooks in a log frame at the edge of the lot. The legs of the log frame are planted in a couple of half-barrel tubs that are bolted to the asphalt. The tubs also contain dirt, which supports several dead yew bushes. Each side of the sign is illuminated by a single lightbulb mounted in an all-weather light fixture that is in turn mounted to the frame. The sign itself is flapping and twisting in the wind as though it were made of cardboard, and the rain lashes violently against it.

At 8:20 PM, the wind grabs the sign and flings it so hard against its frame that it smashes one of the lights. There is a flash and a pop. The one remaining light, and the lights inside the Buck Snort, wink out in sympathy, then, a moment later, come back on.

One of the two people sitting inside the restaurant glances out the window, then grunts. His name is Bruce. The other is named Heather. They're brother and sister. They're both thirty-seven years old. They are sitting, silently, at separate tables, in opposite corners of the Buck Snort. Neither has spoken in three hours. In front of Bruce sits a plastic model of a sports car, which he has been meticulously gluing together for the better part of the day. Arrayed around the model is a debris field of plastic bits and scraps, and pages from an assembly manual. Arrayed around the debris field are a three-quarters-empty bourbon bottle, an empty and very dirty glass tumbler, and four mostly empty plastic snack bags. Heather is slumped behind several piles of old magazines, a stack of eight and a half by seventeen inch construction paper, and a large bottle of wood glue. She is holding a pair of scissors and is using them to cut out the torsos of women from advertisements in the magazines. Her stash of comestibles occupies a paper grocery sack on the chair beside her; it includes a gallon of pulpless orange juice, a plastic tub of garlic-flavored bagel chips, and several jars of pickles.

Heather and Bruce are still here because they didn't know the storm was coming. They don't have a television or computer. They have been living at the restaurant for six months, since their late parents' house burned down. Heather has been sleeping in the storeroom. Bruce has been sleeping in their truck. They're running out of money. They are only dimly aware of this.

There's something wrong with them, but nobody in the county knows what it is. Drugs, maybe. Their parents were strange, too, even when they were running the Buck Snort at full capacity, liquor license and all. Every morning at nine Bruce illuminates the neon OPEN sign in the window, and every night at ten he turns it off. When somebody comes in, he hands them a menu and walks away. If they stay long enough to order, Heather tries to cook what they ask for. Usually the customer doesn't eat it. Usually they leave without paying. Sometimes somebody pays without eating. No one ever eats and then pays.

At a quarter to nine, a car pulls into the parking lot. It's a late-model Toyota containing a diminutive couple in their early fifties. Their faces suggest that they are quite terrified by the rain and wind and are relieved to have found an open restaurant. They both wear glasses and outdoorsy clothes that appear new. They converse for a moment, gesticulating wildly, then, in a coordinated effort, fling open the car doors, leap out, slam the doors behind them, and run for the entrance of the Buck Snort. Inside the foyer, they assess one another's appearance. They have only been exposed to the elements for four or five seconds, but they are drenched. The man holds up the car key fob and presses a button. Outside, the car's headlights blink twice and the horn sounds. Now they turn and enter the restaurant.

Here is what they see: a large, lodge-like room decorated with paintings, or posters of paintings, of bears, eagles, and deer, and furnished with a collection of rustic wooden tables and chairs. A man and a woman sit at two of the tables, each surrounded by a collection of some kind of refuse. The man is heavily bearded and of indeterminate middle age. The woman's hair is long and dirty, and she gives the impression, confusingly, of also having a beard, even though she doesn't. She is also in her late thirties or early forties.

The man and woman look very similar and wear similar expressions of puzzlement at the sight of the diminutive couple.

The diminutive couple detects a foul odor in the Buck Snort, perhaps a number of foul odors mingled into one. They look at each other, then back, out the window, at their car being battered by rain and wind. They seem to arrive at a decision and step fully into the dining area of the restaurant.

"Evening!" the diminutive man says brightly. He removes his glasses and wipes them dry with a cloth taken from his pants pocket. His name is Roy. The diminutive woman does the same to her glasses, with a similar cloth. Her name is Fern.

A few moments pass. Bruce and Heather have not responded, but they are still looking at Fern and Roy. So Roy tries again. "Glad to see you were open," he says. "We were caught out in the storm." He has to shout over the sound of the wind, and because his own voice, even in a quiet room, doesn't carry. His mother taught him this: "You'll need to shout, little Roy! A little man like you will have to work to be noticed." She was right—Roy's loud talking, combined with his small stature, have always made him a figure of fun among his students, but they pay him the necessary respect. He is a professor of veterinary science.

For her own part, Fern usually does most of the talking when they are together, as she is a talker. But not tonight. She is wary. If it weren't for the storm, she would have turned and left immediately upon seeing Heather and Bruce. Fern owns a yarn shop. She believes that it has given her great insight into the human condition. She is correct.

Fern and Roy have been fishing here in the greater Banner area. They live in Pennsylvania. Their fishing trips are frequent and deeply pleasurable, and the only times when they have sex. On this trip, before the storm, they caught many bass and had sex several times. They were so absorbed in these activities that they failed to listen to the weather report. That's why they're stuck here with Bruce and Heather.

Bruce gets up.

Bruce walks to the hostess station, which is right near where Fern and Roy are standing. Fern and Roy both take a step back. Bruce takes two menus from a wooden holder and moves to the table that is at the farthest equidistant point in the room from his and

Heather's two tables. He sets the menus down and then he returns to his seat, where he glues, with great precision, a tiny off-white license plate to the back of his model sports car. Within seconds, he has completely forgotten the existence of Fern and Roy.

Heather has not. She would appear, from Fern and Roy's point of view, to be watching them hungrily.

Fern and Roy walk to the table Bruce put the menus on and sit down beside each other. This is how they sit in restuarants. Some people find this charming, other find it irritating. Roy is bothered by people's judgment in this matter. Fern is not. Eighteen years with her mother, that degenerate witch, taught her that other people's judgment is typically worthless and self-serving. Roy is the only person she trusts, will ever trust. This restaurant, she does not trust. The menus are simple inkjet-printed pieces of paper. They haven't been laminated. Food and drink stains have obscured much of the text, so that Fern and Roy must cross-reference each other's copies in order to read it. Their jerking heads and darting eyes would probably look comic to anyone watching besides Heather, but only Heather is watching.

There is nothing on the menu that Fern and Roy want to eat.

Roy says, "Maybe we should leave."

"The storm."

"We could sit in the car with the doors locked."

"That's true."

"Do you think they're dangerous?"

Fern narrows her eyes. "No. Maybe."

"I think we should leave," Roy says.

"Perhaps. Perhaps we should."

But before they can, Heather stands up and hurries across the room. *Glides* might be the better verb. Heather glides to their table, her heavy dress billowing out behind her. It is a kind of muumuu, brown and burlappy, giant pockets bulging with something or other, even Heather couldn't tell you what, if you asked. Fern imagines that she inherited this garment from her mother, and she is right. Heather gazes at Fern, then Roy, then says, "So?"

"Ah . . ." says Roy.

"We're not hungry," says Fern, and holds out her menu to Heather. Heather does not take it.

"Maybe we could have some coffee," says Roy.

"No coffee," says Heather.

Fern is still holding out the menu and Heather is still not taking it. "How about some tea, then?" Fern asks.

Heather's jaw works. She seems to be chewing on the idea of tea. She emits a low hum, almost a growl, as though something inside her is shorting out. She glides away to Bruce's table, leans over him. They confer in low voices.

Fern has not lowered her arm. It's sticking straight out, holding the menu toward where Heather was standing a moment ago.

Roy says, quietly, "Are they twins?"

"Yes."

Heather returns. She says, "Fine," then takes the menu out of Fern's hand, and the other menu from the table in front of Roy, and then moves toward a darkened area of the restaurant that Fern supposes must be the kitchen. Roy thinks, it's the dress that makes her appear to glide. It nearly reaches the floor and it billows when she walks. She is like a hovercraft. Before she disappears into the darkness he sees her crumple the menus and throw them onto the floor.

In the kitchen, Heather has located a flashlight and is waving it about, intermittently illuminating rusty metal tins, unwashed utensils, countertops filthy with mouse shit. She is muttering oaths under her breath. A careful listener might discern a version of the conversation she just had with Fern and Roy. *Hrm. Nothungry. Maybesomecoffee. Nogoddamcoffee. Maybesometea. Wantsafuckintea. Hrm. Wantteadowehavetea. Fuckinwehavetea. Heresyourgoddamtea.* The flashlight's beam rests, trembling, on a glass canister, furred with grease-adhered dust. There are tea bags inside. At some point, moisture has gotten into the canister, and the tea bags have been stained by their own contents. But they appear dry now. Heather grabs two, drops them into a pair of dirty coffee mugs, fills the mugs with tap water, and shoves them into a microwave oven. As they heat, sparks jump from the staples that affix the tags to the strings. One of the tags catches fire and burns up. The other is merely singed.

A few minutes later two mugs are deposited in front of Fern and Roy, along with a china sugar bowl filled with dead ants. Heather then returns to her table and magazines.

Moments pass. Fern pushes the bowl of ants to the far corner of their table. She leans over and sniffs her mug.

"I think this is chamomile."

Roy sniffs his mug.

"Mine's black. I think. But it smells burnt." He turns the mug, revealing the blackened string with staple attached. "Here, this is why: something burned here."

"Mine's burned too. A little."

"Are you going to drink it?"

"I don't think so."

"Should we leave now?"

"I'm thinking yes."

A sound has been asserting itself outside the restaurant, subtly at first, but now more confidently, a wobbling, droning note that can't seem to decide whether it is deep or shrill. It is both, perhaps. It's the wind. It is picking up strength. The light from the restaurant illuminates only about ten feet worth of parking lot, enough to reveal the dim outline of Fern and Roy's car, which would appear to be rocking, trembling perhaps, in the new, stronger wind. It is now loud enough outside to make quiet conversation inside difficult. There is also a frantic, wooden knocking that Fern and Roy can't discern the source of—it might be close, or it might be something much louder and farther away.

Bruce and Heather know what it is: it's the wooden Buck Snort sign, flapping helplessly in its log frame. They do not connect the sign, however, to what happens next: a popping sound, a blue flash, and the fluorescent lights inside the Buck Snort dimming, flickering, going out. And then, one empty second later, blinking back on, one by one.

Bruce is sanding the seams and corners of his model car with one-thousand-grit wet/dry sandpaper. The comforting sound of sanding is too quiet to hear over the roar of the wind and rain, but he can feel it through the plastic model: it is the feeling of everything is going to be all right. His memories of their parents have become confused, but he is certain, absoutely certain, that their father used to sand their mother every evening before they went to bed. It was a process related to beauty. Their mother sat at her vanity, the mirror surrounded by colored globes of light, and stripped her face of makeup and removed her wig. And then their father would carefully sand down the edges of her face until they were smooth and dully gleaming, and then she would reapply the makeup for bed. Instead of the wig, their mother wore a head scarf to bed, and their father wore flannel pajamas that took the form of a three-piece suit: pants, vest, and jacket.

A new sound reaches Bruce's one good ear (the other became clogged during a bad cold he had several years ago and has not worked right since): a thin, keening wail. He knows it well. It is the sound of his sister crying.

This sound has a galvanizing effect on Bruce. He stands up suddenly, his chair barking out behind him and falling over on its side. Across the room, Fern and Roy react with animal instinct, wrapping their arms tightly around each other. Bruce does not see this. He sees only his sister, hugging herself and trembling before her pile of magazines and papers and scraps.

Bruce is a big man. His heavy belly and stocky upper body belie a pair of long, strong legs. They are clad in overalls. He heaves himself across the room like an ape. His shaggy head descends to his sister's and they appear, to Fern and Roy, to engage in whispered conversation.

Fern and Roy begin their own whispered conversation.

"Is she upset about the tea?"

"I don't know."

"We have to leave."

"But the wind."

"Still."

Heather, for her part, is not upset about the tea. In fact she has, like her brother, forgotten that Fern and Roy are here. She has merely been overcome by futility and exhaustion, and the sense that something has been left unfinished—perhaps many things. She feels her brother's arm around her shoulder and his breath in her ear and is temporarily soothed. She has a memory of the world outside this place. There was a time when she thought she might be able to outrun whatever it was that has made her this way. (She is able, occasionally, to recognize that their existence here is strange and perhaps dangerous. Maybe this is the thing that has been left unfinished.) She went to New York City. She accomplished it by hitchhiking. This must have been nearly twenty years ago. A man picked her up, a man twice her age with a mustache and a Stetson hat, and they drove to the city and he got her to ingest and smoke various things and they spent a week in somebody's apartment having sex, which she liked. Then she got lost going out for cigarettes and ended up crying in a police station and her parents wired the cops money for a bus ticket home. And she was pregnant, and they went to a doctor and got it cut out of her, and then had her insides tied up so it wouldn't happen again. Not much point since she didn't have sex again. When his truck is too cold, Heather and Bruce sleep together, in the mattress in the storeroom. Now he's saying "There there there there," and she can't remember what she was blubbering about.

Fern and Roy are convinced that Bruce is going to turn around and attack them any minute now. He's big enough so that they would be helpless. They have to leave. They have to. Slowly they disentangle themselves and squeeze out from behind the table. Roy leaves a five-dollar bill on it. They are inching toward the door. The wind is screaming, and the mysterious knocking has intensified. Fern is remembering the wooden yardstick, painted red with black markings, that her mother used to punish her for forgetting the words to prayers. You can still see the marks on her behind: the thinnest and straightest of scars, tiny ridges. Roy runs his thumb over them after sex. In their cabin. On the lake. They should have stayed in the cabin. The trunk of their car is full of bass, and she will fry one for breakfast tomorrow if they can get home in the storm. Among their tackle is a filleting knife and she will go for it if the bearded man follows them. On her mother's deathbed, her sister said "I forgive you, Mother, I forgive you," but Fern would not. They are almost to the door.

Bruce notices their reflection in the reflection of a window in the window. He turns. He raises his arm and leans, every so slightly, in their direction.

Fern and Roy bolt for the foyer. Inside, it is like an echo chamber. The knocking and wind are deafening. Then Fern opens the outer door and it is ripped out of her hands and slams against the outside wall and the glass shatters. She screams. Roy screams. He thinks they will go back inside but no, Fern has dragged herself onto the stoop and now is clinging to the wrought-iron railing set into the cement front steps. She is making her way down. She turns back and looks at him, beseechingly, and he follows.

Now there is a change in the noises around them. The knocking has stopped. Roy turns to the absence of the knocking and sees, illuminated by the light from inside, the wooden Buck Snort sign, attached at a single corner by a length of chain and twisting like a flag in the wind.

Roy remembers: being eleven years old, lying on the front porch swing of his parents' house in southern Ontario, the lumpy and moldy-smelling cushion beneath him, *All Creatures Great and Small* in his hands, the summer heat like a blanket over him, making him feel cradled, held, fully embraced by the world. And the squeaking of the chains the swing hung from, deep groans really, as he twitched, invisibly, his muscles in the exact correct order and at the exact correct intervals to set the swing into pivoting, oscillating motion. And then the placing of the open paperback over his face, inhaling its essence from the gutter between pages, and falling asleep. This is what he is thinking of as he follows his wife down the steps and across the six feet of asphalt to the car and when he is struck with crushing force to the back of the head, just below the occipital protrusion, by the wooden Buck Snort sign, which the wind has freed at last.

Meanwhile, Fern has reached the car and wrestled open the door, which is trying to wrench itself out of her hands, and when she turns she sees something, something large and dark, launch itself from the vicinity of her husband's head and wheel off into the darkness, and she watches her husband pitch forward and fall to the pavement on the other side of the car, and she sees that the bearded man is there, on the steps, his beard and clothes ripping in the wind like John Fucking Brown's.

They are all soaked to the bone. They are all freezing. The raindrops hurt as they hit; it is like a rain of gravel. Bruce is trying to tell these people to come back inside, that they could die out here, but then the sign hits the man and he falls. Bruce looks up at the log frame; it is twisting and creaking now, one of the half-barrels lifts up off the ground, and suddenly the whole thing breaks apart and collapses on the pavement. He is trying to scream at the woman to go back, go back inside, but the words are ripped from his throat and carried away.

Bruce feels focused and competent for the first time in years. He needs to bring the customers back inside. He needs to pick up the fallen man and carry him into the Buck Snort and lay his unconscious body prone on a table and cover him with a tablecloth for warmth. This is an unambiguous good. He climbs down the steps. He makes his way to the driver's side door where the man is lying on the pavement.

But Fern has abandoned the passenger door and moved to the back of the car and popped open the trunk with the key fob in her purse. The trunk lid flies up in the wind like a sail and the car bucks. Fern knows where to look. The tackle box. Unlatch it. Move aside the tray of hooks and lures and bobbers. Underneath, there is the knife. She has it. It's in her hand. She peeks around the edge of the bucking, heaving trunk lid and sees the bearded man in motion. He is headed for Roy to finish him off. This is the moment. A snarl uncurls itself in her throat. Go. Go. Protect the husband. Kill the assailant. Your mother's god won't save him now. Do it.

Fern's scream is too thin, too faint to be heard over the roar of the wind, the pounding of the rain, the creaking and flexing of the trunk lid. Only Heather sees the knife: she is standing at the window now, pressing herself against it, her palms white, flattened by the glass, like two captive sea creatures suctioned to an aquarium wall. That's what they look like to Bruce when he glances up. The hands are white fish; the knife is a white flash in the gloom, a will-o'-the-wisp.

None of it seems real to Heather, no realer than anything outside the windows of the Buck Snort. She thinks, hit him in the midsection, that's the spot. You can't kill the limbs, they grow back. Get the torso, the torso. And Bruce thinks, here comes something, what is it? He is three steps from the man, covers one more step against the mad wind, and the thing comes flying over the man's body and part of itself lodges in his chest and Fern thinks, I've done it, I've protected him, and this is something no prayer could ever have the power to accomplish, no prayer can slip a knife between two ribs and pierce the heart, and Mother, I do not forgive you, not now or ever, forgiveness is for pussies, and I am glad you died without my absolution, and I will see you all in hell.

THE WRAITH

Carl Blunt was fully aware when he married her that Lurene was an unhappy woman, and he'd had no illusions about the possibility of her ever changing. She had told him as much when they met: "I'm not happy," she'd said, on their second date, a dinner followed by a walk along the lake, "and I'm never going to be." His response at the time had been a silent nod of understanding. Later she would tell him that this had clinched her conviction that he was the one; he was the only man she'd ever met who hadn't tried to talk her out of it. He still hadn't. His job was to acknowledge her unhappiness, accept it, and attempt, in ways that did not question her right to it, to comfort her in its throes.

Carl was a large man, over six feet and thick around the middle, and he liked being that way. He viewed his physical size as a single facet of a comprehensive personal identity, which also included among its primary features a quiet competence in all manner of practical tasks (filling the dishwasher, making things level, reading maps), an

unerring mental fastidiousness, highly focused and slightly un-
orthodox artistic tastes, and a calm, friendly, unemphatic manner.
He was attracted to Lurene because of her narrow hips, large breasts,
wide face, stooped walk, and pessimistic worldview, and ten years
of marriage had in no way diminished his attraction. If anything,
she was more herself than ever, her hips thinner, face wider, breasts
larger. She stooped no lower than before, but she gave the appearance of doing so, due to what years of unhappiness had done to her
face. It was still pretty, hadn't taken to wrinkling and sagging, but
its flesh had taken on a grave heaviness that levity was powerless to
penetrate. They had agreed when they married never to have children, and he was glad they had stuck to that promise, because it
just would not have worked. They were too self-absorbed. They felt
proud of themselves for knowing this.

Carl was thirty-three. Lurene was thirty-one.

There was one element in their lives that Carl hadn't counted
on when he married Lurene, a single wild card. That was politics.
Lurene hated George W. Bush, utterly loathed him. This was 2005.
She screamed, literally screamed, when she saw Bush's face, which
fortunately was not very often, because they had sworn off television
news after the 2000 election, and because Carl got to the paper before she did each morning and was able to tear out any photos and
throw them away. Lurene nevertheless often growled at the empty
space Bush's face had occupied.

Neither of them had ever been very politically aware, nor was anyone else they knew, back in the nineties. Carl could remember one
or the other of them vaguely disapproving of something Clinton did
now and then, and he could recall them both being very annoyed
by the impeachment hearings of 1998. But nothing seemed of great
consequence. They regarded the world as working more or less as it
should, and concentrated on themselves, earning money, being married, and pursuing their various interests. They were content.

But Bush brought something out in Lurene that Carl hadn't
known existed. When the Supreme Court voted to stop the recount,
Lurene picked up the transistor radio that Carl's uncle had bought

them as a wedding gift four years before, and she threw it against the kitchen wall, where it split in half, spilling electronic parts on the floor. After September 11, which Lurene blamed Bush for failing to prevent, and the invasion of Afghanistan, of which Lurene did not approve, such incidents became commonplace. She swept books off shelves, overturned chairs, and kicked a dent in the sheetrock wall of their apartment. She snarled at passing cars. When Bush invaded Iraq, she stopped having sex with Carl, and then only agreed to resume relations if she could crouch on her knees and press her raving face into the pillow. If he wanted it any other way, he had to catch her before sunrise, before she'd fully woken up, before the horrible world possessed her.

Abu Ghraib made her vomit, and when Kerry lost, she burned her own hand on the stove top on purpose.

For his part, Carl didn't like the president either. Indeed, he disliked the man very much, the whole lot of liars and fascists. But he didn't complain, because he had no intention of doing anything about it. He didn't go to protests or marches, didn't blog his opinions, didn't stage voter-registration drives or man phone banks. His sole rebellion was his vote, which he cast every four years. He didn't think this entitled him to much acting-out. And so he kept his opinions to himself.

But at some point during the era of Hurricane Katrina, Valerie Plame, Jack Abramoff, and warrantless wiretapping, Lurene's misery reached a disturbing new nadir, a state of steady and imperturbable deadness. News of the latest atrocities struck her with the force of stones flung into the sea; they made their mark with a pale splash, and then vanished underneath the monotonous pummeling waves. At breakfast, she and Carl carried on conversations like this:

"If you get out of that meeting before six, let's go to Jason's for dinner."

"—"

"More coffee?"

"Mm."

"You look pretty this morning."

"___"

The fact was, she didn't look pretty this morning. She looked ghoulish. Her hair had gone lank, her face ashen, her eyes sunken into purple calderas of damp flesh. Her lips were bitten raw and her clothes hung crookedly on her body. Several times each day, Carl found her frozen in some prosaic tableau, her mouth hanging open and her lips twitching, one hand flopped like a hunk of rotten fish on the kitchen counter or off the edge of the bed. And then, as if prodded with electrodes, she would jerk, cough, and start up again, ploughing into whatever was left of her day.

One night, Carl tried to talk to her about it.

"You seem different lately," he said gently, his hand resting ajitter on her bony knee.

She shrugged, turned the page of her magazine.

"I'm afraid you're falling into . . ."

"Don't say it, Carl."

". . . that you're suffering from . . ."

"Don't."

He stopped, pulled his hand away, settled back into his little nest of throw pillows. Depression, he didn't say. The word, with all its clinical associations, was forbidden in their house. It cast unhappiness as a problem, one that could, and should, be solved. Depression was a frailty. Unhappiness, on the other hand, was a way of life. Lurene insisted upon the distinction and had lodged herself permanently and immovably in the unhappiness camp. End of discussion.

But not end of problem, because she got worse. She walked around crying. She began taking sick days off work. She smoldered with resentment for Carl and his asshole, cocksucking bonsai trees and 1920s jazz and arugula, and she took to spitting in his path, as if to curse him, or at least make him slip and break something.

And then, on an unseasonably warm morning in the middle of February—three days, in fact, before Valentine's Day, a holiday they habitually, pointedly did not celebrate—Lurene broke through the floor of her misery and into some annihilating subbasement of agony. He heard her fall: she was standing at the kitchen counter in her business skirt and white blouse, pouring milk into her coffee, and her knees buckled, her hands found the countertop, and a sound escaped her, a mortal, creaking gong, like a pair of rusted cemetery gates at long last falling open. And once they did, the furies poured through, and Lurene keened like a dying animal, and tore open her blouse, scraping red lines down her neck and chest.

Carl had been trying to read an article in the paper about third-world debt relief around the ragged Bush-hole he had torn in the other side. He threw the paper down and leaped to his feet. He ran across the room and caught his wife as she fell.

"Let go of me," she wailed, but made no move to push him away. She collapsed into his body, knocking him off balance, and the table barked against the linoleum floor as it jumped away from his palm.

"My God," he said. "Lurene."

She resisted, righted herself, pressed her hands to his chest.

"Let me go."

"I won't."

"You will, you fuck."

"I won't."

But he did. He caught his balance, she caught her breath, and he allowed her to extricate herself from his embrace. For a moment they stood facing each other, panting, unsteady on their feet.

"Maybe you should lie down."

"I'm going to do it, Carl. I am."

"No, you won't."

"I'm going to kill myself," she said. Her face tilted up to his, trembling as if it might shatter, cutting him to shreds with its pieces. This was new. This, he had never before seen.

"You won't. You will not."

Her only reply was a sigh.

"You're exhausted. You need to rest."

Her head shook no, no.

"Lie down. I will be right there. Lie down."

She sighed again and turned toward the bedroom.

"That's it. I'll call in to work for you."

She dragged herself away and disappeared down the hall.

As soon as she was out of sight, he took two swift, heavy steps to the phone where it hung on the wall. He picked it up and pressed 9, and a moment later pressed 1. He heard, from the bedroom, the sound of the bedsprings compressing, and drew breath. He gazed at his newspaper where it lay, the plate of cantaloupe humped below it, and at the dark gray stain limned by its wetness. His finger hovered over the 1.

Then his eyes traveled to the counter where Lurene had fallen and saw the cutting board, covered with the rough husks of his breakfast. It was wrong somehow, and he stared at it. In the bedroom, Lurene emitted a high, pneumatic whine. A chill ran through him.

The paring knife was missing.

He gasped, dropped the receiver. It bounced against the wall, thudding hollowly as an old bone. He spun and lunged into the hallway.

She was there.

For a moment he thought it was someone else. She was standing straight, her shoulders thrown back, her head held high. She was buttoning her blouse back over her unblemished chest and neck. Her eyes were bright, and something was the matter with her face.

She was smiling.

"Lurene?"

"God," she said, with a little laugh, "sorry about that!"

He stared. She shook her head and advanced toward him with a kiss. It made a soft hot smack against his cold lips.

"I have no idea what came over me," she said. There were tears on her face, and she cheerfully wiped them off with a quick finger, as if they'd blown onto her from somewhere outside. "But I feel much better."

She moved past him to the coatrack and shouldered on her heavy jacket.

"I thought . . ." he stammered.

"Me too!" She gawked at him for a long moment, then let out a mighty equine guffaw. "For a minute there, I wanted to die."

"So you said."

"I'm really sorry." She pulled her woolen cap out of her pocket and popped it onto her head. Her hair pressed against her cheeks and five years dropped off her in an instant. "I scared you. I'm sorry."

"It's all right." He slumped back into his seat.

"It was just, you know, everything, it just came down on me all of a sudden." She had her purse now, her keys, her hand on the doorknob.

"I thought you took the knife."

She blushed. Blushed! Lurene had never once blushed, as far as Carl could remember. She said, "I did," and immediately clapped a prim hand over her mouth. Her fingers parted, her lips poked through, and she said it again. "I don't know what I thought I was going to do. But something snapped, and I felt better." She shrugged. "Gotta go. I'm sorry, sweetie."

Sweetie?

She blew him a kiss (blew him a kiss?) and walked out the door. Her sprightly steps clicked on the stairs, and a minute later he watched out the window as she half-ran, half skipped across the street and down into the subway.

———

He sat for a short while in stunned silence, listening to the radiator clanking and drops of water leaking into the sink. Sweat poured down his face and into his collar and he tried to slow his breathing.

Carl worked at home. He maintained various websites. Some of the websites he maintained actually sold web hosting and design. His livelihood was entirely ephemeral, a direct-deposited paycheck wafted on a breeze of multilayered virtuality. Every day he wondered if he really, truly, was going to do it—was he actually going to sit down and work again? It just didn't seem real. And then, every day, he went ahead and did it, and the money mysteriously arrived in his bank account. And often he spent it on imaginary things—music downloads, software. When occasionally some physical artifact of his labor arrived in the mail—a tax form, an invoice—it always gave him a jolt.

But today especially, this sense of unreality permeated the apartment. For the first time in as long as he could remember, he considered going back to bed and sleeping it off. Restarting the day in a different frame of mind. He sighed. The computer waited in the study for him to power it up, and the stain on his newspaper spread. Any moment now, he would get up and do something, anything, to break the spell. And then he heard the bedsprings creak.

He was still for a good thirty seconds. Then, idiotically, he said, "Lurene?"

Of course there was no response. The creak was not repeated. Nevertheless, he couldn't resist saying her name a second time. More quietly now, more to himself than whatever phantom his imagination had inserted into the next room.

"Lurene?"

The nothing that resulted caused him to flush with embarrassment, and his sweating redoubled. He let out a low, quiet chuckle.

It was time to go to work. He would take a shower, get dressed, then call Lurene at her office to make sure she was all right. There—a plan. He was stirred out of his stupor. He got up and walked down the hall and had his tee shirt halfway up over his head before he even got to the bedroom. He stepped over the threshold, freed his ears from the collar, and tossed the shirt onto the bed, where it struck a naked woman in the back.

He screamed. The shirt slid onto the bunched bedclothes. The naked woman didn't move.

She faced the opposite wall, her head in her hands. Beside her lay the paring knife, dark with blood, and blood stained the sheets it lay upon.

For a moment, as he recovered himself, he believed that it was her, that it was somehow Lurene. He knew her shape, the pattern of vertebrae, the curve of her neck and shoulders, and these were those. But as he steadied his breathing, as his eyes adjusted to the brackish light filtering through the curtains, he could see that this body wasn't his wife's. It was scarred, pitted, scraped. It was gray and battered as a sidewalk, and as lifeless. The back was striated, like a stone plucked from a glacial moraine, as if a lifetime of scratches and welts had never healed, never faded; and it did not rise and fall with the woman's breaths. There were no breaths. Only his own, growing quieter in the room.

Nevertheless, when he spoke, it was to say, once again: "Lurene?"

It rose to its feet and turned.

The thing that faced him now was like a statue, a statue of his wife, cast in concrete and left to weather, forgotten, in some abandoned town square. It gave the impression of advanced age and great strength, and it stared at him through flat gray-black eyes that did not blink. It wasn't Lurene, but looked like it was supposed to be.

"Who are you?" he managed to ask.

The thing looked at him. Its stillness was uncanny. It stood with its legs slightly parted, its torso twisted a quarter turn to face him. The wide face, the heavy breasts, the bony hips were flawless facsimiles of his wife's, hewn from beaten old stone.

And now he recognized some of the marks—a deep cleft in the chin where Lurene had a barely noticeable scar. A long gouge that outlined the pelvis, where Lurene had shed a benign cyst. A gravelly rake across the thigh, faded to pink on the real Lurene, the result of a bicycle accident on their vacation in Europe three years before.

And finally, on the inside of the left wrist, a three-inch laceration, following a vein, that corresponded to no wound he had ever before seen.

Carl and the thing stared at one another for long minutes, his eyes ranging in horrified fascination all over this strange body, the thing's eyes locked in place upon his own. It did not speak. It did not move—until, at last, it broke its gaze and sat down, in exactly the position of contemplative misery he had found it.

Shirtless, sweating more profusely than ever, he strode down the hall to the phone. He snatched up the receiver from where it dangled, tapped the hook until he got a dial tone, and called Lurene's cell.

"Hi! I was just thinking about you."

There was a lilt in her voice, a playful chirp.

"Uh . . ."

"I know I don't tell you this often enough," she whispered. "But I love you. I really do."

"Thanks."

She laughed. "'Thanks'? How romantic!"

"I love you, I mean. I do. But . . ."

"But what!"

"Lurene?" he said, low and soft. "Lurene, tell me something. Be honest with me."

"Yes?"

"Did you cut yourself this morning?"

There was a long beat before she said, as if it were the punch line of a joke, "Nnnnno!"

He didn't say anything. From the bedroom, silence.

"Although," she went on brightly. "Although it's funny, I had this idea on the train this morning that I had. I was so upset. I was almost certain I cut myself. But now I feel like it was a dream."

She stopped, but did not sound finished.

"The thing is," she went on, "I didn't. I couldn't have. There's no . . . there isn't any . . . cut. On my wrist. There's nothing."

"Nothing," he repeated.

"No." And now she sounded a bit uncertain. "Why— That is— What makes you ask?"

It was several seconds before he said, again, "Nothing."

———

He might have told her about the thing, but he didn't. What would he say? Besides, he didn't want to puncture her bubble of cheer. She had earned it, after all.

Carl Blunt did no work at all that day. He sent an email to his boss claiming flu. It was so much easier to lie in email than on the phone—he didn't even have to disguise his perfectly healthy voice. Though he made a couple of typos, for good measure.

After that, he got the hell out of the apartment. He walked through the park, hunkered in his coat, his gloveless hands plunged deep into the pockets. He ate lunch at the pizzeria at the end of his block, went to the drugstore, bought underwear and aspirin, and went to see a movie. He was back at the apartment by four thirty. He hung up his coat, put down the Eckerd bag, and took a deep breath before going down the hall to the bedroom.

There she was. She had moved. She was lying facedown on the bed now, her head pushed into the pillow. The pillow was hideously distended, as if she were made of lead. The mattress sagged in the middle.

He plucked up his courage and sidled into the room, staying close to the wall. He edged around the dresser and chair, pressed himself to the closet door, then leaned far, far out to pluck the knife from the bedclothes. It made a little gluey sound as it detached itself from the puddle of dried blood. The thing remained still, and Carl withdrew quickly, scooting out of the room with the knife suspended between his thumb and index finger.

In the kitchen, he washed it, placed it in the dish rack, and sat at the table to wait for Lurene.

Thirty minutes later she walked in the door. She dropped her briefcase on the floor, hung up her coat, did a little pirouette, then came to Carl for a kiss hello. Up close, she looked different. At first he thought it was merely in contrast to the thing in the bedroom. But no: she was different. Her skin was clear and soft as an infant's, her hair thicker, her eyes brighter. It wasn't a question of age. Tiny lines still fanned out from her eyes; her cheeks betrayed the slightest hint of future jowls. It was a question of pain. In her face, there was none. It was a face to which no insults had ever been spoken, that had never been slapped or seen a hooded man with electrodes attached to his arms. The scar on her chin was gone. She was utterly, frighteningly unscathed by life.

"Good day?" she said.

"No."

"No?" She skipped to the sink and began to fill a glass with water.

"I didn't get anything done."

"How come?" She sipped her drink, cocked her head, gave him a little grin.

He didn't answer.

"Maybe you didn't get anything done for the same reason I didn't get anything done."

"What," he asked, "is that?"

She winked. "Distraction."

"Okay . . ."

"I was thinking of *other things,*" she sang.

"Ah."

She put the glass down, came to him, and kissed him. She plucked his hand from his lap and pressed it to her breast. "Sexy time!"

"Well . . ."

"C'mon, don't be a poop," she said, hauling him to his feet. She grabbed fistfuls of his shirt and pulled him to her, pressing herself against him. "Let's go."

"I think you should go in there alone, first."

"You want me to get all ready?"

"No," he said. "I mean—there's something in there."

His voice, he thought, was dark with foreboding. But she didn't seem to notice. She had the cheery obliviousness of a character on television. It was as if he were setting her up for a punch line.

It occurred to him that she was nearly as frightening as the thing on the bed.

"Something special?" she cooed.

"No, Lurene. Really." He gulped. "Something scary. Something you left there this morning."

She let go of his shirt, fell back on her heels, pouted. "Are you try-ing to ruin my fun?"

"Lurene," he said. "You cut yourself this morning. With the knife. And it . . . left something. In the bedroom."

Now, at last, a look of annoyance crossed her face. And perhaps a tiny spark of fear. She held up her hand and unbuttoned the cuff of her blouse.

"Look," she said. "Nothing. No cut."

"There was blood in there."

She scowled.

"And the other thing," he said.

"The knife?"

"No."

She stared at him with can-do intensity, like a fighter pilot.

"Okay, ya lunk," she finally gushed, slapping his chest with a fine ivory hand. "You need a shower anyway. Come to think of it, so do I. I'll go in there and clean up whatever mess I left and I'll meet you in the bathroom, whaddya say?"

He swallowed, nodded.

She spun and marched off. Carl remained in the kitchen, standing, listening. Her hard-soled office pumps clomped the length of the hallway, passed onto the carpet of the bedroom, and then stopped. He bent over, straining to hear. Would she scream? Would she run out?

She wouldn't. She didn't. She was absolutely quiet, for at least a minute. Carl continued to sweat. The wall clock thunked out the seconds.

And then, at last, her footsteps started again. Slowly now, gently, she took three, four, five steps, and again stopped. The silence this time was longer: two, three minutes. And then he heard the bedsprings creak, and a small, guttural yelp, and a ragged release of breath.

"Lurene?"

He moved to the entrance of the hallway, gazed down at the inch of bedroom he could make out through the distant, foreshortened door.

"Honey?"

A groan, movement on the bed. And then Lurene's shoes touching the floor, one, then the other. A grunt, and footsteps. One, two, three, four. And on five, she appeared.

Her hand was wrapped around the wounded wrist. Blood seeped from underneath. Her shoulders were sloped, her back bent, her face a mask of misery. "Carl," she said. "Find the bandages." And she fell, gasping, to her knees.

Every morning for a week, she disappeared into the bedroom to get dressed and emerged cheery and full of life. Every morning she left the thing behind, with Carl, in the apartment. He managed to work with it there—he had to. Sometimes he heard it get up and move around. He had found, on the internet, the word: *wraith*. The ghost of a person still living. He didn't know if that's what it was, specifically; the proper nomenclature hardly seemed important. It was a handy nickname for something that he sure as hell was not going to call "Lurene." The wraith. Sometimes he could swear it was standing in the hallway, waiting for him. But he never budged from the study except for a quick dash to the kitchen for food, or the bathroom. He did not attempt to talk to it. He tried to be quiet, so as not to bother it.

When Lurene came home from work each day, she would draw him into the bathroom, into the shower, and make love to him there. Never before had she taken the initiative in an act that, under ordinary circumstances, she lacked the reserves of joy even to contemplate; he had always demanded (well—requested, really), she had always submitted. Now, though, he found himself shocked and embarrassed, embarrassed by her ardent desire, by his sudden, livid physical response. Her body was so light, so unencumbered by its own corporeality; every motion was effortless and perfect. And then, even before his lust had managed to leave him, she would go—leave the shower, dry off in silence, and return to the wraith. She could feel its need, she told him. She had to go to it, or it would come to her.

One afternoon it was waiting outside the bathroom door.

The next, it was inside the bathroom—behind the curtain when they pulled it aside.

The day after that they locked the door.

Over that weekend, and the next, Lurene stayed Lurene, and said nothing about the wraith, and so neither did Carl. But on Monday morning, he asked her, as she got up from the breakfast table, if he could see.

"See," she repeated, as if she didn't know what he meant.

"See it happen."

Her frown deepened, her eyes narrowed.

"I want to know," he said. "I want to know how it happens. How it comes out."

For a moment he thought she would strike him, but what she did instead was begin to weep. "I don't think I could," she whispered. "I don't think it would work. With you there."

He stood, took her into his arms. He had not made love with his wife, his entire wife, since these strange days began. He missed her. The other one, the happy one—with her it was too easy. His love needed something heavy to hold it down. He said, "Don't cry, don't cry."

"This can't go on," she said.

"It can. It can go on." Though he knew she was right.

They stood in silence for a time, gripping each other so tightly they could barely breathe. Then she pushed him away, walked down the hall, and emerged a new woman.

———

That afternoon, around lunchtime, he was working on some text formatting, trying to convince a client she didn't want blinking letters with sparks shooting off them, when he heard the wraith get out of bed. Its feet thudded on the floor, and he heard them dragging dryly across the room, like a pair of sandbags.

He had grown used to its wanderings, and he tried to ignore it. But after a moment, the footsteps continued into the hallway and down it, to stop right outside his door. His fingers paused over the keyboard, and he held his breath. The door wasn't locked. The wraith had never seemed to show much interest in him without Lurene around.

"Hello?" he squeaked.

The door flew open and crashed into the wall behind it, deepening the depression the knob had dug over years. The wraith was staring at him, its eyes blacker and deeper than ever, and as lifeless.

He jumped out of his seat. "Uhh . . ." he said.

It took three long steps toward him and grabbed his shirt in its long gray fingers. It was right there, right up in his face, holding him close. He was not frightened, not yet, but he understood that he was helpless. The wraith had a smell, not a bad smell, like that of wet stones drying in hot sun. A bit of ozone, a bit of rot.

"What . . . what is it?" he managed.

The wraith pulled his shirt open, and the buttons clattered on the floor. It—she—pushed it over his shoulders and down his arms and tossed it back over her head. She was very, very strong. She reached for his belt.

"Whoa, whoa!" he said, and she stopped. She did not back off. She stared at him. He gulped air. And then took the rest of his own clothes off, without her help.

The wraith pushed him into the bedroom and onto the bed, then settled itself over him like a landslide. Its skin was neither rough nor cold, though it wasn't as warm as living flesh, and certainly wasn't as soft as Lurene's. It had the consistency of scar tissue, rough but yielding. It felt unbreakable. It felt like it would survive for eternity.

And it turned him on! That was certainly a surprise. He touched hips, belly, breasts, and felt as breathlessly eager, as hungry, as lustful, as he had ever felt in his life. He marveled at himself, his breath catching in his throat. How was it possible? But it was. The wraith knew precisely what to do with him, and did it without hesitation. It moved over him, shifting its tremendous weight, sending shocks of pleasure through him. It could kill him in an instant, that was the crazy thing. It could crush him, but instead of feeling afraid, he felt safe. Protected by it. Gentled. Unlike with his flesh wife, he used no condom. It hurt to penetrate and it hurt when he came.

Its eyes remained open, its lips pressed shut, until it was through. Then it heaved itself up off him and flopped over, facedown on its pillow.

It took a while before Carl realized the whole thing was over. When his heart stopped racing, he picked himself up and tiptoed back to the office. He put his clothes back on, realized he couldn't button his shirt, then threw it in the trash. He had to walk past the wraith again to get a new one, but it didn't budge. Somehow he managed to return to work.

When Lurene got home, they did it in the shower again, and the wraith didn't bother them. He could barely keep it up. And when afterward Lurene emerged from the bedroom, fully herself, she gave him a look. But she didn't pursue it. Whatever had happened, she didn't want to know.

———

And so it continued for several weeks, became routine, and he amazed himself at what depths of depravity it was possible to grow accustomed to. The warrantless wiretapping continued, the vice president shot some guy in the face, and Carl got himself off daily with his giggling fake wife and a lumbering clay monster. The new normal! His work increased to full productivity, and the fissure that these strange events had wrenched open simply filled itself in and smoothed itself over. He began to wonder if this was his fate, to be married to a pair of horny half-women, and he decided that there were worse ways to live out one's days.

But then one morning Lurene came out of the bedroom disheveled, stooped, and utterly whole. He gaped. He didn't have to ask, but he asked.

"What happened?"

"I can't do it."

"Well—can't you—did you try again?"

A sharp look. "Yes I tried again, you prick!"

He winced, sunk a bit into his chair. "I'm sorry!"

She looked around the room, as if for some obvious solution she had failed to notice. "Fuck," she said, and pulled on her coat and hat.

"You're just going to go in to work?" he asked.

"Do you have some better idea?"

He shook his head no.

He spent the entire day in a state of mild anxiety, unaccustomed as he had become to being alone in the apartment. Several times he peeked in the bedroom to see if she'd been mistaken, if the wraith was there. But nothing lay on the bed. His palms sweated and he had to change his shirt often. He did things wrong, then did them wrong again.

He slept on it, figuring it would all make sense in the morning. But it was the same the next day, and the next, and all the rest of that week. And then one night Lurene stumbled from the bathroom wearing an expression of horrified epiphany.

"I know why I can't do it," she said. "I'm pregnant."

Unthinkingly, he added himself to the crowded ranks of men who responded to those words by saying "That's impossible." To which Lurene did not lower herself to reply.

He tried again. "We were protected."

She shrugged, lowering herself onto the sofa beside him. They sat in silence, waiting for this new information to settle itself. The television seemed very loud. Carl turned it off.

"Carl," she said.

He turned to her.

"You fucked it. Didn't you."

He looked at her with what must have been an expression of utter forlornness, and he realized what a weakling he was, that he had no volition, he could only do what he was told, he habitually ignored the world's ills because he couldn't abide them, and he had capitulated to her misery, not because it was right, but because it freed him from his own. And then he proved it to himself by saying, "It forced me to. I couldn't stop it."

Her slap was not unexpected, nor was it undeserved. But it was unprecedented. It turned his head with a sound like a splintering plank, and though it didn't hurt, not much, it had all the force behind it of a ton of stone.

His head was hung when she got up from the sofa, and it was still hung when she marched into the kitchen, with what, if he had been paying attention, he would have recognized as her old steely resolve. But the silvery snick of the paring knife being pulled from the block—that he recognized.

He managed to stop her. She meant for him to. Her hand was in the air, the fingers white around the knife; her eyes were trained on the doorway as he stumbled through. He grabbed her by the wrist and she pretended to fight against him, and the knife clattered to the floor. She let herself go limp. He encircled her in his arms and led her back to the couch.

"I want it out of me," she said, through gritted teeth. She threw off his embrace and rocked back and forth, her lip between her teeth.

"We could . . . get an abortion," he said, and regretted it immediately. But she shook her head.

"Not that!" she cried. "The other!"

Her face was wet and livid, the lips trembling, and to his great surprise, Carl gasped and let out a sob. The sound it made was very loud, like a bedsheet being torn in two, and he slumped against the back of the sofa and for a few moments was insensible with grief. When he came around, he was again surprised, this time to find himself in Lurene's arms, to find her kissing his forehead, his ear, his hair; to find her small rough hands caressing his cheeks, wiping the tears away. "Oh, baby," she said, and her voice was deep and unhappy and real. "Don't worry. It'll be all right."

That beautiful lie! She had never before uttered it. He buried his face in her hot neck, and he pressed his lips to the vein there, which pulsed and leaped with blood, and they stayed that way for a long time, as out in the world things were bombed, and polls were taken, and money was allocated, and money was spent. To their child, should it be born, none of this would ever be quite real. All of it—the terrorism, the torture, the scandals—would have the hazy quality of near legend, the actual truth just barely out of reach, like a scary campfire tale about something that, swear to God, actually happened to a best friend's cousin's roommate. The events, though factual, would seem invented, and the characters would be parodies of themselves, rough outlines, without particular depth or dimension.

A tragedy, Carl and Lurene might have said, that the truth was always forgotten, that history was dulled and simplified until it didn't resemble itself at all. But they understood that forgetting was the way people managed to go on. Even they would be forgotten, eventually, and once they were gone, their child would come to wonder what they were really like, back when the world was such a storied mess. The child would recall Lurene as firm and stoic, Carl as decent and shy, and the two would seem long-suffering and impossibly old, heavy with the burdens of their age, like statues come to life.

THE ACCURSED ITEMS

A LIBRARY CARD, from a town he wishes he still lived in

———

A STUDENT BIBLE, received at confirmation, its red plastic cover melted by the radiator

———

LOVE LETTERS, seized by federal agents in an unsuccessful drug raid, tested in a lab for traces of cocaine, exhaustively read for references to drug contacts, sealed in a labeled plastic bag and packed, along with a plush bear holding a plastic heart, into an unlabeled cardboard box, itself loaded into a truck with hundreds of similar boxes when the police headquarters was moved, and forever lost

———

CAR WASH SUDS, evaporating on the pavement

———

A PAINTED EGG, thought to have been broken by the housekeeper, forgotten in the absence of compelling evidence, swept into a cheap plastic tumbler and inadvertently donated, with the set, to Goodwill

———

THE SCRATCHED STONE, covered by fallen leaves, that marks where a previous owner's cat is buried

———

A MINNIE MOUSE DOLL you found by the roadside and brought home, intending to run it through the washer and give it to your infant son, but which looked no less forlorn after washing and was abandoned on a basement shelf, only to be found by your son eight years later and mistaken for a once-loved toy that he had himself forsaken, leading to his first real experience of guilt and shame

———

NUDE POLAROIDS of a thirteen-year-old female cousin

———

A WHITE GLOVE worn through just below the second knuckle of the fourth finger, where she tapped her wedding ring for many years against the brass studs of the armchair

———

THE UNPAINTED PATCH on the hood of the car where vandals scrawled epithets

———

AN ACCOMPLISHED FORGERY of a famous painting lost in a 1965 mansion fire, which now hangs in the largest gallery of a major American art museum

———

THE METAL PAIL from which the last traces of blood could not be scrubbed

———

AN ICICLE preserved in the freezer by a child, which, when discovered months later, is thought to be evidence of a problem with the appliance, leading to a costly and inconclusive diagnostic exam by a repairman

———

A GAY PORNO MAGAZINE thrown onto a baseball field from a car window and perused with great interest by the adolescent members of both teams, two of whom meet in the woods some weeks later to reproduce the tableaux they have seen, leading to a gradual understanding that they are in fact gay: an incident the memory of which causes one of the two, when he is well into a life that is disappointing emotionally, professionally, and sexually, to fling a gay porno magazine out his car window as he passes an occupied baseball field on his way to what will be an unsuccessful job interview

———

A RÉSUMÉ that betrays its author as utterly unqualified for the position for which she has applied, but which, because it smells good, leads its reader, a desperate, experientially undernourished middle manager at an internet-based retail corporation, to invite her into the office for an interview that, although it further betrays the applicant's complete unsuitability for the job, provides the middle manager with a physical impression to complement the good smell, which impression is intensely exciting, forcing him to hire her as a supplemental secretary, much to the bafflement, chagrin, and eventual disgust of his extant secretary, who, during her employer's lunch hour, removes the résumé in question from his files and personally delivers it to the CEO, and who is with the CEO when he barges into the middle manager's office and finds the unsuitable supplemental secretary standing beside him, crying silently with her dress half off, while he sits in his reclining office chair sweating profusely and holding a plastic letter opener in a threatening manner

———

THE MORTAR spilled by the mason, hardened onto the rubberized plastic strips of your chaise longue

———

AN UPTURNED BIRD'S NEST, blown from a tree into a snowbank

———

AN OVERTURNED CAN OF PAINT, unnoticed for months, which when found is lifted whole from the floor, the spilled liquid hardened into the shape of a puddle in an accidental imitation of the fake-spilled-drink gags available in any gift or joke shop

———

MEAT, left out on the butcher block by an unidentified tenant in the eight-bedroom house, which each tenant, insisting that he is not responsible, refuses to dispose of, and which within a day begins to reek, and within three days has drawn flies, and within a week, maggots, but which by now has become a symbol of the mistrust each tenant feels for his housemates and its continued putrefaction a point of pride, so that each tenant eats his meals locked in his room or out of the house, until the meat has nearly been consumed by the insects that have occupied it, and the house fills with flies, and the meat disappears almost entirely, save for a few dried strings of sinew and a dark stain that, at the semester's end, cannot be bleached out by the landlord, who retains the tenants' security deposit to cover the cost of replacing the block

—

SHOULDER PADS her mother tore from an otherwise stylish dress, recovered from the garbage and employed to fill out her bra while she dances to pop music in front of the mirror

—

A TWENTY-FOOT LENGTH OF CEMENT PIPE, ten feet in diameter, abandoned in a farm field, which the farmer has plowed around and which will barely be visible, months later, above the rustling cornstalks

—

YOUR TONGUE, forming forbidden words inside your closed mouth

—

A SET OF JUNIOR BARBELLS, the plastic weights grown brittle and split along the seams so that sand has spilled out, which he cannot bring himself to discard, even though they remind him, every time he works out on his state-of-the-art cable-based bodybuilding system, of a time when he was weak and at the mercy of his father, who was the one who bought him the junior barbells in the first place, and against whom he mercilessly retaliated as soon as he was strong enough to do so, a retaliation that his father, lying prostrate on the shag rug with his face bent and bloodied, seemed, with a wry, knowing, split-lipped smile, to tacitly approve of and even take proud responsibility for

———

TRIPLE-WASHED MIXED GREENS in a plastic bag, on a shelf beside others like it

———

GRIT found encrusted in the tire wells of the suspect's car that, after extensive testing in a forensic geology laboratory, proves to have come from a beach in Oregon the suspect claims never to have visited

———

THE FATHER'S BELT, which the mother matches, as the child sleeps, to the scars on the child's back, scars the child insisted came from falling against a schoolyard fence during a "shirts vs. skins" game of kickball

———

A BISCUIT crushed into the slush of a Kentucky Fried Chicken parking lot

———

THE ORANGE TOBOGGAN whisking her to her death

———

THE CASSETTE TAPE that happened to be in the tape deck when it was stolen from a car and was still lodged there when you bought the stolen deck for thirty bucks from a collapsible buffet table set up on the sidewalk outside your office building, and which contained, as you learned the moment you installed the deck and turned it on, a desperate recorded plea for reconciliation from a weeping woman to the lover who spurned her, which fills you with both pity and delight to hear, pity because of her plaintive voice and the blurred, haunted quality of the recording, delight because the offending lover's tape deck has been stolen

———

A BUMPER STICKER, affixed to the inside of a women's room stall door, bearing the name and telephone number of a rape crisis center that has lost its funding and is no longer operating

———

THE PASSPORT PHOTOS on which your eyes are obscured by little white bars

———

THE TUBE OF UNGUENT tightly rolled at the empty end, which she is just about to realize has been leaking all over the contents of her purse for days

———

THE TEST RESULTS from the genetics lab that his hands are shaking too hard to open

---

SPIDERWEBS that connect her bicycle to the cellar wall, which are severed when, some months after her death, he fills the tires with air, straps on her helmet, which is too small for him, climbs onto the bicycle, and rides as fast as he can through the darkened streets of their town, screaming her name at the top of his lungs, until at last he is arrested for disturbing the peace and spends the night in jail, which he later realizes is exactly the place he wanted to be that night, which is perhaps the reason that he elected to ride, while screaming, the bicycle, which he leaves behind at the police station and never sees again

---

THE QUILTED GRAY METALLIC-NYLON VEST that the Korean exchange student lost outside the Christian Center, on the back of which is printed an incomprehensible English phrase

---

THE NEW MAP on which his hometown is not marked, as it no longer exists, because the state forced its residents to sell their homes so that the new reservoir could be created above them, which reservoir, with its waterfront casinos, has greatly increased the value of the surrounding properties, many of which are owned by the senator who lobbied to have the reservoir project approved

---

A BOTTLE OF PAIN RELIEVER brought on a business trip that proves, at the moment it is most needed, to be filled not with pain reliever but with buttons

———

THE HOUSEPLANT that will not die

———

FIFTY PAIRS OF OLD BLUE JEANS found at secondhand clothing stores and brought, at great expense, on a trip to eastern Europe and the former Soviet Republics, where, rumor had it, old blue jeans could be sold for a lot of money, but where this was no longer true, as so many previous visitors had heard the same rumor and done the same thing, creating a glut of old blue jeans, which were not even all that stylish there anymore, and causing the entire trip to be ruined by the necessity of hauling around these huge suitcases full of other people's jeans, which smelled kind of bad, as if those other people were currently wearing them

———

ACRID MIST that, not long after a crash is heard from the chemistry storeroom, begins to seep out from the under the closed door

———

WORK GLOVES, once owned by the farmer, routinely used for calving and for the slaughter of cattle, and hardened with blood and slime into the exact shape of his hands, that are many years after his death discovered hanging in the barn by the farmer's son, who tries them on and finds that his own hands, though soft from his life of relative affluence and leisure and work behind a desk, fit perfectly

———

THE PHOTOGRAPH of the woman and her children and the children's father that the father has been cut out of, which the woman uses to mark her place in *Valley of the Dolls* when she goes to the window to see what is the matter

—

THE DECK OF CARDS that his children have added extra aces and kings to, because it's more fun that way, but which he is accused of cheating with and is beaten up for during his regular card game, a beating he will have to explain to his wife with some lie, as he has been insisting that he works late on Friday nights, not gambling, an activity she believes he was addicted to but has been weaned from with the help of Gamblers Anonymous, an organization he never joined, despite what he said

—

SNEAKERS hanging from the power line, with one half of a boy's broken glasses stuffed into each toe

—

THE URINE SAMPLE produced for the canceled doctor's appointment and forgotten in the back of the fridge

—

THE UNEVEN HEDGE

—

HAIL

———

SEVEN HATS, knitted by the Retired Ladies' League of Piedmont for a set of septuplets; two of whom die shortly after birth; one of whom grows up to host a nightly TV news broadcast in a small Midwestern city, until she is attacked and her face permanently disfigured one night outside the studio by a knife-wielding stalker, and is not rehired for the next season, because, according to her employers, "of cutbacks across the board," and who in the ensuing lawsuit becomes very rich and endows a journalism scholarship in her dead siblings' names; two of whom grow up to design and market a line of toys, furniture, and multimedia entertainments for the parents of multiples, including a kit, complete with iron-ons, for creating tee shirts that bear the message BABY, with an arrow, many times over, and who claim that the dead siblings never existed; one of whom grows up with some sort of persecution complex and fantasizes elaborate mass slayings of his siblings, then becomes briefly famous for his memoir about growing up as one of the so-called "Piedmont Quints" in which he claims to have been brutally tortured by the others and confesses his fantasies that the two dead siblings had become guardian angels who watched over him through his darkest hours, though a fat lot of good they did him; and one who grows up to become a late-night radio call-in psychologist specializing in sexual problems and who discovers the hats in her parents' attic when her mother dies, including the two that were worn, very briefly, by the dead siblings for a newspaper article she still has a clipping of, but realizes she will never know which two, and so smells them all and crushes each to her breast for good measure

———

MY EYEGLASSES, covered with a thickening layer of dust that I never seem to notice, that I simply adjust to, until at last I clean them out of habit, and discover a new world sharp and filled with detail, whose novelty and clarity I forget about completely within five minutes

———

YOUR SIGNATURE, rendered illegible by disease

WEBER'S HEAD

John Weber, the first person to answer my ad, appeared pleasant enough, tall and round-faced with a receding cap of curls, sloped shoulders, and an easy, calm demeanor. He nodded constantly as I showed him around the place, as if willing to accept and agree with every single thing in the world for the rest of his life. At the time, these seemed like good portents. I didn't like looking for roommates, and I didn't like dealing with people, so I told him he was welcome to the room and accepted his check.

He moved in the next day with the help of a wan, stringy-haired woman wearing hiking shorts, though it was late October and forty degrees outside. The woman did not smile and hauled his boxes in the door with practiced efficiency while Weber began unpacking in his room. I asked her if she wanted any help.

"No," she said.

"Are you sure?" I wasn't doing anything, just waiting for noon to come along so that I could catch my bus.

She said nothing in response, but shook her head vigorously, her hair falling over her face. I returned to my coffee and magazine and left her alone.

When I came home from work that night, John Weber was standing alone in the kitchen with an apron around his waist. Various things were hissing and bubbling in pots and pans on the stove, and he beckoned me over with his spatula. The kitchen table was set with two placemats—they must have belonged to him, because I had never owned any in my life—and there were separate glasses for water and wine. I didn't recognize the silverware, either. It was heavy and bright and lay upon folded cloth napkins.

"Expecting a guest?" I was thinking of the woman from that morning.

"Nope. Just a roommate!"

He was grinning, waiting for a reaction.

"You mean me?"

"You're my only roommate!" he laughed. "Take a load off!"

His manner could be described as bustling. He pulled out my chair for me, took the briefcase from my hand and set it on the floor behind me. He said, "Red or white?"

I looked at the table, and back at him. "What?"

"Red or white?"

"Uh . . ."

He rolled, jocularly, his large, slightly bulging gray eyes, then gestured toward the counter, where two bottles of wine stood, uncorked. One of them, the white, was tucked into a cylindrical stone bottle cooler, the kind you keep in the freezer. I had never seen one outside of a cooking supply catalog, and had never considered that somebody might actually own one.

"Uh . . . red," I said.

"You sure not white?"

"Yes."

"Because the white spoils faster once you open it."

"I'm sorry," I said. "White wine gives me a headache."

He rolled his eyes again, not so jocularly this time, and snatched the white wine off the counter. Into the fridge it went with a clatter, and the cooler into the freezer. He poured my red wine with unnecessary haste, and some of it slopped over onto the tablecloth, which must also have belonged to him.

"How was your day?" he asked a minute later, his back to me, his arms working over the pots and pans.

"Fine." I took a swig of wine. It was not the gamy plonk I usually drank. "How was yours?"

"Exciting! I'm glad to be here."

"Is your room all put together?"

"Sure!" He turned off each burner and began transferring food to a pair of china plates. "I don't have many possessions," he went on. "I don't believe in them."

"Well, what about the napkins and placemats and tablecloth and all that?"

"Oh, someone gave them to me."

With a flourish, he whipped off his apron and hung it on a wall hook that I was certain he had installed there himself for this express purpose. In response to this effort, the landlord would no doubt someday withhold twenty dollars of the security deposit. Then John Weber lifted the two plates high into the air and glided them onto the placemats. With a similar motion, he seated himself, then grinned at me again, awaiting my reaction.

Before me lay a lovely-looking lamb chop, overlaid with a coarse sauce of what appeared to be diced tomatoes, onions, and rosemary. There was a little pile of roasted new potatoes and some spears of asparagus. It was really very impressive, and I looked at it in dismay as the sounds of rending and smacking reached me from across the table. It was quite a sight, John Weber digging in; he yanked shreds of lamb from the chop with his incisors, folded entire spears of asparagus roughly into his mouth. His jaw clicked and popped. He wasn't a slob—on the contrary, he dabbed constantly at the corners of his mouth with his napkin—but his ardent champing had its closest analogue in the desperate feast of a hyena hunched over a still-twitching zebra. It was unsettling. I tried not to make any sound.

"Hey," he said, his pupils dilated, his shoulders faintly heaving. "What's the matter?"

"John," I said. "I'm sorry to tell you this. I already ate."

The fork slowly descended to the plate.

"Why didn't you say?" he wanted to know.

"You'd already cooked it."

"You could have called home."

"John," I said, meeting his hurt and angry gaze. "I don't know you. You moved in this morning. Why would I expect you to cook dinner for me?"

He waved his hand in front of his face, sweeping the question away. "We're roommates," he said. "We have to show one another a little bit of respect."

I should have kicked him out right then and there. But I didn't. How could I? You don't kick a man out of his home for making you dinner. And I had already cashed the check.

"All right," I said. "I'm sorry." And I picked up my knife and fork and went to work.

———

The apartment building in question stood, or rather lay, at the bottom of a mountain. It was a one-story strip of six units, with four arranged in a row and two more at an angle, to accommodate a rock outcropping in the back. Our apartment was one of the ones on the angle, and our back windows looked out at the outcropping. Even at the height of summer, we didn't get a single ray of sunlight until midafternoon.

The mountain was called Mount Peak—a terrible name for a mountain. It didn't even have a peak: it was rounded on top. It was part of the western foothills of the Rockies, and though this all sounds very bracing and natural, the fact is that Mount Peak was, in almost every sense, a thoroughly shitty mountain. The southern third had been completely chopped off to make way for a highway, its western face had been logged and stood bare and weedy. An abandoned housing project jutted out to the north like a tumor. In addition, about a hundred feet above our apartment, the local high school had spelled out the name of its mascot, BEAVERS, in white-painted stones, and a few of these would roll down each week and thump against our back wall. Sometimes one of them would ricochet off a tree stump and crash through a window.

Even the wildlife looked scraggly and sick. Mangy elk could often be found mornings, standing around in the parking lot looking confused. You would have to honk at them to leave, if you were lucky enough to own a car. We once found a dead bighorn sheep lying on our front stoop, and another time we had to cancel a dinner date because a scrawny, insane-looking moutain lion was standing outside our door, growling.

By "we" I don't mean John Weber and me; I mean Ruperta and me. Ruperta was my girlfriend. She left me because we had sex problems—specifically, the not having of it. It was my fault. I didn't want to do it anymore. All I wanted to do was read and reread from my library of books about trains. It was my interest in trains that caused me to rent this place, with Ruperta, five years before; if you hiked to the south end of the mountain you got a great view of the tracks down below. But a few months after we moved in, the only freight company that used the tracks went out of business, and they fell into disrepair.

Honestly, I don't know what was wrong with me. I felt like I was slowing down. I had moved to this town to go to graduate school in environmental and land use law, and I suppose I lost enthusiasm. To be sure, the subject was not very interesting to me. I read a lot of thick, boring books, and went on field trips to see how various ranches diverted creek water. Then, one day, while inspecting a barbed-wire fence as part of a summer internship, I fell into a ravine and broke my arm. When I got out of the hospital, I had lost all desire to return to school, and I started begging off when Ruperta wanted to get it on. She put up with that for a very long time, and this reasonableness caused me to lose all respect for her, respect I regained the moment she left. I missed her terribly.

Since quitting school, I had worked for eight dollars an hour editing the newsletter of a hunting and conservation outfit. The work took about three hours each week, so I spent the rest of the time pretending to do it and posting on internet messageboards under a variety of names. I chatted all day long about knitting, veganism, soccer, scrapbooking, and dog grooming, none of which I knew anything about, nor cared to learn. I was thoroughly debased, and at thirty-two felt like I'd been an old man for a long time. I saw no way of escaping the life I'd made for myself, save for the mountain falling down and crushing me.

———

Weber was also probably around thirty, but his girlfriend, Sandy, looked closer to forty. Forty-two, if I had to make a precise guess. She came twice a week to spend the night in Weber's room, where some kind of new age harp CD was cued up and left to repeat all night long. I asked Weber if he could turn the music off after midnight, and he laughed. "Of course not!" he said.

"Why not? It's hard to sleep."

"Well, Sandy can't sleep without it."

"But Sandy doesn't live here. I live here."

"Sandy is a guest." He shook his head. "I'm disappointed in you. You don't know how to treat a guest, do you. You should be ashamed of yourself."

I actually got to spend a fair amount of time alone with Sandy, since Weber liked to sleep in on the mornings after her visits—he was actually still in school, studying I don't know what—and she, like me, was an early riser. We sat across from one another at the table, me with the paper, she with nothing, drinking from gigantic mugs of coffee. She made cryptic little pronouncements in a withered, weary voice.

"John doesn't like coffee."

"There's a nuclear missile near here, I bet you didn't know that."

"John used to race bicycles competitively."

"It's possible to get certain diseases from fish, you know."

One morning in late autumn she said, incredibly, "John is a genius, you know."

I could not resist. "He is?"

Beneath her haylike skirt of hair, her chin seemed to nod very slightly.

"What's he a genius of?"

"Art," she replied.

"Art?"

"Sculpture. He's a sculpturist."

"I would never have guessed."

It was hard to see what her eyes were up to under there, but I had the feeling they were glaring at me. We drank our coffees for several minutes.

"Don't be an asshole," Sandy said.

———

It was another week before I found out exactly what type of sculpturism Weber was getting up to in his room. He had invited me in there more than once, usually so that I could hear one or another horrible song that he was grooving on:

"Hey, come listen to this!"

"I can hear it from out here," I would reply from the living room.

"No, you can't. You need to get the full audio spectrum."

"John, I can hear enough out here to know I don't want to come in there and hear it better."

A moment of silence that suggested deep puzzlement, and then he would emerge wearing a pained expression. "You mean you don't like it?"

"No."

"How can you not like this?" Gesturing back toward the room.

"By hearing it, and then considering my feelings about it, and then deciding I don't like it."

"You know," he said on one of these occasions, "it really hurts my feelings when you won't listen to my music."

At which point I set down *Small-Gauge Railways of the American Northeast,* carefully marking the page with a magazine subscription card, and said, "One, it isn't your music, John. You didn't compose it or perform it. It's somebody else's music that you happen to like. And two, we don't have to like the same things. Do I keep asking you to look at pictures of trains?"

"No, and maybe you should." He crossed his freckled arms over his scrawny chest. "Trains are cool. I like trains. Why don't you show me your stuff more often?"

"I don't want to."

"Right! There's the problem! Sometimes I think we should see a counselor or something."

"A roommate counselor?"

"A relationship counselor."

"We're not in a relationship."

"We're in a roommate relationship."

And so on. Thus, I had managed to avoid being lured into the dark heart of Weber's personal space, which in my opinion had, in the form of his incessant demand for attention and approval, encroached upon the rest of the apartment enough already. But then, apparently dissatisfied by my resistance to his overtures, he began to borrow my books. I came home from work one night, ate (I had managed to get him to stop serving me meals, though not to stop him demanding grocery money for the meals he would continue to offer to make me), showered, put on my pajamas, and went to bed with a good heavy train book. Then John Weber walked in.

"Hey dude."

"What do you want, John."

He came and sat on the edge of my futon, which lay on the floor in the corner as it had ever since Ruperta took our bed. I scootched my legs over and pulled up the covers to my chest.

"I wanted to return your book," he said and handed me *New Innovations in Rail Travel 1982–1992.*

"Where did you get this?"

"I borrowed it."

"From where?" I demanded.

"Right there, man." He pointed to one of the enormous sagging homemade bookshelves that lined the walls of my room.

"You came in here and took my book?"

"Not took. Borrowed. There's a difference."

I wanted very badly to debate the precise difference between taking and borrowing and establish definitively which of the two he had done. But I also wanted him to leave immediately. For a moment, I was suspended between these contradictory channels of annoyance, and in that weightlessness felt the presence of a terrifying possibility: that John Weber's obliviousness and intensity were, in some twisted way, actually profound. That there was substance to him, a substance that I would forever lack. My heart spasmed and I capitulated. "Thank you," I said and stared daggers at him until he left.

But the next night, when he was at Sandy's place, I couldn't find a particular hobo oral history I was looking for, and I became convinced that Weber had taken it away to his inner sanctum. And so I threw open his door and plunged in, expertly flipping the oddly-placed switch—it was two feet from the doorjamb and about nine inches too high—that I remembered clearly from the days when Ruperta used the room as an office. At which time I saw that Weber was not, in fact, at Sandy's—he was right here in his room. Except he was a uniform medium-gray color, and his body was missing below the neck.

Of course I screamed. You, too, would have screamed. I want to scream today, remembering it. Weber's head. It sat on top of— appeared, in fact, to be growing out of—a miniature chest of drawers in the corner of his room. It was made of modeling clay. John Weber, sculpturist. The head was life-size; it rested upon a sturdy neck, which thickened into what should have been shoulders, but in fact was merely a broad smearing of clay that covered the top of the bureau and extended partway down the sides. This head was extraordinarily, horrifyingly realistic. The flared nostrils, the slightly uneven ears, the chinless chin—they were all perfect. The head was so fabulously accomplished that it brought out details I didn't notice that I'd noticed on the real John Weber—the lines around the eyes, the pockmarks on the forehead, the crookedness of the teeth. He even had the smile down right—that awful half smirk, simultaneously innocent and calculating, relaxed and desperate, brilliant and moronic.

How was it possible that John Weber could see himself so clearly? He was the most obstinately unobservant person I had ever met. Of course, there was his epic, heroic narcissism; that probably explained it. To one side of the head, attached to the wall, was a foot-square mirror where, no doubt, he studied his face as he worked. This, I surmised, must have been the real reason he invited me into his room. The music was a ruse. He wanted me to see—to admire—the head.

When he came home late the next morning, I watched him more closely than usual, hoping to learn how I had missed this hidden talent. He seemed to appreciate the extra attention and became voluble.

"Have a good night?" he asked me.

It gave me a bit of a shock. Did he know, somehow, that I had gone into his room? I was feeling bad about it, as I had later found the hobo book hidden underneath a corner of my futon. "Fine," I said cautiously. "And you?"

"Oh," he said, with a smarmy touch of wistfulness. "I guess so."

"Is something wrong?"

He exhaled loudly, pretended to consider before speaking. "Let me ask you something."

"Okay . . ."

"What do you think of Sandy?"

"Ahh . . . she seems . . . very nice."

"Well, of course she's nice. She's very nice. What I mean is . . . I'm afraid maybe we're a bad match."

"How so?"

I'd been alone on the couch, and now Weber flopped down next to me and swung one leg over the other. He wore a thick fleece zippered sweatshirt and, like Sandy, an unseasonable pair of many-pocketed khaki hiking shorts.

"Well, there's the age difference, for one thing."

I shrugged. "She's not that much older."

"You mean younger. I'm not that much older, you mean. That's it though, I kind of am. I mean, I think she thinks of me as being like a mentor or something. You know? I'm so much more talented and mature than her, it's like I'm like her father. Or actually I'm nothing like her father, I'm like another father."

"How old is she, exactly?"

"She's nineteen."

I could only blankly stare.

"I know, I know, robbing the cradle, right?" He stood up now and began to pace. "Her parents totally hate me. They think I'm corrupting her or something. Which is totally crazy since I don't even believe in sex before marriage."

"You don't?" I said.

John Weber laughed. "No, of course not, are you nuts? That's a recipe for disaster. And don't tell her I told you because this is totally private and secret but Sandy is not a virgin *at all,* and her parents don't know obviously, and that's what's crazy, I'm keeping her on the straight and narrow, not corrupting her!"

"Wow."

"And I am very cool with that. With her having sex, like, in her past. I mean, I still respect her and all. But I dunno, I mean, she wants to have sex and kiss and all that, because she's used to it I guess, but at this point if I did that stuff it would be like doing it to my daughter or something, on account of this being-like-her-father thing. Not like her father," he self-corrected, "like a second father."

"You don't kiss?"

"On the cheek." He blushed. "Sort of neck, too."

That was enough for me. I stood up. "I have to go to work," I said.

"No you don't. It's only ten thirty."

"There are errands I need to do."

"The next bus won't be here for half an hour."

"I am going to walk to town."

His raised his eyebrows. "You are? That's so cool. I am coming with you." He went to the coatrack and shrugged on his jacket. "I have to get some fresh air and straighten all this out in my head."

Did he say "my head" with special, slightly fey, significance? I believe that he did. I did not want to walk the two miles to town, let alone with John Weber, but that's what I ended up doing, and in retrospect it was a good thing, because I bumped into Ruperta. In order to get away from Weber as quickly as possible, I had pretended to need something at the first retail business we passed, a fishing and hunting supply store at the edge of town.

"What do you need there?" he wanted to know.

"Some very strong filament. Fishing line. For hanging something."

Weber seemed to recoil. "Well, I'm not going in there with you."

"Okay," I said, perhaps too readily.

"I don't believe in killing animals," he went on. "That's, like, an animal-murdering supply store, basically."

I couldn't help myself. I asked, "But . . . don't you eat meat?"

He snorted. "Well, yeah, but that's different. That's meat animals. This is wildlife."

I'd be lying if I said I didn't envy him. I wanted what he had: the ability to remake the world on the fly, to force it to conform to his vision. Or maybe what I really envied was his vision: that he had one. In any event, I hated him. I said goodbye and left him to his cognitive dissonance. Then I went inside and gazed back through the window at his hunched form as he slouched toward town. When I turned around, I saw Ruperta behind the counter.

"What are you doing here?" she said.

"What are *you* doing here?"

She shrugged. "Bernice fired me." Bernice was her old boss, the owner of a catering company that Ruperta had managed. "For no reason! She said I was spying on her through her windows at night. Which obviously I wasn't. She's fired half the staff. She'll be out of business by New Year's and in the loony bin by Groundhog Day. Who's the big guy?"

I explained as best I could about Weber, and told her about the head. She nodded, smiling wryly. I was in love with her. And here I thought I had made so much progress.

"Still on those train books?"

"No," I said, "I've kind of lost interest."

"Huh," she said. "Well. Goodbye."

I hadn't intended to leave. But I said goodbye and walked the rest of the way into town.

—

For the next two weeks, I hoped daily that Weber would spend the night at the home of his immoral, withered teen sex addict so that I could go snoop in his bedroom. When he did, I explored every corner, digging through his stuff carefully at first and later with desperate abandon. The room produced more fascinating artifacts than I had anticipated—love letters from various adolescent girls (boringly, they seem to have been written when Weber, too, was an adolescent); photographs of Weber and some other people at a party, in which only Weber appeared sober; several books on sculptural technique (which, oddly, didn't appear ever to have been opened); and, inside a special little carved Indian-looking hinged box lined with crushed velvet, a single, foil-wrapped, six-months-expired, spermicidally-lubricated condom. I could not help but let out a little bark of laughter when I saw it. But I then remembered that Weber was the one with the girlfriend, not me, and I licked my lips in bitter humiliation.

The head, meanwhile, had improved. It had become creepier. It was . . . animated, almost; it had a life force. Weber had turned it, so that now it faced the window and gazed at Mount Peak with admiration, respect, and not a little irony, as if it and the mountain had made a pact. The freckles and blotches that populated the real John Weber's face had been reproduced here, somehow, as slight depressions or perhaps microscopically thin plateaus; their monochrome relief gave them a quality of terrible realness, and I could not refrain from touching them. Then, in the harsh glare from Weber's daylight-corrected lamp, I saw that my fingerprints had marred, subtly, the surface of the head and mixed with Weber's own. I thought of Ruperta and emitted a small whimper.

Have I described her? I don't think that I have. Ruperta was an arrangement of pleasing roundnesses, wide round eyes nestled in wide round glasses, surrounded by black parentheses of hair set atop a full, pink melon head. Her body was all balls stuck to balls: a snowman of flesh. She was my type—indeed, the perfect expression of it. I walked to town every day now in order to pass by the animal-murdering supply store, where she allowed me to speak to her briefly each day, to construct the elaborate illusion that I was leading a respectable and appealing life. She told me that she had learned to fire a rifle and to tie trout flies, and that she liked these things a great deal, and what did I think of that? I liked that very much, I said, and as I said it, it became true. I felt the possbility of reinvention, of reconciliation. Some days I wept as I walked the rest of the way to work.

John Weber, meawhile, did not seem himself. Sometimes, he appeared not to notice me at all. I found him one morning sitting at the kitchen table, gazing out the window at the mountain. In the next room, I recalled, the head was doing exactly the same thing.

"John," I said. "What's the matter?"

"Nothing," he replied.

I stood there, unsure what I should do. Had John Weber just turned down an opportunity to speak? He looked so glum. Or, rather . . . serious.

"No, what?" I persisted.

He turned to me now, slowly, and regarded me as though he were deciding what sort of person I was, whether I could be trusted with what he had to say. After a moment, he came to a decision.

"Well, to be honest, for a while there I wasn't sure about you. You're a little self-absorbed, you know. But I guess we're really friends now, aren't we?"

"Sure." I thought of the condom, nestled in its tiny secret bed, and felt guilty.

"I've decided to ask Sandy to get engaged."

I tried, but failed, not to say, "Really?"

"Yes. And if she agrees, I am going to make love with her."

Regret flooded my body—I had passed up the chance to never hear this!

"I have a plan," Weber said, brightening. "I'm going to invite her on a hike. Up Mount Peak. And we're going to go all the way to the Beavers sign. And I'll propose to her, and if she says yes, I'm going to point down at our roof and say, 'See that? That's where I'm going to make passionate love to you as soon as we get down there.'"

"Umm, you want me to make myself scarce?"

He waved his hand. "Ah, no, doesn't matter, hang around if you want. Anyway, then we're each going to take a white stone from the Beavers sign, and we're going to bring them down here and lay them next to the bed while we do it. That's the plan."

"There's a big pile of the stones out back," I pointed out.

"The stones aren't the point, roommate," he said. "Getting the stones is the point."

"I see."

"And plus," he said, his dark mood utterly dispelled now, "I have something else for her. A very special thing I've been making."

"Wow."

"Do you want to see it?"

"I think that's just between you two."

"That's a good point. I can't show it to you. What was I thinking? It has to be pure. Only I have set my eyes upon it, and she will be the first ever to see it, aside from its maker."

"That's romantic," I said.

He was euphoric now. "Really? You think so?" He stood up. "Oh man, this is so awesome. I am so gonna get engaged to her." And before I could stop him, he came to me and hugged me. "Thanks, man. You're the greatest. I was so wrong about you."

"You're welcome," I said uncertainly and withdrew from our embrace. Weber threw on his coat and marched out the door, presumably to go set up his Big Day.

That day came quickly. The following Saturday morning the two of them set out at dawn on a gear-collecting mission and reappeared a few hours later in their excursion getups: fleece jackets, tan shorts lousy with zippered pockets (new ones, with more pockets than ever before), sleek boots of synthetic fabrics in natural colors, and matching backpacks with a single, diagonal padded strap. Weber looked elated. Sandy looked skeptical. The backpack strap was very wide and kept pressing into one or another of her small breasts, forcing her to adjust it every thirty seconds or so.

"I got us some stuff," Weber said.

"I can see that," I replied.

"It's all for our special day."

Sandy said, "I still don't see what's so special about it."

"Everything," Weber said, taking her hands. "Everything about it is very special." I caught a glimpse of Sandy rolling her eyes.

They turned, walked out the door, and headed for the mountain. But after a moment, Weber came back. He hurried over to me and laid his hands on my shoulders. Even through my oxford shirt I could feel how damp they were.

"I won't be the same when I come back. You need to understand that, roomie."

"Okay . . ."

"Old John Weber will be no more." His face appeared beatific, or perhaps just flushed. "You won't be able to count on my advice— new John Weber might be beyond all that. So I just want to tell you now—you need to change, too."

"Do I?"

"Put it all behind you. The trains and stuff. All your internet groups. Find purpose for your life. That's all." He lifted his hands and brought them down on my shoulders a second time, perhaps a bit too heartily.

"Did you look on my computer?" I asked him.

But he only shook his head, his real head, the less intelligent of the two. "So long," he said and marched out.

Here's what had happened the night before: I strolled into the fishing and hunting shop right before it closed and asked Ruperta if she'd let me take her out to dinner. She said yes. We got into her car and drove east around Mount Peak, and then south behind its much more impressive twin, Mount Clark. Eventually we came to the large log structure that housed Pappy's Best Steaks Ever Grill, where, if you had the money and, more importantly, the desire, you could walk around back and pick out, from a meadow, which grass-fed steer you wished to devour that night. They would slaughter it on the spot, and when you were through eating, they would load the leftover butchered cuts, wrapped in white paper and packed into cardboard boxes, onto the back of your pickup truck.

We did not choose that option, though. Ruperta had some prime rib, and I ordered barbecued chicken.

"You're not going all hippie vegetarian on me, are you?" she asked.

"Chicken's not a vegetable," I argued.

"It's close."

We didn't say much during the meal. Afterward we drove out to the all-night shooting range, and I watched Ruperta spray a man-shaped target with hot lead underneath the arc lights. I was impressed—she was very good. When she was through we sat in the car and made out, and she lay her fat little hand on my crotch.

"Is this real?" she quipped.

"Ha ha."

"You should know I slept with my boss a couple of times."

"Oh," I said. I had assumed, of course, that she would go seeking amorous companionship, but it was hard to imagine it actually happening. I felt very small.

She frowned and removed her hand. "Hmm. Just like old times."

And so all this was on my mind as I sat and watched through the kitchen window as Weber and Sandy scaled the mountain. Now, I am not big on epiphanies. But as their bunched, indistinguishably hairy calves vanished from the frame, I felt a bottomless hole open up in the floor of my soul, and I knew with sickening certainty that, if I did not leave this place immediately, I was going to die here. John Weber would marry his weathered nymph, and they would keep me, like a son or drooling pet, in this hideous little clapboard prison. Or worse yet, Sandy would decline to wed, and then Weber and I would be alone. One way or another, I would never escape Weber. His avidity was more powerful than my aversion. He had a life force—he had *joie de vivre*. All I had was a collection of train books and an intimidating ex-girlfriend.

Maybe he was right about me.

I went to Weber's room and pawed, once again, through his possessions. I had my own things, of course, mementoes of an unremarkable life, stored away in boxes and crates in the closet, but they didn't interest me. I knew Weber's better than mine. The head still stood on its pedestal, gazing out at the mountain's cheesy face, and was I imagining it, or did it look a little smugger these days, a little more smarmy, a little more glib? I don't know what made me do what I did next—some uncharacteristic upwelling of personality, maybe—but I dropped the packet of state-themed postcards I was holding, took three steps across the room, and mashed in Weber's nose with my thumb. I gasped, as if having just watched someone else do it. The face was ruined, of course; the jolly ape Weber had always secretly resembled was revealed in all its glory, with my whorled print in the center of it.

That was that. I was gone. I would leave it all behind. I ran to the bedroom; snatched up my wallet, an extra pair of eyeglasses, and my only pair of clean socks; and bolted for the door, shouldering on my coat as I went.

I made it to the middle of the gravel lot before I changed my mind. The air was chill, the sun was nowhere to be found, and I had already lost heart. I couldn't just leave. I couldn't just start over. What had I been thinking? I was not that kind of man; rather, I was the kind of man who endured, ignored, and took his lumps. Perhaps I could mound the nose back into shape. I turned, drew a deep breath, and took one step back toward the door.

There was a rumbling. Thunder, I surmised—or a big rig passing on the freeway. But I could feel it in my stomach, in my bowels, and I knew that this was something else, a new sound, low and terrible.

A moment later, dozens of animals, their patchy fur standing on end, came pouring around the sides of our building—squirrels, deer and elk, grouse and chukars, a mountain cat and a lone galloping moose—and streamed past me as if I were a rock or tree. I did not understand what it was I was seeing. The animals fled, the rumble grew in intensity, and I looked up to see an avalanche, a white wave fast approaching, scouring the mountain clean: a million little boulders, ten years of Sisyphean teenage ambition loosed from the tyranny of the text. The BEAVERS sign, ruined, and on the rampage.

A hundred lifetimes might have passed in those awful moments, as the stones screamed down the rock face—a hundred of my lifetime, anyway, which might as well have been lived in a second, for all the good it had done anyone—and buried our lousy little shack of a home. Buried is the wrong word, perhaps. Annihilated is more like it. Our apartment unit, all of the apartment units, were crushed. The wave stopped at my feet, half-surrounding me in an implausible arc of apparent magnetic repulsion, and I stood there, blinking at the dusty ruins.

Of course there would be lawsuits, lots of them. There would be resignations, elections, excuses, exhortations. The landlord would flee. The Open Space Committee would be formed. The high school would change the name of its mascot. And, in time, the crushed bodies of Weber and his girl would be discovered in the rubble, and upon her broken finger an engagement ring would be found. This last, of course, is the detail that would be best remembered: a love so strong, it brought down a mountain.

My own life, though, would never be so romantic. I would merely shack back up with Ruperta, regain my potency, and happily resign myself to life as a kept man. When a heart attack claimed her lovesick employer, she would buy the business for a song and open three more across the state. She would become mildly famous throughout the region for her amusing television ads in which she lured whitetail deer with a come-hither glance. And when, in a rare exhibition of initiative, I proposed marriage to her, she would respond by driving us to the courthouse to get it over with.

As for Mount Peak, it still stands, renamed Mount Sandy, thanks to the passionate lobbying efforts of Weber's fiancée's mother and father. (Weber's family, for their part, just wanted to put everything behind them.) Nature has been allowed to reclaim it—the logging roads closed, the housing project bulldozed, the forest reseeded. From our taxidermy-festooned house across town, the new saplings seem to shroud it in a haze of new green, like a girl in a peekaboo teddy. By the time we're old, it will be wearing a heavy coat, like a stout old fellow with a war wound.

This I am looking forward to seeing, from the picnic table on the back deck, where I have learned to tie flies for my boss, my wife. It is a pastime designed to endure, a tedium of infinite small variations. Weber was right about me, that I would be better off with some kind of purpose. I'm not a man, not really, just the gray clammy shadow of one—startlingly realistic at times, sure, but the product of hands not my own. I sit, bent over my vise, under the watchful eye of Mount Sandy, and expect to be here, still doing it, when I drop dead of old age.

ECSTASY

The sitter was asleep and dreaming when footsteps sounded on the porch. Her dream was anxious; it was spring and finals were not far away. Exams had never bothered her before, but now she had decided, in the middle of her sophomore year at college, to major in chemistry, and for the first time her performance was of real importance to her. So, after putting the children to bed, she had spent the evening rereading her chemistry textbook and class notes, attempting to cram this vital information further into her already-packed head. The footsteps woke her: she sat up on the couch, the dream dissolving. What had it been about? No matter, the children's parents were back. Her watch said midnight. Maybe time for another hour of work, when she got home.

The parents were decent people. They tended to shuffle around on the porch a little before coming inside, to spare the sitter the embarrassment of being found asleep. They didn't mind her sleeping—in fact they often told her that she ought to get more sleep—but the sitter liked to be in control of a situation. The parents must have sensed this; they gave her space. She rubbed her eyes and shook her head. Any moment now they would open the door.

Instead there was a knock. The sitter looked at the deadbolt, making sure that it was engaged. A knock, at midnight? In this neighborhood? A man's shadow darkened the curtain over the door. He shifted from foot to foot, waiting.

She went to the door and stood in front of it. Who could it be? A criminal, she reasoned, wouldn't knock. She quickly peeked behind the curtain before the illogic of this thought could sink in. There he was, a young man in a uniform. A policeman. He was gazing to his left, at a screen of clematis blooming on the wrought-iron trellis that enclosed the porch. Beneath the clematis she could see a tricycle, a garden spade, a snow shovel that had not yet been put away. The policeman was tapping his foot.

She unlocked and opened the door. The policeman stood stiffly, his hands behind his back. On his belt hung a radio and a holster with a gun in it. A wire ran from the radio up to his shoulder, where a small microphone was pinned. He looked into her eyes and said, "Miss? May I come in?"

She stepped back and he entered, closing the door behind him. As though it were an afterthought, he removed his hat. The two of them looked at each other. She thought that maybe she had seen this policeman before. He might have been the one who broke up a party she was at, a party where there was beer. She didn't like this sort of party but had gone because her friend asked her. She drank beer from a huge plastic cup and sat near the stereo, listening to the music. Actually she had had a great time, until the police came. This policeman had a narrow face and head and wavy black hair, and brown eyes that blinked. He cleared his throat, preparing to speak. A terrible thought occurred to the sitter.

The policeman said, "You're the babysitter for Mr. and Mrs. Geary?"

"Yes."

"Are the children sleeping?"

"Yes," she said.

"Maybe you should sit down."

The sitter made no move toward the sofa. She could see the depression, the smooth place on the slipcover where she had been sleeping moments before. She said, "What happened? Was there an accident?"

"Yes," said the policeman.

It gave her a jolt—as if she'd just made it happen by guessing. "Are they all right?" she asked, automatically.

The policeman looked down at his feet. He couldn't have been much older than she was. As young as twenty-five, certainly not more than thirty. He said, "They died."

"Oh my God," she said. It didn't seem like enough. She said it again, more quietly.

"She was carrying baby pictures. We figured . . . I had a feeling there would be a sitter." The policeman wobbled back and forth as he had done behind the door. He told her that a delivery van had hit their car head on; they'd been taken to the hospital but couldn't be saved. He said, "I'm sorry."

Now the sitter did want to sit down, but again she made no move. Nothing seemed appropriate. She continued standing before the policeman, continued to gaze at the spot where she'd been sleeping. The policeman's hand was resting on her shoulder now. "We've contacted the victim's—Mrs. Geary's—um, sister," he said. "We found her number in the victim's purse. She's coming up from Scranton. It'll be an hour or two. We were thinking—if you want to go home, you could go. A female officer could come and stay here. But we thought—if one of the children wakes up, you could—that is, it might be better if there wasn't a police officer here. If it was you instead." He took his hand off her shoulder, suddenly, as if he'd forgotten about it.

The sitter looked up at the policeman's face. It registered that she was being asked to do something. "Yes," she said. "Sure."

"You'll stay?"

"Yes."

He asked her name and address and phone number and wrote

them in a small spiral notebook. Then he took out a card with his name and the number of the police department, and he added the name of the female officer who could take over for her, if necessary. His name was Officer Clarke. He gave her the card. His handwriting was severely slanted, almost illegible. She thanked him. A sigh escaped her, because she'd been holding her breath. But he seemed to interpret the sigh as an expression of grief. His hand returned to her shoulder and squeezed it, very gently. "I'm sorry," he said. "Did you know them well?"

"Yes," she said, though she didn't, not really. Hadn't.

"I'm sorry," he said again.

"Uh huh."

After that, they stood there another moment, and then the sitter lost her balance, just a little, and the policeman caught her up in his arms and held her. It was odd, but it seemed like something he wanted to do. She let him. His radio microphone pressed into her forehead. She patted his back, as if consoling him. He smelled very clean, the uniform very new. She sort of squeezed him, to signal the end of the embrace, and pulled away. They stood in front of each other as before. She said, "Thank you. I'm sorry you had to do this."

"I've never done it before." He said this in a quiet, very un-cop-like voice; the embrace had seemed to soften him. His face looked different now, too.

"I'm sorry," she said again.

He straightened, seeming to recover himself. "Well. So am I. Thank you for agreeing to stay. The sister will be here soon, the sister and her husband. Their name is Low."

"Oh," she said, unsure of how to respond. Their name is low? What did that mean? Officer Clarke turned and went to the door. On the way out, he apologized again. Then he closed the door and was gone.

When she could no longer hear the police car, the sitter went to the sofa and sat there, her hands folded in her lap. She thought about what she should do. In a while she got up and began to walk around the house. She played a chord or two on the piano, very quietly, so as not to wake the children. She looked at a painting of some flowers on the wall. In the dining room, on a bookshelf, she found a row of photo albums. She pulled one down and opened it on the dining table. It was dark in the room, but a streetlamp cast enough light to see by. There were pictures of a party in a dirty apartment, people holding glasses of wine and one woman drinking directly out of a bottle of liquor. Here was Mrs. Geary talking to a curly-haired man, not Mr. Geary. On the next page was a bleary photo of the Gearys collapsed into a chair, laughing. A hand belonging to someone outside the frame was pointing at them. The hand, unlike the Gearys, was in sharp focus. Later in the book there were wedding photos, not professional ones, snapshots. The Gearys appeared to have gotten married in a forest. The sitter replaced the album and took down another. Here were pictures of Mrs. Geary, completely naked, giving birth to a baby. Her red anguished face and large breasts were in shadow in the background; in the foreground were her white legs and, beneath a thick patch of black pubic hair, a small red human head, its own thin hair slick and parted, as if combed. There were more pictures of the Gearys together with the new baby. Mr. Geary was fully dressed. The rest of the album consisted of baby pictures; when the Gearys appeared it was in a supporting role. A series of pictures depicted friends and relatives holding the baby. The baby was John, the older child, who was five now. The younger one, Emma, was two; the sitter knew that the other albums probably contained pictures of her birth and infancy. But she didn't want to look at them. She put the album back and returned to the dining table. She realized that all those people—the people at the drunken party, the friends and relatives, perhaps even the obstetrician—would have to find out about what happened. Some of them were probably finding out right now. She imagined their shocked faces and suddenly felt very sad and rested her head on her folded arms. Her face tightened, as if she were about to cry. But she didn't. The feeling passed. Another was coming, she sensed, but it wasn't here yet. She got up from the table and continued looking around the house. The kitchen, the den. She went up the stairs, treading lightly. She did not hesitate:

she went in the closed door of the Gearys' bedroom and switched on the lights.

It was tidy, if a little stuffy. The windows needed to be opened, the linens changed, but there was no one to do this, and no one ever would. The carpet was beige, the bedspread a knitted afghan. Family photos hung on the walls. The sitter took off her shoes and lay on the bed. At each side stood a white bedside table with a lamp on it. One of the tables also held a near-empty glass of water, a full bottle of aspirin, and a stack of parenting books. On the other was a science fiction paperback and a mug with some cold coffee dried to the bottom. She leaned over and opened this table's single drawer. The drawer was full of junk: thread, buttons, coins, papers, breath mints. There was a deck of cards, or rather just the box. The cards were missing. Instead there was a flimsy plastic sandwich bag containing three loosely rolled joints. She held up the bag, sniffed it, set it down beside her on the bed. Then she put the box away and closed the drawer. As she did this she noticed a book sticking out from under the bed.

She knew the book. It was a sex manual. She had a boyfriend last year who bought her a copy and was always trying to get her to flip through it with him while they were in bed together. When they broke up she threw the book out. Now she took it onto her lap and paged through it. After a moment a photograph fell out. It was a Polaroid of Mrs. Geary's face. The picture seemed to be taken in this very bed. Her eyes were closed and her mouth was open, and her hands were tangled in her long hair, which fell across the pillow. The sitter did not know Mrs. Geary to be long-haired: but then again, perhaps she was. Suddenly it was hard to remember. She looked at the picture for a while, then slid it into the pocket of her jeans. She put the book away, this time tucking it more thoroughly under the bed. After that, she lay back and closed her eyes. Soon she was asleep.

A noise in the house woke her. Were the sister and her husband here? No, not yet. The sound was nearer. Footsteps. A door opened. She sat up on the bed. A boy walked into the room.

It was John, the five-year-old. He seemed to have a stunned look on his face, and for a moment she imagined that somehow he had heard the news. But of course he hadn't. He was sleepwalking. This was something the boy did. Once he had brought his pillow downstairs and mashed it onto a bookshelf and went back up again. Another time, when she went up to check on him, she found him curled on the bathroom floor, clutching the bath mat. Now he looked at her without seeing and said, "I can't find my dog." Maybe he was referring to his stuffed dog, Albert, who was tucked under one arm. The sitter got down from the bed and took the dog from him and gave it back. "Here's your dog, John," she said. John didn't smile, didn't change his expression at all, but his voice registered relief. "I found my dog," he said. She put her arm around his shoulders and led him back to his room. He climbed into bed on his own. She sat on his small wooden chair while he closed his eyes and returned to restful sleep. There was a rhythmic sound in the room, and she realized it was her own breathing. She was breathing fast, shallow breaths, and her heart was thumping. She tried to calm down but couldn't. The breaths just came faster. She left John's room, closed his door behind her, and went back to the Gearys' bedroom.

For a short while, the sitter stood there panting. Then she threw open the window. Inside the wall, the sash weights rattled. She picked up the plastic bag and shoved it into her pocket with the photo, and she stripped the bed and carried the sheets down the hallway and stairs. In the downstairs bathroom she emptied the bag into the toilet and flushed away the joints and dropped the bag into the little wastebasket beside the toilet. She loaded the sheets into the washing machine and turned it on. Then she went back to the sofa to wait.

It wasn't long before Mrs. Geary's sister arrived. She didn't knock, she just walked right in. She looked like Mrs. Geary, but older, thinner, with a longer face. The sitter had never seen her before, but clearly the woman was transformed by grief. Her face was wet and frantic and her long hair stuck to her cheeks. The sitter stood and the sister came right at her. At first the sitter thought she was about to be struck, but the sister embraced her, harder than the policeman had done, and let out a cry. The sitter said, "The children are sleeping."

Mrs. Geary's sister pulled back and seemed to search the sitter's face for something. "They're all right," the sitter said. "They don't know."

The sister nodded, backing away. She seemed afraid of the sitter somehow. Her husband had entered and stood behind her now, a lanky Asian man wearing large, wire-rimmed glasses and a wrinkled shirt. Now the sitter understood: their name was Lo, L-O. Mr. Lo nodded as his eyes met the sitter's. She nodded back. The washing machine churned and thumped.

The sitter looked at the two of them, who stood apart, not touching. She wanted very badly to leave. "I'll go now," she said. She bent down and picked up her books and notes from the coffee table. "I'm sorry. Really, I am. I can babysit later this week, if you want. If you need help." She certainly did not want them to take her up on the offer, and they didn't ask for her name or phone number. She said, "I'm so sorry."

"Okay," said Mrs. Lo. She looked at the ceiling, as though the children might be visible through it. The sitter moved to the door. She looked back at Mr. and Mrs. Lo once more. "Goodbye," she said, and walked out.

She walked home in the dark, feeling the photograph bending in her back pocket. It was a beautiful, clear night. A spring smell, the smell of dead things exposed to light and warmth, filled the air. The sitter felt a strange precipitousness, as if a hand were pushing her from behind, threatening to topple her. She jogged the last few blocks to her dormitory, clutching her books in both arms.

It was past two when she got to her room. She had a roommate, but the roommate was out, studying with her boyfriend. She put down the books and went to the sink, where she filled a glass with water and drank it. Then she lay down on her bed in the dark and closed her eyes. She tried to think about the Gearys—it seemed like the right thing to do—but only the children came to mind: Emma's determined walk, the way she pumped her small fists, the sound of her small sneakers dragging across the carpet. She thought about John's obsession with dinosaurs. All children liked dinosaurs, but at this moment his interest seemed incredible to her. All the amazing things he knew, the facts. She thought about this for a while, and then her phone rang. She got up and went to the kitchen, where she had left it, and sunk into a chair as she answered. It was Officer Clarke.

"I wanted to thank you," he said. "Most people would have gone home."

"Anyone would stay."

"Well, thanks anyway. It was a good thing you did. I'm here now and Mr. and Mrs. Lo are seeing to the children."

"Are they awake?"

"No," said Officer Clarke, but he was obviously lying. "They're inside," he added. "Actually, I'm sitting in my patrol car."

"Oh," she said. She felt the invisible hand pressing into her back, and she leaned forward, supporting herself with her hand on the table's edge.

"Listen," said the policeman, "I was wondering—"

"Officer Clarke?" she said suddenly.

"Yes?"

"I have to tell you something."

"What is it?" he said.

"I stole something. From the Gearys' house. I stole a photograph." There, she thought: that's better.

A silence followed. If he asked her to return the photo, she would go back right now and do it. But he said, "I guess that's all right. I guess . . . you just keep it."

"Okay," she said. She stood up. There was another silence between them now, a companionable one, even though she was alone at home and he was sitting in a car in someone's driveway. She listened to him breathing and didn't feel the need to add anything. At last he said her name.

"Yes?" she said.

"I'd like to . . . see you again. Sometime. When you're . . . over this experience."

For a moment she didn't know what he meant. She thought it had something to do with the night's events. Then she understood.

She realized that she wanted him to come over right now. She would give him a cup of coffee, or maybe a beer, even though she was slightly underaged, even though he busted her once for drinking. She was sure he didn't remember the beer party, or at least not her involvement; he had taken one look at her and told her to go home. He said she was getting off easy this time. Now she thought: a policeman, asking me out. Her friends, were she to tell them, would be shocked and amazed. But all she said was, "Yes, okay."

"Is it really okay? I know I'm kind of old."

"You're not old."

"I'm twenty-eight. I was married before."

"Twenty-eight's not old."

He said, "I'm sorry about tonight."

"Me too," she said. And then she remembered something.

"All right, then. I have to go. I'll call you. I think . . . I think you're a very good person. I don't know how I know that."

After a moment she said "Thank you," though of course there was no way he could know that. Anyone would have stayed. Nevertheless she liked hearing him say it. She hung up the phone and went back to bed. She didn't want to get undressed. She lay there, her hand on her jeans, drawing shallow breaths.

What she remembered was the dream she'd been having, hours ago, the one that Officer Clarke interrupted. In it, she was working at a warehouse of some kind. She had to pack some very tall shelves with boxes, pamphlets, bulging envelopes, glass jars. There were so many of them, and they were all different sizes. She wedged them and turned them, trying to fill every inch of available space, trying to prevent the objects from squeezing out and falling on the floor. More objects were piled on a table behind her, and the pile was growing, supplemented by unseen workers. There was no way they would fit.

It was an anxiety dream. The memory of it sent a thrill through her. She shivered, as if with pleasure. It seemed wrong to be so excited; she tried to put the feeling away, to make herself feel the way she thought was appropriate, but the excitement persisted. It was all over her body, the feeling of getting away with something.

TOTAL HUMILIATION IN 1987

We rose at four in the morning—Margaret, the girls, and me—and zombied into the already-packed van to depart on our final family vacation to the little cabin on the shore of Lake Craig. The month was August, the sky was purple and empty, and the trees bowed before the oncoming thunderstorm that, with any luck, we wouldn't be here to enjoy. The drive into the mountains would take five hours, and I had loaded up the iPod with a special family vacation playlist that began with mellow ambient electronica and minimalist classical and gradually ramped its way up to classic rock and big band jazz. If I had calculated correctly, we would hear Duke Ellington's "Rockin' in Rhythm" (the Fargo 1942 version) as we turned onto the winding switchbacked road that, a thousand feet later, would hoist us over the pass between Mounts Ringwood and Edgar and down into our week of isolation from the world.

Everyone but me was asleep before we'd even left the county: Margaret with the seat belt supporting her wan face like a sling;

Lynnae and Lyrae conked identically in opposite corners of the back seat, in their way-too-skimpy hipster duds. Lyn was eleven, Rae was thirteen, and both knew something funny was going on, though neither had dared ask what. Heaped behind them were our possessions—recreational equipment, outdoor clothing, plastic sacks of food, a case of beer, a case of wine. At each of the girls' feet lay a satchel full of personal possessions—Rae, no doubt, her phone, her journal, and the thick romance paperbacks I winced every time I laid eyes on, absolutely contributing to her affection for them. Lyn's bag was most likely filled with gum and candy wrappers, her own music player (probably stuffed with contraband pop), and the nine-hundred-page science fiction epic she was determined to finish reading this week. Margaret's leather backpack was probably filled with work—menus, recipes, staff schedules—and her beloved BlackBerry, fitted into its fetishy leather holster.

I had brought little, and had nothing with me in the driver's seat, save for my water bottle. "That's because," Margaret had said without looking at me, when the previous night I had proudly stated my need for nothing more, "you are uncomplicated," the word signifying a whole collection of shortcomings I was supposed to embody, and which had come, in her mind, to constitute a kind of passive aggression. I did not entirely understand this theory and had vowed to give it some serious thought while we were at the lake. As for keeping a stash of goodies beside me in the car, what was I supposed to be able to do while driving, other than drink water? But this was unproductive thinking, Margaret would say, were she awake and I speaking my thoughts aloud, so I clammed up mentally and tried to focus on the road.

This was a pleasure. I love to drive. When it's early, as it was that day, the road is endlessly interesting, a gift that renews itself mile upon mile, and the few other drivers you pass are all your greatest friends. The road signs, the flashing lights are there for you alone, the state cops in their cruisers your personal protectors. The stars were winking out on my left, the sun rising on my right, and the van clung to every hill and dale as though it were driving itself. From time to time I cracked a window to let the air replenish itself; the girls seemed not to notice, though Margaret stirred, scowled, moved her stiff mouth as though dreaming of an uncooperative employee.

Everyone was awake by six, when we were about to leave the Thruway for our traditional stop at Mister Bip's. The girls were subdued and expressionless, their hair stuck to their faces; Margaret was staring out the window. I signaled and pulled off at the exit.

Rae, newly weight-conscious, had only toast and black coffee. Lyn ordered oatmeal, her breakfast every single morning since she got on solid food back in '96. Margaret chose the Greek omelet, and it sounded so good to me I asked for the same. She glanced at me as though wary of being mocked. I offered a thumbs-up, which she rebuffed with a blink.

"I wonder if this is all from the same part of the field," Lyn said ten minutes later, the first words any of us had spoken to the others in hours.

"What?" Margaret asked.

"Like where it was harvested." She held up a spoonful of the oatmeal. "If I was out there in the field, like, I could see all of my breakfast around me."

"Maybe," I said.

"Do you really need that much brown sugar?" Margaret wanted to know.

"I love brown sugar!"

"You are going to be so zit-infested someday," Rae offered.

"I think it's all from the same corner of the field," Lyn said, her tone indicating that the debate was over. "I think all these oats are friends." She switched to a tiny oat-voice. "Heeey, buddy! Wassup?"

I guffawed. Rae said God. Margaret looked at her watch.

An hour later, with Bob Dylan yammering about somebody's new hat, Rae said, "Damn, I'm hungry, Dave."

"You shouldn't have had just toast and coffee," I said.

"I know." She sighed. "Damn."

"That's enough damns," Margaret said wearily.

"Your mother's right."

I could hear Rae's lips smack. "Sorry, Mags," she said.

Margaret opened her mouth, then closed it without speaking.

"I saw you making love with him," Bob Dylan said. "You forgot to close the garage door."

———

A new alertness overcame us as we crested the mountain pass; everyone sat straight in their seats, on the lookout for minor changes in the landscape. The next fifteen minutes would set the tone for the days to come: was the bait and tackle stand still open? Was the *Adirondack Backpacker's Gazette* still in print? Would the water-stained map still be safely bolted behind cracked plexiglas in front of the defunct post office, as always? Yes, yes, and yes. Tentative good cheer reigned as we bumped and shuddered our way down the gravel road to the water. I glanced over at Margaret and saw the corners of her mouth twitching, as though in pleasure. The final test of our journey's success, however, still lay ahead: the Grimy Fisherman's Bass Shack, our favorite restaurant anywhere in the world. Its owner, Belinda, had become a good friend over the past decade; and though we wondered how many other "good friends" she had, among the many vacationers who wished, as we did, to feel like locals for one week a year, we nevertheless were certain her friendship with us was something special. Furthermore, the food at her Shack was fantastic, and Margaret had stolen, with Belinda's permission, many a fine dish from its modest menu.

It was to Margaret that Belinda's place was most important, and it was her sharp eye that noticed it first, set back in the pines at a bend in the road. "Thank God," she said, and I honked the horn as we passed. The place looked pretty empty, though—it didn't open until eleven.

Our cabin was not far beyond. We pulled into the gravel drive and leaped out with a collective cheer, the girls hugging one another the way they used to all the time when Rae was seven and Lyn was five. Margaret inhaled deeply. "Seems the same," she said.

"It'll be like always," I assured her.

To this, she had no response.

The key was under the stump behind the trash hutch, as usual, though it was a new stump: I had noticed the old one going rotten last year. We crowded around the door as I unlocked it, and tumbled in like a pack of stray cats.

The cabin was of rough-hewn, unpainted logs, and consisted of one large common room and two bedrooms, each containing a bunk bed. The four of us fanned out, sniffing around our favorite objects and areas, making sure they were as we left them. Dozens of visitors occupied this place every year, but we always got the impression, upon returning, that it had been empty since our last visit. There were always small differences—certain decades-old magazines missing, sheets that bore the scent of a new detergent, a favored dishrag retired from service—but rarely any of substance. One year there was a new refrigerator, which we all stared at in shock for some seconds. Another year, a woodstove appeared in the corner, presumably in order to draw late-season customers.

But this year, nothing much. The lightbulbs had been replaced by energy-saving compact fluorescents, and the bathroom was filled with new towels and washcloths—overall, though, our cabin was the same. GUESTS PLEASE PROVIDE BALANCE OF RENT AND DEPOSIT AT OFFICE THANKS, read the familiar manila envelope, twice-laminated with packing tape, that was affixed to the fridge by a (surprisingly powerful) Mount Rushmore magnet. The sight of it loosened something in my chest, and I went off to the kitchen window to gather myself.

When I came to, the girls had run down to the lake in their swimsuits, and Margaret was out on the path, taking her annual Inaugural Stroll. I went to the bedroom. Her backpack, suitcase, and straw hat lay on the lower bunk, staking their claim. My own suitcase had been heaved onto the top, along with my plastic grocery sack of rock and roll biographies. She was a small woman, Margaret, and it had probably taken a lot of effort to get that stuff up there. I climbed the wooden ladder and lay facedown beside it.

Margaret was the owner and head chef of Chez Maggie, a popular bistro in Nestor, the college town where we lived. She was extremely popular there, and was featured in the restaurant's print and TV ads, flashing her trademark wink and "waggling OK" hand gesture. She wrote the "Feedbag" column for the local paper, a kind of half-recipes, half-entertaining-philosophy thing, which she was in the process of trying to get into syndication. Indeed, after nine years of running Chez Maggie, Margaret had acquired ambitions. She was prone to making snarky comments about Nestor and its smug hippie attitude, and had been doing a lot of research on up-and-coming American cities (Portland, Denver, Salt Lake) for reasons she declined to provide. She attempted to enthuse me about these places but never explained why I ought to be enthused, and seemed annoyed and unsurprised when I failed to follow her lead.

I say this to establish that I did know that something was coming: some theatrical reveal of the whole plan; some kind of prim, professional report that I would receive one night, over wine and an elaborately simple knockout dessert. And so I can say with confidence that I was not entirely surprised by the moment when it came. But there was no wine, and there was no dessert, and the girls weren't just in bed, they were in bed forty miles away at Margaret's mother's place, where she had dispatched them under the pretense that we would get to have an "intimate" "time alone," which I thought meant wild nude abandon, but which actually meant something else.

"I'm leaving you," she said.

"Nooo," I replied, automatically, in a kind of friendly/skeptical tone, as if she'd gotten something slightly wrong.

"I'm in love with Allan. He's leaving his wife. We're going to live at his lake place, and he will be investing in the expansion of my business."

I don't know how I must have looked, staring at her like that across the brilliantly lit dining room table. After a time I was able to say, "I don't understand this."

"Of course you knew, David. You're just too simple and straightforward to know what you know." She made a face. "I mean that as a compliment. The fact is, you don't need me. What you need is sex, music, and food. I need more than that. I need somebody with a vision. Allan understands what I want, and he wants to help me get it. He admires my ambition."

There was so much to digest and refute in that little speech, so much that, on one hand, made no sense whatsoever, and on another explained so terribly, terribly much of Margaret's behavior around me since we married, that I could only sit there, staring, with my mouth agape. Allan, I should add, was one of her investors—the big one, I guess. I'd met him—he was just some rich guy. Or so he seemed to me. I must have missed something.

"I do need you." It was hardly the most important of her assertions to refute, but it was the thing I managed to blurt.

She shook her head. "I'm sorry, no."

"I'm ambitious!"

This drew a sigh. "David, what have you done for the past decade?"

"Raised our daughters," I said.

"Yes." She nodded, as though conceding the point. "Yes, and good job. But look at what's happened to you. What about your music— you could have been great. But you gave it up."

She was referring to the guitars and amplifiers, the tape machines and synthesizers and drums, which once I had used to record albums of instrumental music for independent films and television shows, and which I had gradually sold off, until all I had left was my trusty Gibson acoustic, the one I had found in a pawnshop in Nebraska during a road trip with an old girlfriend in 1982. It was true that I had sacrificed my ambitions. I had done this so that Margaret could go to cooking school, and then to open a restaurant, then run the restaurant while I raised Lyn and Rae. The money I got for selling those things, I gave to her.

Of course she was right that I might have continued to write and record. I might someday have achieved considerable fame and fortune, won an Emmy, an Oscar. What I had managed to achieve instead was happiness—at home, with our girls, bringing them up while Margaret labored in the trenches. I know, I know, it sounds like cold comfort, and at times I had wondered if that was how I should see it myself. But I didn't miss what I used to do. My work, the trappings of it, had become a burden to me. It stood in the way of the simplicity that, however annoying it was to hear Margaret ascribe it to me, I nevertheless strove for. Lack of ambition had become my ambition.

In any event, ever since the I'm-leaving-you conversation, she had been going on a lot of "little trips," the destination and purpose of which she refused to say. And then she would come home and stay with me and the girls for a couple of nights, and then she would leave again. And each time I figured she wouldn't be back, and each time she returned as though she'd done nothing more scandalous than run down to the supermarket.

After two weeks of this, I asked her, Hey, what are you doing here? Are you staying with me? Or are you leaving me? And she wouldn't answer, only stare over my shoulder, blinking. I continued to ask her every few days for another two weeks, and every time got the stare, until at last, a week before our vacation, she turned to me and said, in much the way she had the first time, "Okay, I'm leaving you."

"Okay."

"If you're demanding I decide, that's my decision."

"Oh," I said. We were back at the dining room table, with the girls in bed upstairs. Margaret looked thinner and more tired. "So you're leaving me now because I keep asking you if you're leaving me?"

She covered her face with her hands. I was angry. And at the same time I felt bad for her, really bad. "I'm leaving you," she said, "for the reasons I previously stated."

It was then that we agreed the lake trip would be the end, and when we got home, we would tell the girls. Or I would tell them. Or something.

We spent the afternoon in separate spheres, Margaret on the porch with her BlackBerry, me on the lakeshore tossing stones, the girls out in the middle of the lake lying on inner tubes in the bikinis their mother had bought them and I wished to hell they had held off a few years before wearing. Their names had been Margaret's idea, which, like most things, I went along with. But the nicknames were my innovation—Lyn and Rae—and those were the names they seemed most comfortable with. I was aware that Margaret resented me for this, but resentment fueled a lot of her most productive activity, and I was happy to provide it. Not that I had ever striven to do so—Margaret would have found something to resent regardless of what I did—but I figured that, like other bad habits, it was best kept in the home.

Listen to me—trash-talking my wife. She was not all bad, Margaret. There were good times, moments of profound sweetness and fun. We were a team: us versus the fools. Nothing had changed, really, except that I wasn't on the team anymore.

That night we went to eat at the Grimy Fisherman's. Though we hadn't yet seen another soul down at the lakeside, the place was packed. Belinda was heavy but agile, with a round fleshy face, lively eyes, and cascading piles of gold hair. Honestly she was pretty hot, and I loved her place, the pleasure of her patrons, her pleasure in them, the dim brown light and deafening noise. She kissed the girls, called them by name (my versions, of course), told them they were absolute heartbreakers, brought them special treats they hadn't ordered and which wouldn't show up on the bill.

At one point Margaret got up to go to the ladies. She brought her BlackBerry. Belinda showed up at our table in seconds, as if by chance, slipping into Margaret's seat and resting a fishy hand on my shoulder. "So how are you doing?" she said seriously, and it was clear that somehow she knew everything.

"Oh, fine!" I chirped.

"Good," she said seriously. "Good."

Lyn was buried in her paperback—she always brought something to read for the dull moments in life, and I found this habit both endearing and highly respectable—but Rae looked up with shy, alarmed curiosity.

"We're so glad to be back," I offered.

Belinda nodded slowly. "You are always welcome here. You know that."

"I do."

"Don't forget," she said, and tousled my hair, as though I were a child.

When I looked up, Rae was staring at me. I smiled. She quickly bowed her head and moved the scraps around on her plate.

"I wonder what's taking your mother," I said.

Rae shrugged. "She brought her phone."

"Ah. Did she now."

A nod. At this moment Lyn looked up from her book and glanced at us both. "What?" she said. "What'd I miss?"

"Nothing," I told her. "We're waiting for your mom. Then we'll have dessert."

"No, thanks," Rae said from under her hair.

"I think I'll pass too," I agreed.

Margaret returned, looking flushed and concerned. I ignored this. She didn't want dessert either, but Lyn did of course, so we all sat for ten minutes watching her alternately eat an ice cream sundae and read. When she was through, she said, "You people are freaks," and for once, none of us disagreed.

———

That night Margaret and I lay awake. The moon was new, the sky had clouded over, and the only light in the room emanated from the bottom bunk, where she was tik-takking away, answering her email. I was thinking about a night long ago, when the girls were babies and asleep in their beds, and I was alone in the studio, writing a song for Margaret's birthday. I turned off the lamp and played guitar, whisper-quiet, illuminated only by the moonlight through the window and the glowing LEDs and VU meters from my equipment racks.

Oddly I don't remember if she liked the song, or even how it went. I suppose I have it somewhere, the recording I made, but it hardly matters. It was the doing and the being that I loved, the experience of making something I liked. The perfect moment.

How is it that I gave it up so easily? What was it in me that needed to sacrifice that pleasure? Margaret didn't need my gear money. I could have gotten a night job. Maybe, I thought, she was right about me. Maybe ambition frightened me. And maybe there was something the matter with that, and maybe not.

"Margaret," I said to the darkness, "we are going to have to tell the girls something."

No answer, other than a pause in her clicky thumb-typing.

"If you leave it to me," I added, "I don't know what I can say, other than that you've left us for Allan."

This time the typing stopped entirely. I heard her rolling off the bed, and a moment later, her thin face glared at me between the slats of the top bunk.

"How dare you bring them into this," she said, her teeth clenched.

"But Margaret—"

"You would dare to harm your own daughters for your petty resentment!"

"Am I fucking Allan?" I asked her. "I don't think it's me doing that, is it?"

"You bastard," she spat.

"No, sorry! That's you, fucking Allan. I'm the one who still loves you and wants to keep our family together, sorry!"

For a moment it appeared that her head might explode. Then, like Neptune descending into his kingdom, the sea, she withdrew from sight and settled back onto her bunk.

Five minutes later, the clicking resumed.

———

On the afternoon of the third day of our visit, the girls were sitting on the beach, poking the sand with sticks and talking. Margaret was in the house, working. I was in the boat, fishing. Not really. I'd grabbed one of the fishing poles from the bucket on the porch, stuck a worm on the end, rowed out to the middle of the lake, dunked the line in the water, and lay back to look at the sky. Thank heaven for small miracles, it was still blue.

I must have fallen asleep, because my reaction to the commotion on the shore was to open my eyes. I sat up, blinking. The sun had tightened and probably burned the skin on my face, and I felt really old.

The girls were pointing at a hole in the sand that they had dug. They were talking a mile a minute and sort of dancing around the hole in their little bikinis, as if as part of some exotic preteen summoning ritual, an effort to make an anti-zit djinn pop out of the ground. Margaret stood in the shade of the porch, looking on in stern curiosity. Lyn saw that I had sat up in the boat, and frantically motioned me in.

It took me a couple of minutes, by which time Margaret had ventured onto the sand and was peering into the hole with the girls. At the bottom of it was a curved section of smooth metal about three inches in diameter.

"Whoa!" I said.

"Should we dig it out? Let's dig it out!" That was Rae.

"Mom says it might be dangerous," Lyn said, trying not to sound accusatory.

"It could be some electrical junction box," Margaret offered. She seemed to doubt it herself.

We stared at the object for a few silent seconds. Then I got down on my knees and cleared away more sand.

What was revealed was the approximate size of a loaf of Wonder bread, the shape of a gelcap, the color of a toaster. It was bisected by a thin black line of rubber. The metal was corroded, but not too badly. I took hold of both ends, lifted it out of the hole, and gave it a shake. Loose objects clattered around inside.

We all glanced at one another. I gripped one end in my crooked hairy arm and the other in my veined sweaty hand and gave it a sharp twist. It opened with a small groan of what sounded to me like relief.

Immediately something fell out and landed on the sand at Lyn's feet. It was a Pez dispenser, with the head of Papa Smurf on the end.

"Huh?" she asked no one in particular.

The end of the object I held in my arm contained a collection of papers, toys, shells, stones, and other objects. I reached in and pulled out a folded piece of construction paper. The words on it were printed in a neat, steady hand, using a marker. They read:

> THE HARRIS FAMILY
> VACATION 1987
> NOT TO BE OPENED UNTIL
> THE YEAR 2000!!!!

———

The four of us sat around the dining table, the contents of the time capsule spread out before us. There was a strong sense of waning enthusiasm, which we were desperate to artificially prop up: frankly, it was all a little disappointing. There was the obligatory newspaper, of course: fallout from Reagan's nomination of Robert Bork to the Supreme Court was big news, as was a tornado in Alberta. And people were fighting in Mecca. There was a Pac-Man keychain with no keys on it—Pac-Man was old news in 1987, if I remember correctly, so the keychain probably seemed a small sacrifice to make for posterity. Ditto the Elton John cassette ("Sad Songs (Say So Much)"? My God, what had become of him?), the Danielle Steel paperback, the deck of Star Wars playing cards that I bet had been stolen from the cabin, and which come to think of it might fetch a nice little sum on eBay.

More interesting were the family artifacts that had been provided— a sun-soaked Polaroid of a small and homely family, Dad with his bald spot and paunch; Mom with her squint, her puffy do, and her short shorts; and son and daughter, approximately the girls' ages, appearing sullen and standing as far apart from one another as possible. There were also neatly folded personal statements from each member of the family, printed in pencil on lined three-hole paper, which we solemnly passed around.

Dad went in for brevity. "A great family, a great vacation. Here's to 1987. Phil Harris." Mom was wordier, yet circumspect, as though trying, gently, to ward off future unhappiness. "Thru good times and bad, the Harris family indures. We are loving and friendly and happy to be together on this beutiful lake, in this beutiful time of year. May the finder of this time capsule have peace in their life and happiness on the earth. Sincerly, Ruby Harris."

The boy had written, "BEN HARRIS. MY SISTER IS A WHITCH. THIS LAKE IS BORING. BE WARE! BEN HARRIS." Lyn found this note to be hilarious, and laughed until tears rolled down her cheeks.

The girl's note, on the other hand, sucked the life out of our little party.

I am Natalie Harris, and I want to say I hate my brother and I hate my dad, and I don't hate my mother but I hope I never grow up like her and let somebody treat me the way my dad treats me here which is like shes an idiot or a child. He is creepy and mean and ruined the whole week by walking in on me when I was in the bathroom, and I was having my period and putting in a tampon and he laughed at me and wouldnt leave the room saying I had to say pretty please. It was TOTAL HUMILIATION and I called for mom and she didnt even bother getting up off the chair and who could blame her, my dad would just yell at her that she has no sense of humor because shes too dumb to get a joke. I cant stand it anymore and I am going to leave this place (home I mean) the second I am old enough to get a job. Or maybe even before, I could go live with Pam whos parents are dead and she lives with her aunt whos barely college aged and totally cool. I cant stand this lake and this cabin its like a jail and I dont understand why we cant just go to disney like normal families and stop pretending we like each other so we can actually have some actual fun for one time in our stupid lives. So if you find this thats a good thing, because that means its the future and I am grown up and having a real life somewhere with real people instead of this stupid fake family. Thats all I have to say and lucky for you to not be in 1987 at the dumb f—k cabins at dumb f—k lake craig new york. Natalie Harris

The note circulated around the table, and when we had all read it we sat in silence, listening to the dumbfuck lake creeping up the beach outside. Rae studied her fingertips, and I noticed that her fingernails, usually painted with care, were bitten and bare; Margaret stared into her coffee mug full of red wine. Lyn had been the last to receive the note and she continued to hold on to it, pressing it with both hands against her belly and gazing in mute wonder at the objects spread across the table.

I broke the silence by suggesting we fill the capsule with our own artifacts, and this gave everybody something to do. While Margaret and the girls prepared the contributions, I gathered up the Harris family's stuff and shoved it all into a plastic freezer bag. I used a ball-point pen to write "1987" on the bag in a near-illegible scrawl, then tucked it into one end of the capsule. Our shitty lives would be interred together, I figured.

Lyn requested that each of us get to be alone while we said good-bye to, as she put it, "our parts of ourselves," and so I brought our half of the capsule outside and set it on the ground next to the hole it had come from, and one by one we paid it a visit in solitude. I was made to go first, but personally, I couldn't think of anything to add. I traveled light, and what little I had, I wanted to keep. My life, after all, was the way I liked it, or at least had been until a few weeks before. And look what was happening to me! Look at my punishment, for the crime of contentment! In the end, as a gesture of solidarity, I stripped off my Timex and dropped it into the capsule. Who cared what time it was? It would be better, in the months and years to come, not to watch what remained of my fragile youth drain away into the future's reeking maw. Now I wouldn't be able to monitor my descent into bitterness and decrepitude, thank God!

Margaret went next, and was back in a flash: either she'd flung her contribution in irritated haste, or she hadn't participated at all. The girls went out together, bearing something or other wrapped in a plastic grocery sack. When they were through, I carefully fitted the Harris half of the capsule onto ours and screwed them tight, before calling my family out to the burial. They came slowly, purposefully, their faces grave. The girls were holding lit candles—not sure where they found those. Margaret had her hands shoved deep into the pockets of her shorts, and in the moon- and candlelight appeared to have briefly been crying. This surprised me, and I gazed at her with a question in my eyes, but she never looked up to answer it.

I knelt on the beach and pressed the time capsule to the bottom of the hole. Rae took the initiative of pushing the sand back over it. When she was through, her sister stamped on the mounded sand with surprising vehemence, then she turned on her heel and marched back into the house, her arms straight down at her sides.

"Can we go home tomorrow?" Rae asked Margaret and me.

"We still have a couple of days left!" I protested, but I wanted to leave too.

Rae sighed and crossed her arms over her chest.

"I do have a lot of work to attend to," Margaret said, the only words she'd spoken since we'd read Natalie Harris's note. It occurred to me, suddenly, that we hadn't left a family statement in the capsule, identifying ourselves. The future wouldn't recognize us. I grew depressed.

Rae and Margaret waited, not looking at each other, not looking at me.

"If it's what your sister wants," I said, and Rae went inside to share the good news.

For a few minutes, Margaret and I stood facing each other across the packed sand, before I turned to face the lake. I wasn't even sure if she was still behind me when, some time later, I said, "If you're still planning to leave, I'd like you to do it as soon as we get home."

There was no answer, though I thought perhaps I heard a small motion, perhaps that of a woman covering her face with her hands.

"Are you still planning to leave?" I asked her.

And again, no reply, and I considered that good news, if in fact she was still behind me.

"I still love you," I added quietly, and this time the silence was a bad thing, and I wished I hadn't spoken. I should have turned, to see if she was standing there, if she had heard me—it would have been best if she'd left between "Are you still planning to leave" and "I love you"—but instead I sat down on the damp beach, then lay down, then curled up and went to sleep.

———

The following morning we drove away in silence. I had prepared a playlist for the ride home, too, but it didn't seem very fun anymore, and both girls had their headphones on, and each stared out her respective window at the passing scenery. I didn't think we would ever see this road again, not the four of us anyway, not together. We passed Belinda's place, and though I tried to peer in the windows, I couldn't see her, and I thought maybe someday I could come back alone, and Belinda would still be there, and would sit down beside me the way she had the other night, and put her arm around me, and whisper poor baby, and I would see for the first time the little apartment behind the restaurant, the little bedroom where she slept.

We made good time and found ourselves at Mister Bip's before the menu changed from breakfast to lunch. We ordered the exact same things we'd ordered on the way to Lake Craig and ate them listlessly, saying little between bites. I happened to glance at Margaret's hands as she ate. Her wedding ring was gone. Halfway through her omelet she excused herself, grabbed up her satchel, and headed for the ladies'.

Lyn and Rae watched her leave with what appeared to me undue interest. They stole a glance at one another, and then at me, and then quickly returned their attention to their meals.

"What?" I said.

Rae didn't look up. Lyn gazed at me innocently and offered a puzzled shrug, but her hand snaked over and found her sister's, and they came together in a white-knuckle clutch.

A moment later, Margaret emerged from the ladies' and headed straight for the exit. We watched through the window as she opened the trunk of the car and began rummaging around through our things. After a while, she opened the passenger door, and then the driver's, and then the rear doors, leaving them all open. She appeared to be searching under the seats for something.

I wiped my mouth and went out to see what was up.

"Okay," she said, "where is it." The expression on her face was one of barely repressed anger and panic.

"What are you missing?"

"My BlackBerry, Dave."

"Oh. No. Where did you have it last?"

Her eyes flashed like broken glass; her body was a tree bending in a gale. She said, "Fuck you, Dave! Give it back to me!"

Across the parking lot, an elderly couple ducked their heads and hastened their progress from their Cadillac to the entrance. I raised my hands.

"Whoa, take it easy. I don't—"

Margaret reared back and hit me in the head with her satchel. Something in there really packed quite a wallop—an eyeglass case, maybe?—and I staggered a couple of steps to the side. I could see the girls through the window, staring at us with huge round eyes, and half the rest of the patrons besides.

"You infantile, jealous piece of shit!" she shouted. "This is so like you! So like you! Do you think this will make me love you again? You fucking moron!"

I stood perfectly still, my hand to my head, as Margaret trembled, buckled, and slumped to the ground, sobbing.

A man was standing beside me, holding a piece of paper. "Here's your bill," he said. "We'd like for you to leave immediately. So the police don't need to become involved." His mustache and eyebrows were epic. They looked like props.

I dug out my wallet and handed him two twenties.

"Sorry about all this," I said.

He didn't ask if I needed change as he returned to the restaurant, passing the girls on their way out. I suddenly recalled their mysterious plastic-wrapped package on the beach and felt a wave of love for them as perfect and as melancholy as a song. They gave their mother a wide berth and slipped in the open doors of the car.

I helped Margaret to her feet and took her into my arms. "Let go of me," she cried, but she didn't resist, and I held her there, in defiance of the mustache man, in defiance of her disgust, of my lost ambitions, of the unraveling of my family. I ought to have gotten angry, I know, but I couldn't. I just couldn't. She was so sad, and it was summer, and tomorrow was another day.

FLIGHT

I was heading east through central Washington in my rented car, hours behind me and hours ahead. The land was flat and brown all around and the trees very small, set far apart from one another a great distance from the highway. The sky was clear and dark blue and wallpapered with tiny weird clouds. So intent were my eyes on the incessant approach of road that the stationary world inside seemed to race away when I looked at it, and I felt like I was falling helplessly through space.

At a desolate exit I stopped for gas and bought a frozen something-or-other, which I heated in the microwave in the gas station and ate standing while I looked at boxes of rental videos. Back on the road, I drove until night fell. When I got tired I pulled over at a rest stop and dozed next to an idling tractor trailer. For what it was worth, I was more than halfway home.

A telephone woke me. When I opened my eyes I was surprised to find myself in a car. It was a cellular phone, bolted to the hump between the seats. I hadn't asked for it at the rental office, but they had provided it gratis, as if it would be of some use. Outside, the rest-stop parking lot was illuminated by streetlights around which no insects swarmed. Beyond the light there was only blackness. The glowing digits on the dash read 1:25.

The phone kept ringing. I picked up the receiver and pressed a button marked START.

"Hello?"

For a moment I heard only shallow breaths.

"Hello?"

"It's me," came a woman's voice.

———

"Don't hang up," she said. The voice was hoarse and slow, a night-time voice, the sort heard when everyone else has left the party and the floor is littered with half-empty plastic beer cups. "Okay, good," she said. "Don't. Hang up. Please."

"Okay."

"I don't know why I'm calling. I know it's late." She let out a long, acid sigh that ended with a hitch, and I thought she'd cry. But the moment passed. "First of all, I want to say, I want to apologize, and please don't say anything, please, I would like to finish before you say anything or hang up on me. First of all, I am very, very sorry, and I know that may not mean anything to you right now, and I under-stand that, but I am sorry. I just got home and all I could think about on the drive back was what a terrible mistake I made and that I would do anything, anything in the world, to be able to take it back. Okay. Just let me finish. Second of all, I just want to say that I know you won't take me back and I don't expect you to just because of this phone call, but if it's any consolation to you for what happened I am never going to forget this and I will probably go to my grave thinking that it was the worst mistake I ever made. I mean, and I can barely imagine this, I guess there will be somebody else someday"—she was sniffling now—"but even so I think that no matter what happiness comes to me I will always remember this unhappiness and think how much better my life would have been if I had thought . . . I mean if I had thought for even a second, but there's no point in saying that now. And the third thing, I guess there is no third thing, except just that I love you and I know that means nothing to you now, or maybe just makes you angry thinking it's a lie or maybe even if it isn't a lie it just doesn't matter to you anymore, because you can't love a person you cannot trust. I shouldn't sit here and tell you—but I will, I'll tell you because I have to say it—you can trust me, if you took me back, which I know is out of the question, you would never hear a lie out of my mouth again." A pause. "So I'm sorry," and her voice broke on "sorry," before she lost it to sobs.

I was still not awake enough to realize that I'd been asleep for some time, and my mind tried to peek around this monologue and find the missing hours. I was awake enough to know that this voice on the phone belonged to no one I'd ever spoken to.

—

The day before had been my thirty-sixth birthday. I was supposed to fly from Newark to Minneapolis, then connect to Marshall, Montana, where I lived alone in a two-room apartment in a crumbling part of town known as West Hill. I had been in Newark to attend my mother's deathbed, which failed to work out: by the time I arrived, less than twenty-four hours after she had called to tell me she was dying, she had already arranged for a car to take her home from the hospital.

Choppy air roiled over the East Coast, and some kind of accident in Denver had delayed flights across the country, so my plane idled for hours on the runway, stuck in traffic. To save myself the trouble of carry-on luggage, I'd foolishly packed the books I'd brought into my duffel, which was checked through to Montana; now I had nothing to read. Instead I listened to my fellow passengers cobble together a narrative from the fragments of crash rumor they'd overheard back in the terminal.

"It was a UPS plane. The crew escaped, but all the packages were burned up. Guarantee my J.Crew stuff was in there."

"I think it was a military transport. Some general or somebody got killed."

"They saw it go down in the mountains but can't get to it."

"It was a private jet. I hope it was Bill Gates's."

I checked and double-checked my arrival and departure times in Minneapolis and the gate map in my on-flight magazine, try-ing to calculate the latest the plane could take off and still allow me to meet my connection. I saw myself sprinting down a crowded concourse, unencumbered by luggage, toward a far-flung terminal. Outside, men and women in dayglo jumpsuits zipped around on their little vehicles.

"There's a massage station back on concourse B," somebody said. "For fifteen bucks you can get a half-hour back rub. I ought to have done it."

"In front of all Newark!"

"I'm not ashamed."

We took off with apologies from the pilot at about the time we were supposed to have begun our descent into Minneapolis–Saint Paul. I fell asleep, ate dinner, fell asleep again, and disembarked in the muggy and lake-spangled Midwest.

"Flight 157 to Marshall?" I asked the ticket agent.

She laughed. "Long gone."

"Put me on a later flight?"

"No such thing. I can get you out at nine fifteen tomorrow morning."

"Will you get me a hotel room and a ride to it?"

She reached under the counter and pulled out a coupon: 10 per-cent off at the Super 8. "We can give you a discount," she said. "No accommodations for weather delays, sorry."

I refused the coupon. "I thought it was a crash. In Denver."

"That was O'Hare. And I wouldn't call it a crash."

I persisted. Could I get out of Minneapolis that night? I didn't know anyone in Minneapolis, and didn't want to sleep huddled against the refrigerated terminal air on an ass-worn seat in the waiting area. She asked how about Seattle at 9:00 PM, then Marshall at 2:10 in the morning, and I said okay.

———

I had time to kill. The airport had a little mall, and the shops had themes: winter, health, wholesomeness. But it was August, and weary, begrimed travelers from all quarters haunted the unswept concourses. At something called High Plains Brewhouse I bought snob coffee and drank it over an abandoned *USA Today*. I read over and over, without comprehension, a graph charting the consumption of watermelon in America since 1954. I must have slept, because when I woke my flight was boarding.

Everyone on the plane to Seattle seemed to be drunk. They were possessed of an odd solidarity, as if they had all been friends for ages, though they lacked any common feature save their booze-fueled ruddiness and good spirits. I asked the slumped, frayed-looking woman sitting next to me what was going on. Her face fell into a happy leer as she remembered. "You see that guy?" she said.

"Him?" I was pointing to a thickset man wearing a big hat and waiting in line for the first-class bathroom a dozen rows ahead.

"He is a top-notch oil-and-gas lawyer from Fort Worth, Texas, and he has been buying us drinks for the last two and a half hours." Apparently they had all been booked onto a flight scheduled to depart some time ago, but while taxiing their plane bumped a wing against a moveable ladder left out on the tarmac. Maintenance crews had to examine and possibly repair the damage. "They put us all on this flight, but we had to wait. So this guy gets up and says the drinks are on him. I put away a half-dozen margaritas with some high school teacher." At that moment a bespectacled man wearing a loosened Mickey Mouse necktie shambled past and pointed at the woman with both hands. The two burst into giggles and the man moved on. "Oh, my," she said.

"Did you hear about the crash in Denver?" I asked.

"That was in Omaha, I heard. You know, the plane was full of zoo animals from Africa, isn't that terrible? Although no more terrible than a zoo. I believe they are inhumane, the zoos, not the animals. The animals ought to be let go."

People were boarding the plane to cheers and applause, ducking in embarrassment or making jokes, exaggerating their drunkenness, staging pantomimed pratfalls. Nobody seemed to recognize specific seat assignments: they just stowed their carry-ons and stood around, as if at a cocktail party. Flight attendants touched their shoulders and spoke quietly and were met with roars of laughter.

In time, we took off. Passengers quieted, falling into boozy sleep. The new silence, backed by murmured conversations and the ambient rumble of the engines, reminded me of my mother's hospital room, the sharp evening light softened through tan shades. She was telling two nurses a joke when I arrived. "So Moses says, 'I'll take a mulligan!'" They laughed together.

"Mom?" I said.

"Paulie!"

"How are you?"

The nurses bustled out past me, averting their eyes. "Actually, Paulie, I'm feeling much better."

She looked like a party clown on a three-day weekend, her skin sallow from long days under makeup, her eyes tired and shifting.

"I'll be out of here tomorrow," she said.

"That's great." I riffled through the list of comforting phrases I'd compiled in my head. Had I misunderstood? Come right away, Paulie, she'd said, and I maxed out my credit card buying the ticket.

"Have you gotten your birthday present?" she asked me.

"No."

"It's coming. You'll love it."

"Terrific," I said. "Thanks." I wanted to sit down, though not necessarily here. The only furniture in the room was her bed and a nightstand, which a lamp shared with a paperback novel and her reading glasses. "Maybe I'll go find a chair."

"Why don't you do that? Then we can talk."

All along the ward I peered into rooms, looking for a free chair. There were a few, but the beds they stood by were occupied by sick people languidly manipulating their television remote controls or fitfully dozing. At the end of the hall I turned a corner and found an empty room. I went in. There was a neatly dressed bed, half-curtained and in shadow, and beyond it an unmade one under bright light. Two chairs were arranged at its foot. As I picked one up, preparing to carry it back, I noticed that the unmade bed was unmade because somebody was lying in it: a very old man with skin the color of Elmer's glue. A discreet translucent tube was taped across his face, branching off into his nostrils, and he breathed in a rhythm so slow that I thought he must be in hibernation.

Except that his eyes were open. They were dark brown and brilliantly alive, like shiny coins half-buried on a desolate beach. He lifted his head—barely—and moved his lips. Words escaped in a whisper. I couldn't understand them.

"I'm sorry?" I said, moving closer. "Sir?"

His hand had snaked out from under the sheet and he beckoned to me. I went to his bedside. "I didn't mean to walk in like this," I said. "I thought the room was empty."

He shook his head, dismissing the apology. Closer, said his fingers. I brought my ear to his lips and smelled the bitter dryness of him, something like baking soda.

"Take it," he said.

"Sir?"

"Take the chair," he said. "Nobody's using it."

When I returned to my mother's room with the chair, I discovered her chart hanging on a little hook outside her door: "Hemorrhoidectomy," it said. Surgery performed by a Dr. Martinez, and a touch of codeine prescribed for the pain.

———

My flight to Marshall had been canceled. In fact, there was even some doubt it had ever existed. "I know we used to fly to Marshall at that time," the ticket agent told me. "But I don't think we have for quite a while." His appearance put me briefly at ease; he wore his hair short and unkempt and he had a little black goatee: exactly the way young men in Seattle were supposed to look in 1995. I explained that I'd been booked on the flight; it had to exist. I gave him my name and he looked it up.

"You're booked to fly to Madison, Wisconsin," he said.

"Marshall. Marshall, Montana."

He shook his head. "Look," he said. "I can let you use the phone." He reached beneath the counter and pulled out a receiver with a glowing keypad. "If you know anyone in town, have them come get you and bring you back in the morning. We'll get you out of here then."

"That's all you're giving me? A phone call?"

He frowned. "Take it or leave it," he said.

———

Janine arrived in the same Ford Escort we'd shared when we lived together in Marshall. Idling, it made a new sound, as if a man were crouched under the hood sharpening a large knife. She leaned across the empty passenger seat and pushed open the door for me.

The back seat was full of cardboard boxes with what looked like all her winter clothes spilling out. She was wearing a Greek fisherman's cap and a couple of large crystal pendants around her neck. I knew the hat but not the pendants.

"I really appreciate it," I said. She eyed me with a kind of dispassionate destructiveness, as if I were a walnut she was about to crack open.

"There's a patch of cold floor with your name on it," she said.

"Well, thanks. It's a far cry from the airport."

She took a cigarette from a crumpled pack on the dash and stoked it with the lighter. Look! she was saying. You drove me back to smoking! We listened to music without speaking for most of the ride back to her place. It was a mix tape of some kind, a compilation of songs that were popular before we knew each other. "This is a good tape," I said.

"Somebody made it for me."

"I see."

She put out her cigarette. "So where were you flying back from?" she asked. A car moved into traffic behind us, illuminating the interior, and our eyes met, reflected in the windshield.

"Newark. My mother was in the hospital. She's better now." I considered telling her the whole story, but she interrupted the pause to tell me that her sister, whom I'd totally forgotten had been sick for a long time with bone cancer, had finally died last month.

"Oh my God," I said. "I'm so sorry."

She shrugged. "It was only a matter of time. There was a memorial service. Everybody read a little something they wrote. I know everybody says this, but she would have really loved it."

"It sounds like—"

"In fact I suggested to her that we do something like it while she was still alive. It would be kind of a party, and her friends and all of us would be there, and we'd tell her how much we loved her and everything. But she would have none of it. She was too proud."

We were silent for a little while. She clenched and unclenched her hands on the wheel. I tried to imagine what this would be like, hearing everyone telling you they love you, knowing that they can say nothing else, because you're dying . . .

"That would have been very powerful," I said.

"I don't remember asking your opinion," she came back.

Janine lived in the basement of some rich people. They had fixed things up pretty nicely down there—a terrific kitchen with a tile floor, a fold-down Murphy bed, and some built-in bookshelves— but none of it could dispel the gloom. The air was clammy. Shrill sounds emanated from a clock radio sitting on an upturned milk crate. Janine threw her coat on the bed. "I'll get you a blanket," she said, heading for a closet.

"So what have you been doing?" I asked. "For a living."

"Computer shit," came her muffled voice. "I commute half an

hour." She walked out into the room and threw two rough army blankets and a stained pillow on the floor at my feet. "Don't you want to know what I've been doing with my free time?"

"If you want to talk about it, I . . ."

She waved a dismissive hand at me and walked off, down a little hallway. I saw a light go on and heard water running. I spread the blankets out in a neat rectangle, set the pillow at one end, took off my shoes, and collapsed. I rolled to one side and stared at the carpet a while. It seemed to be moving. Squinting, I could make out a shiny black millipede. I reached for it, but it burrowed down into the weave.

Janine came out wearing a pair of pajamas I gave her for Christmas one year. "Don't get up," she said. She sat on the bed with her legs crossed and watched me. "How long has it been? Since we last spoke?"

"I'll bet it's six months," I said.

"More than two years. Do you know I've been married and divorced since we broke up?"

I didn't think she wanted me to answer, so I didn't.

"I married this guy practically on a whim, about five months after I moved here. He had a house in Queen Anne and bought and sold art for a living. He traveled a lot to Europe and didn't invite me along. I went to work, you know, and would come home to this enormous house with all this art on the walls. Then one time he brought this painter home from Poland, this gigantic kid who did these stupid splatter things, and the kid moved into one of the upstairs rooms and did his thing in there, and Ernest, that's the husband, sold his paintings. And then one night this Polish kid got drunk when Ernest was away and beat the shit out of me and tried to rape me, and when Ernest got back and I told him about it he kicked me out."

"God," I said.

From her breast pocket she produced another cigarette and a lighter. She smoked quietly and continued to look at me.

"I cannot believe you called me and asked me to come get you," she said. "I absolutely cannot believe it."

Obviously this had all been a mistake. Of course I'd been think-ing, somewhere in the back of my mind, that one thing might lead to another and we'd end up having sex or at least sleeping in the same bed. I sat up. "I'm sorry. You're right. Maybe I'll just get a cab back to the airport, and—"

"Oh, chill out, please." She leaned over and switched off the lamp, and I could see the cigarette's tip gently rising and falling in the dark. "You can get your cab in the morning."

The flight to Marshall took off without difficulty and with me on it, exhausted. I was eager to get home and go to bed, my own bed, and sleep for a great many hours, without regard for the time of day. I'd arranged to take several days off from my job—I worked for a tele-marketing company, listening in on the conversations of the telemar-keters, making sure they said the right things—and I figured I would just keep a low profile and pretend I was still with my mother.

I wondered if Janine remembered that I, too, had lost a sibling. His name was Richard and he'd lived to the age of twenty. I was eighteen and had graduated from high school about a week before he died. He was in the back seat of a car driven by a drunken friend that careened into an abandoned quarry filled with about thirty feet of murky water. The other two people in the car died too. It was an event of unequaled notoriety in our town, and one that cast upon me a tragic air that followed me all that summer, wrecking my re-lationships with the very friends who might have been able to make me feel better. In college I occasionally used Rich's death to get girls to sleep with me.

Richard was a careful and serious person. It is inconceivable that he would have been in this car, with these people, drinking. All the same, there he was. Our father was never the same; he died in his six-ties of a heart attack sustained while trimming the hedge. But Mom didn't crack. She contained her grief, promptly screwing the lid on it and meting it out in private over a period of years. By tomorrow night she would be back in our old house, lying on the couch in her robe, telling her dog how happy she was to be home.

I carried the chair into her hospital room but never did sit down. "Hemorrhoids?" I asked her.

She smiled as if she thought I'd known. Her lips moved a little before she spoke, uttering the ghost words that haunted the things she really said. "Paulie, you can't imagine the pain."

"You told me you were dying."

"I said no such thing."

"Do you know how much it cost me to come out here? Do you know what it's like trying to get off work with this kind of notice?" I conjured the image of my boss, mush-mouthed reprimands pouring from his face, to rally around. "You lied to me."

"If it's the money that bothers you, Paulie, I'll pay for your ticket."

"It's not the money. I don't care about the money."

"I said I needed you."

"You lied."

"I wasn't lying," she made herself say. "I wasn't lying."

She lay back, spreading herself across the bed like a jelly. Tears welled in her eyes. But still I persisted, not yet sorry for what I was doing. "You could ask me. You could ask me to come, and I'd come."

"Not true," she whispered.

The crackle of an intercom brought me back to the plane. "Ladies and gentlemen," the captain was saying, "welcome to flight 2195 to Marshall, Montana. I'm sorry to have to tell you that we're not going there. There's been some kind of incident at the Marshall airport, nothing for us to worry about, but it looks like they're not going to clear us to land, so I'm taking us back to Seattle." A groan went up around me.

"He's lying," someone said nearby.

"What's there to lie about?" someone replied.

"God only knows. I don't want to know."

In a moment we were banking back toward the coast.

"Rent me a car," I told the ticket agent, who was young and alert, had probably had a good night's sleep followed by several cups of hot coffee.

"The car-rental offices are right—"

"I know, I know. I want you to rent me a car that I can drive to Marshall. I want it instead of a plane ticket."

"I can get you on the next—"

"Just the car. It costs less than the ticket, right? You're getting a great deal."

I was the first bad thing to happen to the clerk so far that day, and I suppose I felt a little sorry for her, but not really. She stared ragged smoking holes through me. Her hands were poised above the computer keyboard. I stared back.

"Come on," I said.

"I can't."

"You can. You can. You'll be commended for doing it. You'll get rid of me and from here on you can have a normal, pleasant day."

She rolled her eyes. "I wish," she said, and I knew I had her.

———

I listened to her breathing over the car phone. Through the windshield I saw the lights of a plane pulsing; they rose in my field of vision, dimmed in the shaded strip of glass, and disappeared. How long would she have waited for me to say something? Maybe forever.

I said, "Don't. It's all right. Don't."

"I might as well just die," she said, not so sure of herself. "Maybe I should. Die, I mean."

"There's no reason to die. Don't say that."

I believe she was realizing that I was not who she thought I was and deciding what, if anything, to do about it. I had to say something, otherwise she would hang up. At that moment a trailer truck came roaring into the parking lot, slowed briefly as it passed my car, then sped up again, barreling down the exit ramp. I watched its red running lights shrink into the distance.

"What was that?" she said.

"Big rig."

I could hear her licking her lips. "Please forgive me," she said. I tried to picture the room she was in: a sloppy twin bed, maybe, the sheets half pulled from the mattress and leaving a bare corner exposed; dinner plates with crumbs on them stacked on the carpet. A roommate sound asleep behind a thin wall. I was starting to understand what a jerk I was, why I lived alone in a hick town, in a silent apartment, where no neighbors ever visited and no cries of passion ever sounded.

"I'm sorry," I said. "I'm sorry for what happened."

The blackness outside seemed to expand, taking on the shape of something huge: if I opened the car window I could touch it. I found myself gripped by terror and pressed the phone closer to my ear.

"Do you love me?" she whispered.

"Yes."

"Take me back," she cried. "Will you take me back?"

"Yes! Yes!"

"Come home to me!" she was saying, but I could barely hear.

———

When I woke again it was still dark, and the phone lay silent on the passenger seat of the car. I opened the door and stepped out. It was cool, the air fresh, my fear gone. I walked to the low brick building that housed the restrooms and peed to the sound of quiet music. When I came out, I saw, for the first time, an illuminated booth in the parking lot, staffed by a clean-shaven middle-aged man watching a small television. Had he been there all this time? How had I failed to notice him? He presided over a narrow wooden counter under a sign reading FREE COFFEE.

"Free coffee?" he said. His words carried across that scant distance with perfect clarity, as if ferried by swift small birds.

I went to him. Crickets were exploding in the weeds beyond the blacktop. A plastic basket of broken cookies lay on the counter.

"Okay," I said. "And the cookies?"

He nodded. While he fixed my coffee, I tried to rearrange, with gentle fingers, some of the fragments into one whole cookie, but they didn't fit. I picked up a few of the larger pieces. "What time is it?" I asked.

"Nearly three," he said, handing me the coffee. He had made it with cream, which is not the way I drink it, but it seemed important to accept what I was given.

The man didn't seem real to me, and because I thought I might be imagining him I never thanked him. For the rest of the drive, even with the radio going, I struggled to convince myself that there wasn't someone else in the car with me, hiding behind the driver's seat or maybe in the trunk.

———

My building was quiet when I arrived, and I couldn't get in because my keys were in my duffel bag. I wondered if I would ever see the bag again. I walked around outside, trying the windows, which were locked, and I noticed a blinking red light inside: there was a message on the answering machine. Finally I went to my door. A box lay on the hallway floor, with my mother's return address scrawled in her florid hand. I sat down and leaned against the wall, to wait for dawn and for the landlord to wake up.

THE FUTURE JOURNAL

I had a brilliant idea for my classroom bulletin board, but when the principal scuttled it I knew that I wasn't going to be able to teach second grade this year, or perhaps ever again. The bulletin board was going to be an evolutionary chart, starting on the left with some chemical symbols meant to represent amino acids and progressing through single-celled animals and amphibians and apes all the way up to man, who would not be a man at all but a seven-year-old child wearing a mortarboard and holding a scrolled-up diploma. I was going to get Gwen, the art teacher and my significant other, to draw the child in a way that evoked the development of reason through natural selection. Each student would have his/her name markered onto the left-hand column, and with each book he/she read over the course of the year a promotion in evolutionary rank would be awarded by me. I was very excited about this and couldn't wait to get my hands on some construction paper. And then, in an exuberant aside in the break room, I described my plan to Doug, and Doug told me that this was a Christian community and that while evolution was part of the curriculum there was no reason to ruffle any feathers by emphasizing it unnecessarily. Also, while he had me, my practice of encouraging extraneous reading tended to make self-conscious those students who didn't like to read, and since we were on the subject, from now on we would be referring to students as *learners* and to teachers as *facilitators,* at the request of the parents' association. I tried not to cry right there, and in fact I made it into the parking lot before I broke down, flinging my empty briefcase at my car and cursing the day Doug was born while tears streamed down my face. I cry easily, for a man. I'm not ashamed of this.

Once I'd caught my breath I picked up my briefcase and got in behind the wheel. It's a little car, a Volkswagen Golf, red, with a bumper sticker depicting a businessman smugly chattering into a cell phone beside a message reading DRIVE NOW, TALK LATER! A few people have honked at me after reading it, or given me the finger. Let them! I say. I am not afraid to voice my opinions; in fact I believe that to do so is absolutely vital for the advancement of the democratic ideal. It was noon, and I was hungry. My briefcase was empty because I had been eating my lunch during Doug's little speech, and I had left the lunch, largely uneaten, on the break room table when I ran out. It was hot: there was still a week before school was to start. A few of the custodians were hanging around in the parking lot nearby, smoking, though Doug had insisted that all smoking take place off the school grounds. Perhaps the rule wouldn't take full effect until classes began. Anyway, it wasn't my problem. Get fired, gentlemen, if you wish! Die of lung cancer!

I fished in my slacks pocket for my keys and started the Golf. Hot air blew in my face, and the radio blared show tunes. *South Pacific.* I would be playing clarinet in the pit band up at the high school this fall, and there was no reason to put off getting ready. But suddenly the musical, all musicals, seemed shallow and pointless. I switched it off. You're supposed to take the tape out first—the capstan can permanently indent the pinch roller, creating flutter and wow—but for the moment I didn't care. I rolled up the windows and turned the fan on high.

"Fuck! Fuck! Fuck! Fuck!" I shouted.

I drove down to the strip and got in line at Wendy's. Behind me was a giant Oldsmobile containing what appeared to be two identical men, pale, heavy, large-headed, with wispy blond hair and gigantic jaws and necks. I studied them in the rearview. The driver was alert and erect and blazingly illuminated by afternoon sun. The passenger wore a ball cap and his head hung low, so that his entire face was deeply shadowed; he seemed to be asleep. I'm no Chinese cosmologist, but there certainly seemed to be a yin-yang thing going on here, the driver bright, dry, robust; his passenger dark and weak and damp. Which was I?

The passenger, of course. The passive passenger, laboring in darkness, unrecognized and misunderstood, wet (with sweat, as the AC seemed to be completely broken), and subject to the whims of a higher and utterly arbitrary authority. To think that I just sat there nodding at Doug, taking it! Just taking it! I began to feel shaky all over again and kneaded the steering wheel. Sticky black stuff came off it and rolled itself into little cigars under my hands. Evolution, indeed. How very foolish of me, of all of us, to imagine there was constant and inevitable movement toward greater intelligence, efficiency, physical perfection!

Pretty soon my turn came. I accepted the food with a nod. Then I realized I was out of money.

"Do you take checks?" I asked the kid.

"Credit cards?"

"Checks."

"Checks?" he said. I nodded. "Let me talk to my manager."

Like all fast food managers, this one was slight of stature and frowned with a practiced authority. He had the requisite small black mustache. "What seems to be the trouble?"

"I'm sorry," I said. "I'm out of money. I just realized. I don't do credit cards. Can't. The check is local, it's all current, I'll give you my driver's license . . ." I handed him the license and he looked from it to me four or five times, his frown deepening. At last he said, "We don't normally do this, but I'll make an exception."

Whew! I borrowed a pen from the kid and wrote out the check. "Wendy's," I wrote in the PAY TO: line. Somehow, that act made me sadder than anything that had happened yet that day. Behind me, yang honked. I waved and pulled around to the lot.

When I was finished with my Cajun chicken sandwich and Frosty I closed my eyes and tried to meditate. How hard could it be? I thought. I took off my shoes and pushed the seat back and crossed my legs, then placed my hands palms-up on my knees. I said "Ummm . . . ," which did not sound quite right. I pictured a big naked bald man doing the same thing. In a little while a feeling of peace and well-being washed over me. Soon I was dreaming: I was a medicine ball, like the one they had in the school gym, simultaneously heavy and buoyant, girded by flexible metal rods. The children cheered as they propelled me through the air!

I woke to a tap. It was a girl wearing a Wendy's hat. The atmosphere inside the car was stifling. I rolled down the window and the air billowed out. "Yes?"

"They sent me out to see if you were all right?"

"I'm fine."

"They said I should tell you no sleeping in the parking lot?"

"Okay." I looked at the time. Two thirty! How'd that happen? I pulled out onto the street.

———

I didn't want to go back to Betty Shaver Elementary. I couldn't endure the humiliation, and besides, I had nothing to do: my plan had been to work on the bulletin board all day. I'd been planning to drive Gwen home, but she actually lives very close to the school and could comfortably walk, especially on a nice sunny day like this. So, exiled from Wendy's, I drove around, looking for hidden neighborhoods I'd never seen before. In a hilly town like ours, such places really exist, carved out of mountainsides or tucked away behind copses of trees. But my search was in vain, as the last few had been. I had found them all long ago. Disappointed, I tooled around on pot-holed country roads for fifteen minutes or so, until one led me to Route 13, which gave way to the Southern Tier Expressway. I revved it up to seventy, and the whole car hummed, or maybe shuddered. I switched the radio back on and began to sing. What in God's name was I doing? The road unscrolled before me like a medieval decree: the king of my subconscious had spoken.

I drove several hours until the sun dipped into my path, then I switched my glasses for the prescription shades that were stashed in the glovebox. That was better: the mountains and highways and clouds all sharpened and browned, as if they'd just come out of the oven. After a couple of hours I pulled over and got on the horn to Gwen, still at school.

"I was just about to leave. Where are you?" In the background I could hear a ditto machine, which in this age of electronic reproduc-tion the Betty Shaver Elementary still maintained. Only a few ancient teachers used it, hooked as they were on the smell, that of fresh-baked cookies laced with acetone.

"That isn't important," I said importantly. "I just want to tell you I won't be back for our dinner date."

"Really? Why not?"

"It isn't important."

"Can I tell you something? About an idea I had? Or is this a bad time?"

"No, now is just fine," I said. I have to admit, I was a little bit put off by her acceptance of my dismissal. Couldn't she have pressed the issue? But that was just not her way. You can imagine how de-lighted I was to find her, five years after my divorce, trying to lift a graffiti'd desk-chair-combo thing into the trunk of her car out in the BSE parking lot. Can I say that she is beautiful? Can I mention her golden tresses, her too-large face, her twitchy little schnoz? I had thought I might never make love to a woman again.

Her twenty or so thin bangles chimed as she settled herself in the school office; I could imagine her hips shifting on the simulated-woodgrain surface of the buffet table where copies were collated and where people talked on the phone. She said, "This being the year 2000 and all, I was thinking about how everybody's thinking about the future? You know, with the internet and everything, it's all future, future, future."

"Yes."

"So I'm going to ask the kids to paint the future! First they'll mix up their own colors and put them in Tupperware and make up names for them, Millennium Red or Future Blue or some such happy horseshit"—and here I noticed that the dittoing had stopped, and that Gwen was alone in the copy room, else she would not have said *horseshit*—"and those'll be the colors they use all year. And then I'll ask them to paint the future. Like what the buildings will look like, and the people, and the trees and plants and insects—"

"Probably they'll all be dead."

She tsked. "That's exactly why I am not giving you this assignment, Luther, because you have no hope. But the good thing is that whenever I run out of ideas I can just whip out the whole future theme and make them paint that. And maybe we can do a storybook—like get Mrs. Greitz to have them write a futuristic story together—"

"Hah! Greitz! Good luck with that!" I said.

"—and then in my classes we can illustrate it, with our fancy new colors and all that. I wonder if it's possible to get metallic paint? Since, you know, there are metallic crayons . . ."

She went on for a while in this vein, and I grew more and more jealous of the idea and more and more bitter about my own crushing defeat that morning. How was it that this woman, this gawky young thing, could bob so blithely down the rapids of life's river? And how was it that my canoe was forever snagged upon its tangled flotsam? I thought, the hell with it. The hell with it all!

"So do you like it?" Gwen said.

"I do. Like all your ideas, it is brilliant. But listen—"

"Oh! Maybe you can help me in reading and science! You can

have them read a science fiction book and teach them about rock-etry or computers!"

"Listen, I have to tell you something."

A silence. "What, already?"

"I'm quitting. I'm not coming back to work."

She laughed. "Whyever not?"

"You can ask Doug. Tell him I quit. Tell him no hard feelings. He'll know why."

More silence. "You're serious!"

"Yes."

"Luther, where are you?"

"That's not important. I'll be back soon, I promise. But tell Doug it's over. I'll see you."

Hanging up, I did not feel the kind of masculine personal tri-umph I'd hoped to, and when I turned and regarded the Golf it seemed a trifle of a car, a mere toy, incapable of taking me anywhere, literally and metaphorically. Yet I climbed in. I had no choice!

The Expressway emptied onto Route 90 and Pennsylvania, and pretty soon I was in, you know, Ohio. More hours passed. It got to be around dinnertime. I ate at another Wendy's, exactly what I'd eaten for lunch. It seems to me that if you eat something once in a day, it is simple nourishment, but if you eat the same thing twice it is a motif. As I polished off the last of the Frosty and endured the sudden headache, I found myself cheered. A motif! I stopped in the men's room (surprisingly clean) and, when finished, used a match from the box I habitually carry to burn away all evidence of my efforts. This small act of propriety and self-negation felt right on the money, as did having quit. It was all for the best: removing myself from the future. I was a throwback, a species meant to at-rophy. Back on the road, fully warmed up by *South Pacific* (now dormant), I began to sing in the operatic style, narrating my day in rhymed couplets:

> I finally got fed up with BSE
> I quit my job, albeit cowardly

Ne'er again shall I have to say this:
Plants make food through photosynthesis!

Mundane details took on ominous musical meaning. The major players earned their own melodies: a few plodding tones in a minor key for Doug, a staccato trill for Gwen, a repeating tritone (or "devil's interval") for me. In this manner I passed the last half hour of my trip and exited the highway at Toledo—or, more specifically, Northwood, the leafy suburb that was my ultimate destination.

It was not yet dark. I motored the quiet streets, slowing now and again for ballplayers, cyclists, joggers. Everyone was getting their last breath of summer; children frolicked with a desperate urgency; adults congregated at the ends of driveways, anticipating the blissful absence of the children. Somewhere, I supposed, teachers were growing tense, worrying about guns and drugs and standardized tests. Not me!

Once I'd found the house I wanted, I parked across the street. For a few minutes I sat in the car, reconnoitering. A white mock Tudor with an apron of sculpted yews. In a patch around a dogwood tree, tiger lilies grew impossibly tall. A cat sat in a window, staring. Nobody seemed to be home, though the garage was open and toys spilled out. I reswitched glasses and climbed out and stretched and unstuck my shirt and pants from my back. My necktie was still tightly knotted: duh! I loosened it and instantly felt ten times better. I crossed the street and yard and walked in the unlocked front door.

"Hello!" I called out. A thud: the cat jumping down from the sill. I scratched its head. It was a new one, barely past kittenhood; the old cat must have died. No, here he came, lumbering along like a sack of potting soil with legs, mewling in a very boring way. I couldn't stand cats, but I felt a subtle solidarity with these two. I went to the kitchen and filled their bowls from a large glass jar obviously bought from some specialty shop (with a metal scoop inside, no less!), then I opened a cold beer and sat down to drink it. The clock read eight fifteen. People were finishing their dinners out and heading home . . .

but they pass the ice cream stand . . . they sit licking their soft serve, watching cars speed by . . .

The beer went straight to my head. I stood, swooning, and made the rounds of the first floor. It was very tidy, but not the kind of tidy that you could say is concealing some sick personal shortcoming. The television was discreetly hidden in a painted pine cabinet, but the compact discs (mostly pop) were right out in plain sight. Books and magazines were neither at right angles to one another nor to the tables they lay open upon. They were not fanned in an attractive pattern. An empty tumbler, encrusted with the residue of some drink, stood on the floor beside an easy chair. I picked it up and gave it a whiff. Fruit smoothie. Banana, strawberry—something else? I fit it back into the depression it had made on the carpet.

It was dark outside now; the VCR read 8:52. I took a deep breath and went upstairs. A bathroom (more magazines), a little boys' room (bunk beds, a basket of sports equipment and plastic trucks). The master bedroom, a little frillier than I might have chosen for myself or Gwen, but comfy-looking. I went in and sat on the bed. Yes: where did they get this wonderful comforter? Out in the hall again—I peeked in the linen closet and at last entered the girl's room. Perfect. Storybooks everywhere, stickers, a transparent plastic purse containing Smarties, fruit-flavored lipstick, an electronic game, and a ring of discarded keys, perhaps twenty in all. The bed was made and turned back, the pillow fluffed, a pink nightgown casually tossed over the post, ready for slumber. I sat down on the bed. It creaked. Excellent. No boyfriends sneaking in here at night, a few years down the road. I closed my eyes and smelled the room's stale sweaty candy-corn scent. Downstairs the door opened. I remembered my empty beer bottle and felt a moment of panic, but relaxed when I found it in my hand.

Quietly, I got up and shut the door. I returned to my place on the bed. A television switched on downstairs. Laughter, the whining of the boys. Footsteps sounded on the stairs and hallway and my heart quickened. The boys entered their room, father in tow. Honest-to-God twins, no fertility drugs, three years old. The father dressed them, led them to the bathroom, supervised the brushing of the teeth, read them books in bed. A fine father, by the sound of it. He left and the boys giggled and talked unintelligibly until they slept.

Then there was only the television until a familiar voice said, "Anna, why don't you go get your jammers on?"

"Can I stay up?"

"For a little while."

Light footsteps skipped every other stair. The door opened.

She gasped but didn't cry out. I had my finger to my lips. Her hair was longer, hanging free, fine and light, though clearly less fine and light than it once was. She stepped in and closed the door.

"Hi Daddy," she whispered.

"Howdy," I said.

Anna came to me and let me hug her. I stifled a sigh. She said, "Why are you here?"

"I wanted to see you."

She frowned, glanced over her shoulder. "You can't come out, I don't think."

"I know. Will they come in?"

"No. I'm a light sleeper. Remember? I get goodnight kisses before I go to my room."

My God. "Yes, I remember," I said.

She shook her head, awfully ruefully for a ten-year-old. She said, "I have to go down." She took the nightgown off the bedpost, looked around the room, and entered the cluttered closet. I heard clothes sliding around on their hangers, and her small body brushing against the hollow-core doors. Whence this shyness? I would never again dress her for school. When she came out she seemed to be glowing. I suppose it was the light, what there was of it from the street.

"You look like an angel," I said.

"Whisper."

I said it again, quiet this time.

She went downstairs. "Comfy-girl," said her stepfather. "Come," said my ex-wife. To the sofa? They watched television for a long time. Please, Anna, I thought, don't fall asleep; don't let them carry you up here. Sitting on her bed, it was easy to remember being her age, being in my room, the only place I truly liked, where nobody would bother me, and where all my books were. Weather! I loved weather; I had dozens of books on the subject. I made my own hygrometer and barometer, which were fastened to a ledge outside my window. I kept careful records of temperature and pressure and wind speed. When I told my fourth grade teacher, he said, "Well, Luther, if your instruments are right up against the house, none of the readings will be accurate. A house exudes heat and blocks the wind." He was right. I put my notebooks away but left the instruments outside, where they remained until they were blown into the shrubs during a freak summer windstorm. Why was I so sensitive? Why did I give up, give in so easily? I could pay a shrink a small fortune to find out, but I never will.

Anna came back. The Winnie-the-Pooh clock on her desk read 9:45. I had given the clock to her, for one birthday or another.

"They let you stay up late," I whispered.

"Sh." She climbed into bed beside me and bent her body around my seated form. I wasn't sure what I was supposed to do, so I stayed where I was and found her hand under the covers. I held it and she held back. She fell asleep so quickly, with the speed of a child: it still takes me the better part of an hour. Yet I must have fallen asleep, too, for when I next looked at the clock, Tigger's tail had swished nearly to eleven.

"Anna," I had told her five years before, "your mother and I love each other very much." It was the first and only lie, or at least the only one I remember. Since then my record has been unblemished. "But we can't live together anymore. It isn't because of anything you did, in fact you're the best thing in our lives, and we love you more than anything in the entire world. Mostly you'll stay with Mama but sometimes you'll stay with me, too. We'll have a good time together, I promise."

I practiced so hard, really I did. But Anna cried and cried and said, "I'll be good!"

I pulled my damp hand out of hers. The television was silent. Out in the hall, there was no noise and little light. The master bedroom door was shut. I wanted to go in, I wanted to see my ex-wife sleeping, but of course I didn't. That is just not something people do. I tippy-toed down the stairs and out the door. No alarm, of course. They are convinced they are safe, and they're probably right. The world is not as dangerous as we like to think. The odds are good, really, if you've got a few bucks and don't smoke and live in a decent neighborhood. I don't think there have been better odds ever, in the history of man.

I got back at about five thirty in the morning. I don't think I was awake all the way. Oh, I had my eyes open, I stayed inside the lines, all right: but I believe I dreamed. In my dream, my waking dream, it was the future. Not much looked different. The cars were a little sleeker, that's all, and people wore their collars turned up. And I was older, and so was Gwen, and we had two children, daughters, twins, as old as Gwen was now. And they looked just like her! Their wide faces like suns, warmth-giving, powered by unimaginable forces. And the three of them could read each other's minds, but they didn't do it when I was around, out of politeness. It was a good dream.

When I was nearly home I got to thinking that I could use Gwen's idea after all. I could have my students write a future journal. We'd start out easy: What will your life be like tomorrow? To give them a quick success, to get them motivated. Then the next week it would be: What will your life be like next week? And then: Next month? Next year? Where will you be in twenty years? Fifty? What will your children, your grandchildren, your great-great-great-great grandchildren do? Who will they be? Maybe I would do the assignments with them. In my journal I could follow the lives of the dream-twins, and of Anna, and make all kinds of outlandish predictions that would amuse and delight the children and fill me with a sense of goofy well-being.

Of course, I had quit my job.

I parked outside Gwen's condo and let myself in with my key. She was still asleep. Today was to be a special day for us: a trip, a dip in the lake, a romantic evening at her place. I slid into bed and put my arms around her. She stirred, turned.

"Hmm? What time is it?"

"Almost six," I whispered.

She sat up. Hair stuck to her face. And the smell of her! Like a clump of hot grass that had grown here in the night. "When'd you get in?" she said.

"Just now."

"Luther. Where the hell were you?"

We both waited for my answer. Instead, I said, "You didn't really tell Doug what I asked you to tell him, did you?"

"Besides your having quit?"

"No, that. That I quit."

"Luther, you asked me to."

"You don't mean you told him."

"I did what you asked."

Daylight was gathering. Her arms were crossed over her lovely breasts. What could I do? I burst into tears. "Oh God," I said, "what have I done?" I fell against her: how wonderful to be here, wracked by emotion, in the arms of my lover! A question formed in my mind— Marry me?—but I held it.

"Oh, baby," she said, stroking my hair, "no, I'm sorry, I was kidding—I didn't say anything at all to Doug, nothing at all. No, no . . ."

Okay, that was a mean trick. But I deserved it. Asking her to quit for me was lame, I knew that all along. I kept on sobbing, and let her rock me until her back hurt too much and she had to get up. For a time, while she showered, I was alone in her bed. Posters covered the walls, she'd had them since college. Monet, French movies, kittycats. The woman I love has cat posters, I said aloud. I heard the water turn off, saw the bright flash of robe as she passed in the hall. By the time she returned with the paper I was ready to tell her what I'd done.

FAREWELL, BOUNDER

The dog who died was his once. Flop-eared, hang-tongued, the color of television static, Bounder had appeared to him at a highway Gas-n-Go near (but not in) Mitchell, South Dakota, home of the Corn Palace. Owing to his matted locks and his tee shirt with the word BULLSHIT printed on it, he'd been refused the men's room key and so was forced to piss in the weeds out back, behind the propane tank, while the Christian-fundamentalist proprietress glared at him through a torn screen door. I've never felt so free, he told himself, and said it aloud, to the giant spun-sugar sky: "I've never felt so free!" But it wasn't true. There was a woman waiting for him in the car. He was trying to dump her but she wouldn't let him. "Don't be ridiculous," she'd said in their motel bed, then rolled naked onto him, which had the time-honored effect.

God, he thought, shaking off his thing. The open road was a prison, love was a prison, the car, the five-hundred-dollar Datsun, was a prison. Prison was also a prison—he'd spent two nights there in the past year, once for being drunk and once for being liberal—but not as much of a prison as love was.

He carefully tucked himself away and buckled his belt, and it was then that the dog appeared, sticking his head out from under the propane tank: a puppy. He bent and scratched. Cute. No tags. A stray. Yes! he thought: Not the girl, a dog! He walked to the car slowly, to see if the dog would follow. It did. He opened the driver's side door and the dog leaped in.

"Hello, Bounder!" said the girl.

The chains rattled on his cell door. Jesus Christ, he thought. She has to name my goddamn dog. They drove off into the prairie night, the stars unnecessarily bright, Bounder curled up in the back, perfectly content, as if he'd come with the car.

Ah, those days! Now he can't even remember her name. Wait a minute—it was Francis (not Frances, she was named after an uncle) Jean Sheppard. Her phone number was 455-6171. Her birthday was, and probably still is, September fourth. He ought to have married her.

Instead he married Ellen Meeks, now Ellen Meibusch, which is his name, though they are no longer married. Ellen took to Bounder in a big, big way. He licked her face and she licked his. She taught him how to dance and sing. She combed his speckled fur and he tipped and tossed with mad pleasure. After Ellen, Bounder treated him with a distant, perfunctory respect, as if he were any old human. They still played catch, or hide-the-tennis-ball, but he had to bribe the dog with meat-flavored snacks.

Ellen comforted him at regular intervals, like a prescription. "He loves you so much, Ray." She hugged him and patted his back.

There was little question of who would get Bounder in the divorce. It never even came up when they lunched with their lawyers. Besides, Julia, his then-lover and new wife, is allergic.

It is Julia who now shouts to him from the tub. "Anything good?" she says.

She is talking about the mail, which he has come to the front door to get. It is a lovely spring day. His old house, the one Ellen still lives in, is visible from here just a few blocks away; there is no evidence of life inside. The mail consists of a single cream-colored envelope that contains a cream-colored card, on which are printed the following words:

FAREWELL, BOUNDER

A GOOD DOG
Join Ellen and Ryan in a celebration
of the long, happy life of our beloved mutt.
Friday, April 14, 7:00 PM

"BOUNDER"
1987 (?)–2000

Ryan is their son, Ray's and Ellen's. His name was a compromise. Ray had wanted to name the boy Ray. Ryan was Ellen's suggestion: "It rhymes with my name, and yours is in it." It made a kind of sense. Very little about Ellen does, any longer.

He didn't know the dog was dead.

In answer to her question, he brings Julia the invitation. She's lying there, naked and wet. Of course—she's in the tub. But he loves the words, the practical filthiness of them: *naked* and *wet*. Her hair is spread all over the tub's rim and floats on and in the water, over her shoulders and breasts. It's very long, this hair. She hasn't cut it since they married, two years ago. If he'd known she would do something so arbitrarily sentimental, he might not have married her, so he's glad he didn't know. She takes the card from his hand with wet fingers and the envelope flutters into the water, and Ellen's nutty all-caps hand-writing begins to blur and the ink streams off in tiny ribbons.

Ray works at NYTech, the renowned local university. He is director of something called Distance Learning. This used to consist of setting up VCRs in classrooms and taking them down again after the videotaped lectures were shown. Now it involves the internet and consequently a great deal of money. (Ray personally takes home a healthy chunk.) He travels to faraway places and tries to convince people that computers will make them smarter. This isn't hard to do, it's something people want to believe.

Julia hands back the invitation. "Have fun," she says.

"You won't come?"

"Ellen will hug me."

"She hugs everybody."

"She hugs me harder."

It's true. When Ellen found out he was getting married, she marched right over to their house and took poor Julia into her arms. Ellen was already a hugger, but now the hugs have come to define her for others. You never know which innocuous personality traits will grow cartoonish.

He looks down at Julia and wonders if she'll have sex with him. Probably she will. When they first had it, he hadn't had any for a long time, and she still feels bad for him, though that was a long time ago. He sits on the toilet seat and pushes his shoes off with his toes. "I didn't know the dog was dead," he said.

"She hasn't been walking him."

Apparently Ellen walks Bounder past this house daily. According to Julia, she cranes her neck as she passes, peering through every window. Julia works in the attic—she paints watercolors of flowers, birds, and cats for a greeting-card company, and watercolors of people screwing for a self-help publisher—and waves to Ellen when she passes, and Ellen waves enthusiastically back.

"Really?" Ray says, removing his socks. "Why didn't you tell me?"

"Because you don't care."

He removes his shirt.

"What are you doing, there?" She is frowning.

"I was thinking we could—that maybe—since I need to get a shower or a bath anyway—" He stands and continues to undress.

Julia sighs. She reaches down and pulls the drain plug to let some of the water out, so that it won't overflow when he gets in. He gets in.

———

That was Saturday. This is Wednesday. The boy, Ryan, is at school. He is in the second grade. At the moment he sits cross-legged on the asphalt at the edge of the kickball diamond, talking with his friends Darren and Philip. A kickball game, of which they are a peripheral, almost theoretical, part, goes on ten feet away. Ryan examines his no-longer-new sneakers, streaked and roughened with coarse dirt. Two weeks ago, when he first wore them to school, they were brilliant white, blinding white. During recess the bigger kids came roaring up and scuffed them with their giant brown boots. These were farm kids, bused in from the other side of the college. When he got home, his mother flew into a rage and called the school, staying on the phone for a good twenty minutes, by Ryan's reckoning, and the following day the farm kids told him he was dead meat. So far he hasn't become dead meat. But at least once a day one of the farm kids points at him and mouths the words. He isn't worried, though: soon they will abandon their threats and simply remind him, as they always did before the sneaker-scuffing, that his mother is a loony.

Ryan's mother is again the topic of conversation. It's Philip who taps his shoulder and points to the parking lot beyond the game. "Here comes your mom," he says without malice. Indeed, his mother's Volvo is careening into an empty space, her rectangular head framed by the rectangular window framed by the rectangular car.

"What's she doing here, man?" This is Darren. There is a hint of threat in his voice, but this is habitual. He is bused in from downtown, where the tough people live.

"I think she's doing story time today."

"What is she, man, is she a teacher or what is she?"

"She's just a helper."

"Man." Darren shakes his head. Ryan likes the way everything is astonishing to Darren.

His mother climbs out of the car and begins to make her brisk and direct way to the cafeteria door. On Wednesdays she reads to the kindergarten. Monday she plays guitar and sings songs, Tuesday she helps with bulletin boards. (On occasion she has left Ryan secret messages on the bulletin boards—a rocketship with his face sketched in the window, his name spelled out in a jumble of alphabet blocks—so he always gives them special attention.) Thursday and Friday she types in the main offce. She goes on every field trip, not just the ones Ryan's class takes. Of course she isn't at the school all day; she also goes to meetings downtown and writes letters to the newspaper. The paper also runs photos of his mother, usually of her speaking into a microphone or holding up a painted sign. Once a new teacher clipped such a photo from the paper and posted it on the wall. The teacher announced that Ryan's mom was famous. The following week another, nearly identical, photo appeared in the paper, but instead of posting it the teacher just took the first one down.

The boys turn to the kickball game. There are too many out-fielders because there were too many boys, but the rule is that all the boys must be picked. A fly ball drops with a percussive wheeze onto the pavement near a cluster of such boys. The big kids get angry as the runner rounds the bases.

Bounder loved kickballs. He used to somehow get his narrow jaws around them, to carry them in that proud dog way without puncturing them with his teeth. There are half a dozen in the yard at home, mostly airless, to give the ailing Bounder a good grip. He liked to make a little pile of them, to half-bury them in the sod. He liked to bring them into the house and nibble and paw at them as if they were babies.

The dog's decline has not been easy for Ryan. Of course he will miss Bounder, the games of fetch, the couch-sprawling, the scrap-tossing, the squirrel-chasing. And death itself—the specter of it, its inevitability, whether or not it has taken or will take notice of him, Ryan, personally—this is grounds for some concern. But it isn't himself he's worried about. It is his mother, what his mother is going to do without the dog. Who will she talk to after he, Ryan, has gone to bed? Already she asks him questions he doesn't understand, questions that don't seem to have answers but to which she neverthe-less expects some response. *How could they do this to us? What kind of nation do they think we live in? Are they serious, Ryan, I mean are they fucking serious?* She gets upset about simple, faraway events that don't have anything to do with her: the construction of a certain highway, something somebody said in a foreign country, some numbers read over the radio. She screams and cries and grips her hair in her fists. Ryan's tack so far has been to gently embrace her rigid body and then go outside to play.

Now he sees that she has noticed the kickball game. She stands on tippy-toes, shading her eyes with her hand, looking for him. Philip scoots forward to hide him from her; he's done this before, which is why he is Ryan's best friend. But it doesn't work.

"She's got you."

In the bright sunshine Ryan's mother marches across the playground, waving as she comes. The asphalt-baked air distorts her image, so that she looks like a spelling test, a C-minus, uncrumpled from a booksack, flung by wind.

Last night they played a game she made up, a game in which Ryan pretends to be her, and she pretends to be Bounder. She went into the kitchen like a normal woman but emerged on her hands and knees, pushing the empty dog dish along the floor with her nose. With the same nose she poked Ryan in the shin. That's how the game starts. Ryan fed her. She ate some of the food. He scratched her back. It wasn't totally crazy—she was laughing the whole time, she always does, so does he, it's like a kind of joke—but it was a little crazy. Last night it stopped when she brought him the leash in her mouth. He said No, Mom, we're not going outside. She whined. He said he didn't want to play anymore. After a while she stood up and went to bed.

When he was sure she was asleep, he went down the street to his dad's. The bedroom light was on and he thought he could see him and Julia moving around. But no one answered when he rang the bell.

Now she is here. She says, "Hello, boys," and the boys say hello.

"Will you two be attending our party on Friday?" This in a fake English accent.

Darren looks at Ryan in astonishment, but Philip only hangs his head. Darren says, "What party?"

"A farewell to Bounder," says Ryan's mother. "To see him into the next world."

"I'm there, Mrs. Meibusch," says Darren. "I am all over that."

"You too, Philip," she says sternly.

"Yes, ma'am."

She gives Ryan a look: Why didn't he invite his friends? He gives her a look: Because it's a freaky-ass dead dog party, that's why.

When she's gone, Darren says, "Dude, I didn't know your dog died."

"He didn't," Ryan says.

———

Julia had a dream one night, the autumn after the summer she started sleeping with Ray. She dreamed that she woke up and went to the window and saw something moving in the yard below: Ellen, dressed in a black catsuit, digging holes in the grass with a trowel. There was no apparent purpose to this exercise; it was methodical and uninspired and rather boring to watch, and Julia wondered why she was dreaming about Ellen and what the dream could mean. Then she dreamed she went back to bed and had a dream: a nice sensible one, something about flying and screwing; they (it was an old boyfriend she was screwing, but she would tell Ray it was him) were on a carpet or raft or something, and birds flew above and below them while they did it. She woke up and called Ray at work and described the dream, leaving out the part about Ellen. Then she forgot about it for a long time.

Ellen and Ray had been her landlords, that's how she met them. They lived right down the street. Occasionally they came by on the weekend to pace the yard and look things over, and Julia had heard them argue from time to time, right out in the open. They didn't seem to be arguing about anything personal. It was mostly Ellen doing the arguing, actually. *How could they let India get nukes?* Julia heard her shout once. *Jesus fucking Christ, Ray!*

One night a storm window blew off in a winter squall and the next day Ray came over to replace it. She invited him in for coffee. The next time he came it was to put mouse poison in the cellar. They had more coffee. On his way out, Ray fixed her with a piercing look and reached out and smashed a glass doorpane with his hammer. He said, "I'll have to come over tomorrow and fix that."

"Don't you have a job?" she said, eyeing the glass shards scattered around their feet.

"I'll take the morning off."

She at last returned his gaze. "Take the whole day," she said.

When he came, she led him up to her studio. At the time, she was hard at work illustrating a book called *Self Esteem Through Self Love*. The easel, walls, and floor were covered with photos, drawings, and paintings of attractive men and women getting themselves off. He turned to her and said, "So tell me about your work." It was four months later that she had the dream. Not long after that, Ray filed for divorce. By March it was all over: joint custody of Ryan; one house for Ellen and one for Ray. Ray chose the house that already had Julia in it.

On one of their first semi-legitimate mornings together, Julia threw open the bedroom curtains and looked down at the yard. The newspaper lay soaking in a patch of melting snow. Nearby, yellow crocuses were blooming, forming patterns in the grass. Recognizable patterns, actually, spelling out the words FUCK YOU. She remembered her dream.

Her initial response to the crocus affront was to hand-deliver to Ellen, gaily wrapped with a big red bow, a freshly printed copy of *Self Esteem Through Self Love*. As Ellen tore away the heavy paper, Julia saw how cruel the gesture was, and she had to restrain herself from grabbing the gift from Ellen's hands. But Ellen's reaction was curious: a quickening of breath, a biting of the lip. A slow fanning of the pages. She raised her face to Julia's (Ellen is so much taller, but it didn't seem that way at the time) and said, "I'd invite you in for a drink, but I'd like to be alone now." And the door swung shut.

She was beginning to sort of like this Ellen.

Of course they had to come in contact; Ryan sometimes had to be fetched. And so Ellen and Julia have become friends, after a fashion. They sit in one kitchen or another and have chats. Ellen doesn't offer anything to eat or drink, she simply sits down and begins talking. Julia wouldn't call her self-absorbed; in fact, she rarely says anything about herself at all. Instead she pours out whatever's occurred to her that day or hour in the form of rants. She asks herself pointed questions and answers them. Julia's role is to nod or say "Of course you're right" or frown or laugh in order to keep her going, like one of those people who stand on the sidelines of a marathon and hand the runners little cups of water. In the wake of these chats Julia likes to listen to the silence, the myriad sounds that comprise it. Sometimes she thinks of her MFA thesis defense. To every question the committee asked her, she responded by holding up a small landscape she'd done, with blue sky and a cloud and a hill and a farm. She never spoke. They awarded her the degree with less than five minutes of debate.

It is now Friday afternoon. Ray is due home any minute. Of course they'll go to the party together; to do otherwise would be to betray her sort-of-friend. She is dressed in black: black jeans and a sweater. Her hair is tied back and she wears no jewelry, except for her wedding ring. She designed the rings herself, silver bands engraved with creeping roses. They had a reclusive silversmith from out of town execute the designs. They were married in a fire tower in the NYTech Experimental Forest, among the genetically altered pines. Only about ten people could get up there at once, and Ellen was one of them. Yes, she was stunning: even in her hiking boots, she had the cold beauty of a metaphor, a Lady Liberty stamped on a coin. Ryan wore a tux and seemed very afraid, though of heights or his father's remarriage, there was no telling.

When something stands between Julia and Ray, it is usually Ryan. It isn't that she's jealous of the boy; on the contrary, she loves him. It is the way Ray treats him that hurts her, his sickening attunement to Ryan's every eccentricity, no matter how slight. It is Ray's antipathy for the half of Ryan that is Ellen's: his lurching forehead-first walk; his pencil-gnawing and scab-picking; his tendency to say things, lots of things, in some weird concocted foreign accent. These things are not Ryan's fault, and what's wrong with them, anyway? She herself had a few bad habits when she was a kid. She smoked. She pulled long strips of skin off her lips and dried them in the pencil trough of her desk. She masturbated during social studies: and look how lucrative that turned out to be!

The other night Ryan came to their door. It was nearly midnight. He rang the bell and turned his waxy divot of a face toward their bedroom window.

"I'll go let him in," Julia said.

"Please, no," said Ray from the bed.

"No?"

He buried his face in the pillow. They still smelled of each other, from sex. "Please. It's Ellen's night tonight. He should be at home."

At home, she thought. The sting made her say, "You are a cold-hearted man, Ray."

"Please don't give me that. He's seven years old. He can't treat our house like a room down the hall. I know how it sounds, but trust me."

She wondered if he really knew how it sounded, how completely awful. She stood watching until Ryan was gone. She watched him pick up a soft drink cup that had been tossed in the yard and stuff it into the trash can at the end of the driveway. After that he went home. He didn't seem broken up about the snub.

She went to the bed. Ray was on his back again. She reached down and feigned grabbing at his crotch. Then she made a fist and pressed it to her own.

"What the hell was that?" he said.

"I took the sex back."

He laughed, though he wasn't supposed to.

Now she can see Ray approaching, walking back from the college. He is too far away to hear, but she can tell by the set of his shoulders, the tilt of his head, that he is whistling. When he passes Ellen's place, he bows his head a little and jams his hands into his pockets. That's Ray's problem: he is terrified of his ex-wife. A sudden rush of affection threatens to topple the tower of chilly detachment she has so carefully erected. He mounts the front steps and shouts her name, and she goes down to greet him.

"I saw you whistling. What was the tune?"

He frowns at being reconnoitered. "I'm surprised you couldn't tell by sight," he mutters.

She sits at the kitchen table arranging toast crumbs into floral patterns while he leans against the sink eating an apple. He is forty and she wishes he had a little gray. She likes gray, she likes the idea of his being an older man. But he neither looks nor acts like the older man he is. When he's finished eating he makes a loop of his arm and she hooks hers through it. He kisses her forehead. The tower crumbles. They walk to the party, already late.

Through Ellen's windows, the town's activists can be seen affecting solemnity, their caftans and rimless spectacles and gaunt, squirrel-like bodies moving through the emptied front room. Here is Lydia Speyer, who lies down in front of idling bulldozers. There is Paul Waller, architect of the local scrip, earned in local health food stores and restaurants and redeemable at same. Julia knows these people from the paper. She drags Ray through the open door and into the shaggy crowd. They are all here, the editor of the anarchist newspaper, the brewer of medieval beers, the used bookstore owner, the wan naturopath. Where is Ellen? Nowhere to be seen. A low table in the center of the room is covered with a white cloth but not with food. The food and drink are on a wheeled cart parked against a wall. There is something ominous about the empty cloth, she can't put her finger on it. Her throat begins to itch: dogstink. She fortifies herself and Ray from the cart and endures the overtures of the alternative dentist, then excuses herself and sneaks out the kitchen door to the backyard.

The children are here, hard at play. They seem to be running around randomly, waving brightly colored objects and hollering nonsense words. From time to time one of them collapses in gales of laughter. She is surprised and unsettled by the realization that they are being ironic, "playing in the yard." She stops one of them—it is Ryan's companion, Philip—and watches his smile deflate as he removes himself from the game.

"Where's Ryan?"

Philip points to the back of the property: the doghouse. He hoists a plastic replica of the Empire State Building in the air and leaps back into the fray.

The yard is full of halfhearted holes and uninflated kickballs. Weed-tufts sprout everywhere, and maple saplings form a ragged border. The doghouse is surrounded by bare dirt, the grass having succumbed to Bounder's years of puttering. She bends over and peers inside, but the house appears to be empty.

"Ryan?"

"Hi."

Ah. There he is: a gray blob in the darkness, crouched against the far wall. She sticks her head in farther. Her eyes adjust, and she can see he is playing solitaire, the cards splayed before him on the ground. Wedged into a far corner is a shredded plush toy and a pocked rubber ball.

"What are you doing in here?"

He looks up and smiles at her, a smile full of understanding and patience. Not the smile of a child. Her heart dislodges for a moment and swings free from a vein, and it occurs to her that Ray should not fear the half of this boy that is Ellen, but the half that is him. He says, "Same thing you're doing in here. Getting away from those cuckoos."

"Can I come in?"

"Sure."

She fits easily; it's a big doghouse and she is a small woman. She says, "Do you miss him? Bounder?"

"I will, I guess."

A jagged splinter juts from a ceiling beam, and she reaches up and plucks it off. "He was a good dog," she says. "Farewell, Bounder."

He looks up at her. God, what a look! It's the spitting image of Ray, this thing he does where he focuses suddenly on her face as if he has just now noticed it for the first time, and he reaches out and touches her cheek, and some small emotion floods his eyes. But Ryan doesn't touch her. The look grows quizzical.

"Do you know what my mom is going to do in there?" he says.

"No, what?" Her sinuses are filling up.

"With Bounder? Did she tell you?"

"Tell me what?"

He leans past her suddenly and pokes his head out. Sunlight screws his pupils to pinpricks. When he ducks back inside, he puts his hand on hers and says, full of concern, "Just stay here." It is no expression of need, but a kind of warning. She has no choice but to heed it. Her nose clogs and begins to run, and as if anticipating this very problem, Ryan reaches into the pocket of his pants and hands her a tissue.

————

Through the closet door Ellen hears Ray arriving: arriving Ray, with her rival Jane, Julia rather, who remains alive, having survived the rivalry. It's time for meet-and-greet, it's time for beat-the-band, it's time to dive into the light and await the vet van. Bounder's in a ball on the closet floor, boring, no not boring, snoring, or rather heavy breathing, wheezing, heaving, sneezing. Dying. Crying. No: crying's all done now, it's out. Out like the light. And now it's time for the dying. All right: she's ready: what's the time?: okay, ready: out.

Hi! She says Hi!, making rounds, shaking hands, taking names, rounding friends. The holy whole of them is here, LydPaulTomSyd-MattPatJanetBob, seeing off the hound, the mutt, the mound in his hut. Except he's in the closet half-asleep, hurting. No—pain is ending, heaven pending, heart is mending! Breathe in, breathe out. That's it.

"I'm so sorry to hear—" It's Lovely Fat Lydia, anti-development maven, swimming in her muumuu, beautiful, they hug, they kiss, It's okay, His time has come, That's old for dog years, Thankyouvery-much. And now the dentist with his giant choppers, size and shape of postage stamps, grips her shoulders, gives them a little massage, "We'll have to get together, come to my place for dinner some night— " Imagine!, a come-on at a time like this—

Wait. Close eyes. Calm. Yes. Better.

"Hi, El."

Open eyes. "Hey, Ray."

She can see herself in the set of his face, the way she seems to him. Poor man. Never understood. She tried to be the girl he thought he saw when first he saw her. Attractive, productive, what they call vivacious yet not in the least bit dumb: she was a catch. Loved, loves him. But he never knew what he was getting; she kidded herself that he did. One night at the copy shop it came out. She was pregnant, it was almost their second anniversary, they were xeroxing invitations to the party they were throwing themselves. Next to her in line was a punk rocker with a poster for his band. That poster: so intricate, so patient, she had to say something. She placed her finger on it on the counter and said what came to mind.

"Pretty-pretty."

The punk swiveled. He clearly didn't like her finger on the poster but didn't ask her to remove it. He said, "I beg your pardon?"

Ray placed a hand on her shoulder, half-protecting, half-restraining. She was going to say it again, she knew it. Here it came: "Pretty-pretty."

The punk looked at Ray for some instruction. She still doesn't know if Ray gave it or not. "Thanks," said the punk, and pulled his poster out from under her finger.

That night he said to her in bed, as proto-Ryan exerted itself in her belly, "What was that all about? In the copy shop."

"What in the copy shop?" The invitations sat addressed and stamped on the mail table, just inside the door.

"What you said to that kid."

"What'd I say?"

"You said, 'Pretty-pretty.'"

Yes! It was succinct, instinctive, perfect. One pretty because it was, and the other because the first wasn't quite enough. But she replied, "Is that what I said? I thought it was a nice poster."

"Maybe you shouldn't do that," he said.

"Say nice things?"

His "never mind" came much later.

The first pretty was not enough, that was the trouble. And since then nothing has ever been enough. And all that came before, that was not enough either. It is not enough to speak against fossil fuels; one must walk two miles to the doctor's office, three to the grocery, four to the library. It is not enough to protest development: fire-bombing bulldozers, that might be enough. It isn't enough to cry, one must rend one's garment. It is not enough to love, one must give everything.

Bounder loved, Bounder gave everything. And when the cancers chose him, Bounder accepted his suffering. It is not enough to let him die. No, she has to make him a gift of death; the dog would have done the same for her. And let them all see her mercy, let them watch him accept bliss into his heart.

Those anniversary party invitations disappeared, but not into the mailbox. The party did not occur. The marriage did not end there— really, it didn't seem like a big deal at the time—but it would, it would.

"I have to tell you something," she says now to Ray. He actually winces.

"What is it?"

But first: "Where's Ryan?"

"I don't know," he says. "With Julia? I can't find her."

"I need him."

"What is it, El?"

"Something is going to happen."

The doorbell rings. His doorbell, Ray's. He rigged the chime so that its factory-installed major triad became the minor seventh that sounded now. How they laughed to hear it, that enigmatic, unresolved chord that transformed every meter reader, every petition-monger and Mormon elder into an omen. Now Ray reacts with a sort of horror, as if the precipitous notes have burst a spore in his memory and let their marriage out. For the first time she sees what a terrible thing she's about to do. Yes: let Ryan stay away.

She opens the door. The vet is there with his awful box. He's a shorty, five five tops, with a confectionery smile that congeals on his jaw when he takes note of the crowd. The crowd, in turn, takes note of him and grows silent. There is a moment of calculation, which is cracked by a whine. The whine is Bounder's. The closet door has fallen open. The old dog drags himself out.

His fur is halfway gone and coarse as twine, the skin studded with cysts. His back legs no longer support his meager weight, and a trail of urine appears, smeared over the floorboards behind him. He is like a bride as the activists part to clear his path. No, Ellen thinks, no, no, no!, and she rushes to him and lifts him off the floor. This seems to hurt him—he howls—and her will weakens. But when she turns back to the vet it is with renewed resolve. Now, she thinks, now.

The tiny doctor says, "Are you kidding me, lady?"

In answer she moves to the table and lays Bounder upon the brilliant sheet. Another yip as he settles, and then a sigh. He closes his swollen eyes and assumes the work of drawing breath.

"Please," she says, "hurry."

The vet looks around, a smirk playing at the corners of his eyes. For him, it is already over, and he is telling the story to his friends at their favorite bar. Let him! she thinks, and she nods at the supine dog. He approaches, sets down his box.

"This the dog?" he says.

Someone unforgivably snickers. "Yes," says Ellen.

It doesn't take long for him to prepare. The syringe is produced, uncapped, and filled with medicine. She ought to look around at her friends, but instead closes her eyes. She has prepared a speech, but it slips her mind. She is disappointing herself. The sounds of the children playing outside fill the room. Now someone (same someone?) catches her breath and lets out a sob, and from elsewhere in the room comes another, and another. Some of the sobs are her own. A hand has found her shoulder. It is Ray's.

"I'm sorry," he says, helplessly, and she leans into him.

"Hold your pet, please," the vet tells her, compassionate suddenly, and she falls to her knees, and Ray joins her there. It is just like their wedding. Her knees had hurt for days; the vows seemed to go on forever. Sometimes it seems like they still are. She and Ray lean over Bounder and take him into their arms. She tries looking in the dog's eyes, but like Ray's, they are shut.

"Don't worry, poochy," says the vet, "this won't hurt a bit."

ACKNOWLEDGMENTS

I'm grateful to everyone who helped me revise and publish these (and other) stories over the past fifteen years. These people include, first and foremost, Rhian Ellis, but also Jennifer Barber, Ira Glass and Starlee Kine, Brian Hall, Bill Kittredge, Ian Jack, Michael Koch, Cressida Leyshon, Amy Grace Lloyd, Halimah Marcus, Fiona McCrae, Ben Metcalf, Ethan Nosowsky, Ann Patchett, Jim Rutman, Ben Samuel, Denise Shannon, Ed Skoog, Ann Vandermeer, Matt Weiland, and Virginia Zech. Finally, I want to thank everyone at Graywolf Press for valuing short fiction in general and mine in particular. I've never been treated better by anyone in my life.